Dear Readers,

We have put together some of the hottest street authors in the game to bring you *Soft: Cocaine Love Stories*. We appreciate all of the support and love from our fans and readers. You guys helped us reach a level that was unimaginable and we are forever grateful—real shit. You, the readers, helped us reach the *New York Times* bestsellers list twice in a row, and we don't plan on stopping now. All the real niggas and real chicks fuck with us, and that's all we need. It's us and y'all against the world.

Now we are trying to take street literature to the next level, and we hope you show these amazing authors the same love you have shown us. We promise to deliver another classic series with *Murderville*, and we are following it up with a page-turner entitled *Murder Mamas*. We love you all, and there would be no us without you. Always Love!

To Caroline McGill, JM Benjamin, Boston George, and T. Styles—thank you for contributing to this anthology. We wish all of you guys the best of luck. We handpicked all of you, knowing that you would write great hood stories.

—Ashley & JaQuavis

Ashley & JaQuavis Present:

Soft

Cocaine Love Stories

Ashley & JaQuavis Present:

Soft

Cocaine Love Stories

T. Styles
Caroline McGill
J.M. Benjamin
& Boston George

www.urbanbooks.net

Urban Books, LLC
97 N18th Street
Wyandanch, NY 11798

ISBN 13: 978-1-60162-588-5
ISBN 10: 1-60162-588-X

First Mass Market Printing March 2014
First Printing September 2011
Printed in the United States of America

10 9 8 7 6 5 4 3 2 1

*This is a work of fiction. Any references or similarities to
actual events, real people, living or dead, or to real locales
are intended to give the novel a sense of reality. Any simi-
larity in other names, characters, places, and incidents is
entirely coincidental.*

Distributed by Kensington Publishing Corp.
Submit Wholesale Orders to:
Kensington Publishing Corp.
C/O Penguin Group (USA) Inc.
Attention: Order Processing
405 Murray Hill Parkway
East Rutherford, NJ 07073-2316
Phone: 1-800-526-0275
Fax: 1-800-227-9604

Luxury Tax

by

T. Styles

" . . . there's a luxury tax when you fuck wit' rich niggas. You don't get to floss wit'out a price, and it's time you recognize that shit."

—Nicky

Ginger

Back It Up

Kentland, Maryland was hot as shit the day Trixy Greggs stepped her funky ass up to me. I was sittin' in front of Carmen and her sister's house smokin' a blunt when she walked up with some bullshit. You'd never know it, but six months ago, we were cool; that is, until I bumped my head after returning home from vacation one night, resulting in a memory loss. When I came to, my best friend was missin', people were mad at me, and my boyfriend, Milli, was actin' different.

"That's fucked up what you did to Quita!" she said, sweat pouring down her face, causing her makeup to streak. "Just 'cause she spanked your daughter for pissin' on herself."

"Bitch, that's between me and Quita, and you ain't got shit to do wit' it."

"What you gonna do, slice my throat too?" she taunted.

"If that's what you want!" She took a step closer, and I said, "Trixy, I'm warnin' you. Step outta my face."

She laughed and said, "And what kind of mother are you? If my baby was taken by Child Protective Services, I'd be tryin' to get her back, not outside runnin' my mouth."

"Bitch, get your rotten-pussy ass outta my face."

"Come on, Trixy," her best friend Shonda said while pulling her arm. "This bitch ain't worth it."

"Fuck that!" she said, shaking Shonda off. "I wonder if Milli feel the same way." She smirked.

Bitches loved sayin' Milli's name outta they mouths. He ran Kentland, and every bitch in Kentland wanted him, but he chose me.

"What you tryin' to say, Trixy?" My True Religion jeans were damp with sweat.

"Come on, Trix." Shonda interrupted again, her light skin flushed. "You don't want shit to go too far." The look on their faces told me they knew something I didn't.

"Why don't you just move the fuck from around here? Don't nobody even fuck wit' you no more!" Trixy said.

"I wanna know what you meant by saying Milli's name outta your mouth," I said, ready to drop her ass.

She laughed and said, "All I know is, you betta not kiss him on them sexy-ass lips of his anytime soon."

I snapped. When I came to, half of the cheap-ass weave she had in her head was on the ground by my feet, and she had bald spots in places her hair shoulda been. I had beaten the brakes off of her ass in a pair of black Dior heels.

"You think I did somethin' now, you betta be glad my Benz wasn't parked on the curb. I got shit in my trunk for bitches like you!"

I saw my friend Nicky push through the crowd. "Come on, Ginger. We gotta go—now!" She pulled my arm as the police sirens grew louder. They were close.

"You ain't did shit but make me mad!" Trixy said. "And before the night is over, you gon' see me again."

"Bitch, take your bald-headed ass in the house and look in the mirror! I did more than just make you mad!"

Trixy was right about one thing: After that shit she just pulled, she was definitely gonna see me again.

Me and Nicky were on the way to my house when about fifteen kids blocked our path. Five of them belonged to Nicky's cousin Stevie, and they all looked dirty and nasty, but Crystal's fresh seventeen-year-old ass was the worst of them all. I couldn't stand that little bitch, and I think she knew it.

I caught her sitting on my car one day and asked her to get off. She rolled her eyes, and later that day I saw scratches on my paint job. She was just like her mother—a little whore in the making.

"Hey, Aunt Nicky, you know where Mama at?" she said, resting her hand on her hips.

She was talkin' to Nicky but looking at me.

"I like your shoes, Ginger."

"Thanks," I said nonchalantly.

Everything I wore was designer, including the Fendi shades I propped up in my shoulder-length hair and the white Armani T-shirt that clung to my back.

Crystal's younger sister, Melli, who I believed was slightly retarded, stood next to her. She never said much but hi and bye.

"I want some sunflower seeds and a pickled sausage," Melli said outta nowhere.

"Shut up and wait!" Crystal said, yanking her arm. "Aunt Nicky, we hungry and can't find Ma."

"Well, she ain't with me. When I see her I'ma give her your message," she said, pushing past them.

Crystal stomped away, yanking her sister by the arm.

"That's sad. Stevie ain't get Melli no help yet. She act like she retarded."

"She ain't retarded!" She laughed. "Just slow."

"Y'all keep thinkin' that shit if you want to, but something's wrong wit' that li'l girl."

When I turned around, I saw Melli looking at me. Oh, well. I was too hot and mad to give a fuck if she heard me or not. I just had my third fight for the week, and Milli was gettin' tired of my shit.

"Why you and Trixy beefin'?" Nicky asked.

"I wish I knew. I know if she don't keep Milli's name outta her mouth, I'ma put somethin' to her ass, Nicky. I'm all the way serious 'bout that shit."

"You ain't got to tell me." She laughed. "Everybody in the neighborhood know you got a temper." I put my shades on and she said, "She ask you if you remember again?"

"She ain't ask me, but I'm sick of people not believin' I don't remember shit. What I gotta lie for? If anything, I feel like people keepin' shit from me. Nobody understands what it's like to lose your memory, only to wake up and have your best friend missin'. You heard anything about Leona?"

"Naw, but you know I'd tell you if I did," she said, searching my eyes.

"Shit just don't feel right," I said. "I feel like me falling and Leona being missin' connects somehow. It don't help that her parents think I had somethin' do with it."

"Ginger, I don't know about her parents, but people around here are upset. It's been six months, and the police be around here every other day askin' questions. And her father being a police officer makes shit worse. You ever thought about moving?"

"What, and leave Milli?"

"Take him with you."

"He don't wanna move, even though we don't really live together anyway. Plus, he make too much money over here." I swallowed hard because I wanted to ask her somethin' I didn't want to know the answer to. "You think Milli cheatin'?"

We stopped walkin' and she said, "Ginger, there's a luxury tax when you fuck wit' rich niggas. You don't get to floss wit'out a price, and it's time you recognize that shit."

"I hear you, but there's a luxury tax when you fuck wit' a bad bitch too, Nicky. It ain't like I can't get another man to do for me what Milli do."

"Can you? And if you could, why would you? All rich niggas cheat, Ginger. It's their right. Just one bitch ain't enough."

She just said some bullshit, but I said, "So you sayin' he's cheatin'?"

"I think he's a nigga, and niggas gonna do nigga shit."

"Nigga shit or not, if I find out he's fuckin' around on me, I'd cut his ass off quick. And he betta hope that's just it."

"That's on you—but it wouldn't be me. Look at your arm. How many bitches you know wit' a four carat diamond bracelet? You should let some shit pass."

She was referring to the diamond bracelet Milli got me when we first got together. I cherished this bracelet because it was the first thing he ever bought me.

Nicky knew a lot about rich niggas 'cause hustlers loved her. She let 'em do what they wanted as long as the money flowed. A little shorter than me at five foot four, she had a big personality and big-ass titties. It didn't hurt that she was a cute redbone.

"I know you twenty-six years old . . . one year older than me, but you talk old as shit sometimes," I said.

"I just know niggas. But to answer your question, I don't think he fuckin' Trixy."

Maybe that's why she let her cousin Stevie fuck her ex-boyfriend Raheem, who she was wit' for two years, and get away with it. Nicky was all about the money, and nothin' else mattered, not even love.

"Now, if you want somebody else to have him, then let him go," she continued. "He wouldn't be on the market long."

I wish I would see another bitch wit' Milli. That nigga had me in a new Benz every six months. His name wasn't Milli for nothin'! At twenty-six he was already a self-made millionaire.

"Come on, Nick. That ain't even in the talk."

"Well then, drop that shit and focus on gettin' your daughter back. When you gotta go to court for slicin' Quita anyway?"

"Next week."

"Umph. Well, I would steer clear of trouble if I were you. Let me go in the house real quick. I'm comin' back later to hit a jay wit' you," she said, runnin' up the street.

When I walked up the steps in front of my house, I tensed up seeing the dark brown blood stain. It was the place where I fell and lost my memory. No matter how hard I scrubbed, it never went away; and no matter how hard I wished, my memory of that night never came back.

Once inside my house, I was lonely. Lately, Milli hadn't been the same, and I missed him. What was the use of havin' money if you alone all the time?

It didn't help that he was so damn sexy. Who works out in no shirt and a pair of jeans? He looked like Columbus Short from the movie *Stomp the Yard*, but a few years older. He had the same full lips and smooth caramel skin and body.

We had a funny kinda relationship. I used to be able to talk to him about anything, but after I fell, even he treated me differently. I went over his house a couple of times to talk to him, to ask if he remembered anything about that night, but he kept saying he didn't know anything. I think he was lying.

I took the lid off the can and acted like I didn't see him when he said, "You up there fightin' them cluckin' bitches again?" He stopped doing his sets and stood up.

"You talkin' to me?"

"I never stopped talkin' to you. I just ain't wanna talk 'bout what you wanted to talk about."

"How you hear 'bout the fight?"

"I know everything."

And then he looked at me with those eyes—the eyes that almost get me in trouble whenever I'm around him.

"Stop lookin' at me like that," I said.

"Why? You finally admittin' you want a nigga?"

"Not even. We could never take it there, 'cause I have a boyfriend and you a stick-up dude."

"Come on, Ginger!" he said, patting his face with a white towel. "First off, you don't know what I do to earn my paper." He breathed heavily. "You goin' off what these muthafuckas 'round here say. Have I ever hit that nigga you wit'?"

"Naw."

"A'ight then." He smiled slyly. "Now, come on over here so I can taste that pussy."

My heart jumped. He never talked to me like that, and it made me wonder why. Part of me was angry, but the other part was turned on.

"Oh, so what? Now you gonna disrespect me?"

"That's disrespecting you, by askin' can I taste your pussy?"

"What . . . what you think?"

He laughed and said, "Yeah, a'ight. Then why you still out here?"

"Boy, this my house, and I do what I want to."

He laughed. "Look, bottom line, you wit' a nigga who could care less about you, yet you push away a nigga that's been feelin' you from day one. But you gonna need me one day." He put the gun that was sittin' on his step in his waist and threw his white T-shirt over his shoulder. "I just hope it ain't too late."

I hated his ass! Don't get it twisted; Gerron was sexy, but not sexier than Milli. Milli's six foot two inch frame floated over my five foot six inch frame just right. Plus, Milli could afford me, and Gerron's money was too iffy. You could make but so much robbin' other niggas.

When I went into the house, I got me a bottle of water and decided to call Milli, since I hadn't spoken to him all day. I grabbed my cell outta my Gucci.

"What it do, babes?" he said, answering the phone after the third ring. His voice was raspy and sexy as usual.

"I can't wait to see you tonight."

"Why you sound like you stressin'? That cop been 'round the way again askin' 'bout Leona?"

"Naw, not today." I sat on the couch and flipped my shoes off to rub my sore feet. The air from the open window cooled me off. When I saw my hands were red with blood from beatin'

Trixy's fat ass, I went in the kitchen to wash them.

"Let me send you on that vacation."

I walked back into the living room and sat on the sofa. "I don't wanna leave if you not goin' wit' me."

"I told you I can't get away right now, but I still want you to enjoy yourself. Shit, take Nicky wit' you."

"Maybe," I said, not feelin' like bein' stuck wit' her for a whole week. I think he wanted me gone for a while, too, because the cops were hassling me. But if I left, what's to say the cops would have too?

"Man, let me know when you ready," he continued. "And why you ain't answer your phone when I hit you earlier?"

"The house phone?"

"Yeah. I told you I was gonna call you back."

"Oh . . . uh . . . I was up the street."

"What you doin' up there?" he said as if he knew I was in another fight.

"Talkin' to Carmen. They invited me to a party."

"Oh. They ain't still talkin' 'bout the fall, are they? I'm tired of niggas gettin' in your business."

"Not really."

"You know I'm diggin' all the way in that pussy when I see you, right? You been playin' wit' yourself lately?"

"Yeah, but I want you to do it for me." I figured I might as well tell him about the fight since he was in a good mood thinking about my pussy. If there was one thing he loved to do, fuckin' was it. I caught him several times jacking off. I thought he had a sex addiction.

"Baby . . . I fought Trixy today."

"What the fuck happen this time?"

"She said some shit I ain't like."

"Why you can't walk away from the ordinary and step up when necessary? You actin' young and dumb, always believin' these bitches when they tell you I fucked them. Your temper is outta control, Ginger. You gotta get that shit right. It's gonna get you in a lot of trouble."

I was just gettin' ready to plead my case when someone threw a bottle with fire through my window. When it hit my hardwood floor, it broke and the flames spread. I threw water on it and smothered the rest with one of the couch pillows. Then I ran to my front door, opening it up to see some skinny bitch with black shorts running up the street. She was one of Trixy's friends, and I couldn't wait to catch that bitch later.

"Ginger! What the fuck is up?" I heard Milli yell.

"Tell Trixy her ass is as good as dead!" I screamed.

I was so mad I didn't care if Milli was on the phone or not, but now I had to deal with him. I put the phone to my ear.

"What the fuck is goin' on, Ginger?"

"Some hatin'-ass bitch just threw fire though the window!"

I looked at the shattered glass on my living room floor and flopped down on the sofa.

"I heard you scream. You a'ight?" Gerron asked, coming through my back door.

I put my hand over my cell and whispered, "Yeah, but Milli's on the phone. You gotta go."

He frowned and walked out.

"Ginger, maybe you should move. Shit gettin' serious."

"I'm not lettin' no dumb-ass bitches run me from outta my house."

"Who you talkin' to, baby?" I heard a woman say in the background on the phone.

Click.

"Hello?"

I called him back four times, and each call went to voice mail. I was so mad I felt like fightin' again. He waited five minutes before calling back.

"Milli, what's up? Who was that bitch in the background?"

"Nobody. Tracey playin' too much."

My cell phone beeped because my battery was running low. I wanted to say I'd call him on my house phone, but I needed to know the truth first.

"Your cousin?"

"Yeah. Who the fuck you think I'm talkin' 'bout?"

I didn't believe him, and for the first time ever, I tested his loyalty. "Milli, put her on the phone."

Although I'd never met Tracey because she didn't like me and I didn't like her, I knew her voice when I heard it. And that was only because whenever she watched my daughter, I always called to check on her.

"So, you don't trust me?" he said with an attitude.

Normally I back down, but this time, I was standin' my ground. "I wanna talk to her."

A few seconds later, Tracey got on the phone and said, "What the fuck you want wit' me?"

It was her.

A second later, Milli returned to the phone and said, "You gonna wish you never doubted me."

Click.

What the fuck was I thinking? If Milli cut me off, how was I gonna take care of myself?

I put my shoes on and stood up. Glass was everywhere and crushed under my feet. I plugged my cell phone up to the charger and decided to call him back on my house phone, but when I picked up the handset, someone was on the line.

"Milli. Is this you?"

"H—hello. Can Reneè talk on the phone please?" a little girl asked.

For the past two weeks, this little bitch got my number mixed up with Shonda's next door, and every time she did, it got on my fuckin' nerves. If I spoke to Shonda, I would have told her to set her ass straight.

"How many times I gotta tell you, you callin' the wrong number?"

"I'm sorry," she said softly.

"Don't be sorry, stop fuckin' callin' my house!" I slammed the phone down and rubbed my aching forehead.

After I hung up, I called Nicky because I needed somebody to talk to. She would probably give me that luxury tax bullshit, but she was all I had since Leona left. I missed Leona so much. She was so good with things like this.

When Nicky answered I said, "When you comin' back over?"

"Fifteen minutes. Why?"

"Hurry up. I'm blown and I need to hit that jay."

"I'm gettin' dressed now. Rico just stopped by and we beefin', so give me about twenty minutes," she said, referring to her boyfriend.

"A'ight . . . and I'ma tell you 'bout the fire somebody threw in my window when you get here."

"See, this what the fuck I'm talkin' 'bout. Every time I come over here, your ass is on the phone. This why our relationship ain't workin'. Everybody else more important than me," Rico said in the background, sounding like a stone cold bitch.

"I'll talk to you later," I said. "Before you come, can you bring the money you owe me? Me and Milli beefin', and he might cut me off like he usually do when he mad, and I need to build back up my stash."

"Yeah, I'll ask Rico for it," she said with a slightly different attitude. I hate when people make you feel bad for askin' for your money back. "Me and Stevie will be over in a minute," she said, hanging up.

Damn, I wished she'd just leave Stevie's ass home so I could talk to her alone. Who hangs out with somebody who fucked their man anyway, cousin or not?

When I got off the phone with her, I prepped the rest of my dinner for the night. Through my window I could see the back of Gerron's house, and I started to walk over there to talk to him, but knew that would turn into somethin' else.

I swept the glass up from my floor and made me a glass of Bacardi Limon, straight up. I had to refill my glass four times. After that, I turned my stereo on and Usher's "Love You Gently" blasted from the speakers; then I put on Lil Wayne's *Tha Carter III* CD. I decided to wait outside for Nicky, but hoped I'd see the bitch who threw somethin' in my house. I swear these bitches wouldn't be satisfied until I killed somebody.

I was lookin' at a group of kids fighting each other when my phone rang again. I ran into the house, grabbed it, and walked back outside.

"Hello!" I said, hoping it was Milli. I missed him already.

"Can Renee talk on the phone?"

"Why you keep callin' my house?" I sighed.

"I keep gettin' the number mixed up. I'm sorry."

"How come I don't believe you?"

Silence.

"What's your name?" I continued.

"Rhianna." I laugh, knowing she's lying. "Are you busy, Ginger?" I thought it was weird that she knew my name, but figured if she caught my voice mail, she could've gotten it from there.

"So, now you wanna talk to me instead of Renee?"

"Yes."

"And what do you want to talk to me about?"

"I wanted to tell you that I heard my mommy say that some man in a red car is gonna set your friend Nicky up."

My heart drops. "Fuck you talkin' 'bout, set her up?"

"My mommy be playin' Spades wit' her friends, and I heard them say that yesterday."

"Who's your mother?" I stand up. "'Cause if you knew me, you wouldn't be pullin' no bullshit like this!"

Click.

"Hello! Hello!" I screamed into the handset.

"Who you yellin' at now, girl?" Nicky asked, walking up to me. She sat on the step beside me, and her cousin Stevie sat a few steps down from us, singing along to the music in my house.

I put the phone down, tryin' to decide if I should tell her about the call or not.

"Ain't nobody, girl. They must've h—had the wrong number, I stutter.

Nicky was wearing a cute green Gucci tank top and a pair of Bulgari shades. "Here's the money I borrowed from you last week," Nicky said, handing me my cash. She would probably borrow it back before the week was out.

Stevie looked at the money Nicky handed me, and I saw a twinge of jealousy in her eyes. She gave me a lot of twenties, but it was cool. I tucked all three grand in my pocket.

The moment I sat down, I saw an unmarked police car pull up. He might as well have driven a marked car, because we'd seen Officer Harvey Chance so many times 'round here, we could smell him miles away.

"How are you doing this evening, ladies?" he said as he approached us. He wore a pair of black designer slacks and a black shirt. His black-and-grey Fendi glasses sat comfortably on the bridge of his nose. Although he irritated the fuck out of me, he was very attractive.

"Ms. Spellman, have you heard anything about Leona Clairmont?"

"I already told y'all I ain't hear shit and don't know shit. She was my friend. Why wouldn't I tell y'all if I knew somethin'?"

I saw a few people lookin' at me talkin' to him, and hated that this was the main reason my neighborhood wanted me gone. With the cops comin' around all the time askin' me questions, it made it hard to sell drugs, and customers were going to other blocks.

"We don't know, but it seems unnatural that she'd disappear off the face of the earth without anybody knowing anything. You were the last person she called, and she hasn't been seen or heard from since."

"Well, like I told y'all before, I was out of town when she called me, and y'all already checked the cell records."

He looked at me, Nicky, and then Stevie. "Well, I'll be in touch again," he said, walking toward his car.

Sometimes I think he asked me the same questions just to see me go the fuck off. A few of my neighbors shook their heads at me and walked in the house. I thought it was kinda funny that they were mad at me because they couldn't do illegal shit because of the cops. I mean really—get a fuckin' job!

When Officer Chance got in his car and waved, I threw up my middle finger.

"You talk to Milli about the fight yet?" Nicky asked, looking at the cop go out of sight.

"Yeah, but that window shit got me fucked up now."

Nicky stood up, dusted the dirt off her ass, and looked in my front window at the burn on the floor. She sat back down and said, "I don't see how you stay around here. Unless they find Leona, shit not gonna go away."

"So maybe they'll find her."

"Yeah, right." She laughed, looking at Stevie.

That hurt. I wanted nothin' more than to see my friend's face.

"I mean really, Ginger, what's so good about Kentland anyway? Why not just move?"

"It's the principle, plus, I ain't do shit to move."

"I heard some bitches up the street say they gonna step to you again, Ginger," Stevie added with a smirk on her face. "You don't want 'em fuckin' wit' your car next."

"Who said that shit?"

"I ain't gettin' in it. I'm just lettin' you know 'cause we cool."

I was thinking, *Why even say something?*

When Crystal spotted her mother at my house and ran up to us, a rack of kids followed. The moment they got in my space, I could smell the sweat and dirt from their skin and wanted to throw up.

"Ma, can I have five dooooolllllaaaas?" Crystal asked, dragging her words.

"What you 'bout to buy?"

"A hot sausage and some nacho cheese sunflower seeds."

"Bring me some seeds back too," Stevie said, reaching into her pocket, just like she did whenever she pretended to have money. When her hands came out empty, she patted her pockets as if some would magically appear. "You got any money on you, Nicky? I'll give it back to you when I get my check on the first."

"I ain't got shit but a C-note. I just gave Ginger all my money," she said, looking at me.

No, bitch, you just gave me all my money, I thought.

"Please, Miss Ginger!" Crystal whined, the other kids chiming in too.

I started to tell them broke-ass bitches to get the fuck off my step; instead, I dug in my pockets and pulled out twenty dollars. I handed the bill to Crystal and said, "Buy everybody somethin'."

She snatched the money out of my hands and ran. Do you know this nasty bitch ain't even say thank you, and her mother didn't make her either?

"She said buy us all somethin'," one of the boys reminded Crystal as they ran down the street. "It ain't just for you."

"You bring the jay?" I asked, shaking my head at the foolishness.

"Naw, a friend of mine on his way to see me. He usually got smoke too."

"I thought you had one rolled up already."

"I did, but somebody decided to help themselves to my shit," she said, looking at Stevie and rolling her eyes.

"Shit, you was takin' all day, so I fired up."

"Fuck that shit, Stevie! I was lookin' forward to blazin'. Now you got us out here on a natural."

"I told you I got money on the next pack," she lied. She never had money on shit.

"You ain't even have money to give your kids," Nicky said, saying what I was thinking.

My attention was briefly taken off her and put on the group of girls who walked by my house. They hung with Trixy.

"Is it hot in there?" one of the girls said.

"Bitch, what you say?" I yelled, standing up.

"Take that shit down the street," Nicky jumped in. "Y'all don't want to see Ginger go off."

They all looked at me, laughed, and walked away. I was contemplating running up to them, but my phone rang. I didn't want to answer. That girl had me shook. But what if it was, Milli?

"Hello."

"Is Ginger Spellman available?"

"Bitch, you called my house. Who the fuck is this?"

"Ms. Spellman, this is Lucy Cunningham from the office of Child Protective Services. Is now a bad time?"

I stood up straight, threw on my professional voice, and said, "Oh . . . uh . . . no. I thought you were somebody playin' on my phone."

"I see. Well, can you turn the music down in the background a little? I can barely hear you."

I rushed inside the house, turned the music down, and stood inside at the front of the glass door.

"That's better," she said. "I'm calling about Denise Knox. Is she your daughter?"

"Yes, ma'am."

"Well, I'm calling to tell you that we have detected crack cocaine in her system."

"Fuck you talkin' 'bout!"

"Like I said, crack is in the child's system. We tested her because she was exhibiting behavior befitting a child who has been exposed to drugs. She wets the bed frequently, her behavior is irrational—"

"She's a child!" I interrupted.

"Ma'am, we've seen enough children to know the symptoms, therefore, we have scheduled an appointment with you on Monday of next week."

"Ma'am, there's been a mistake. I don't even know anybody on crack."

"We'll see about that when we meet you. You'll also have to submit to testing yourself."

There was no use reasoning with this bitch, so I said, "Okay, but where is she right now? I been callin' all over, but nobody seems to know nothin'."

"I'll get to that in a minute, ma'am." She paused. "Now . . . we need you to bring us proof of employment when you come, so that we can make an evaluation on Denise's placement, that is, in the event things work out for you in criminal court. You are facing very serious charges."

This bitch made my blood boil. "I got all that, but can you tell me where they have my baby?"

"She's with—" She paused and I heard the sound of papers shuffling in the background. "Let's see . . . she's at Terrod Knox's cousin's house. Her name is Tracey Knox. Terrod is the child's father, right?"

"Yeah. When did she get there?" I asked, confused. "And why couldn't she stay with my mother like I asked?"

"Because your mother works two jobs and is unable to care for her. The only other alternative is foster care, and I know you don't want that. So she was sent to Tracey's house about an hour ago."

Milli probably didn't know where she was when I spoke to him earlier. I was just happy she was with family, even if it was Tracey.

"Now, if everything is in order after my evaluation, she can be back in your custody. Bring the documentation I asked for and work things out in court."

"Okay. I should be able to do that."

"How are you supporting yourself?"

"I have a job."

"Well, I need verification from your employer. You must understand, Ms. Spellman, the kind of violence you exhibited in front of those children at the daycare center was very serious. It's a wonder you're not still in jail. The child care provider could have died."

"That dumb bitch Quita hit my baby!" I blurted out, causing Nicky and Stevie to look back at me. "I don't play that shit!"

Silence.

"Ms. Spellman, I'm going to also recommend that you attend anger management classes. Now, I hope you have a nice day, because the woman whose throat you cut probably won't."

I threw the phone into the wall, but it didn't break.

I was just puttin' my thoughts together when I saw a red Acura pull up in front of my house.

Nicky smiled at the driver and trotted down the steps toward him.

Was that the car Rhianna was talkin' about on the phone? I pulled open my door, bolted down the steps, and yelled, "Nicky, wait!"

Milli

"What is you doin', nigga? You put the bakin' soda in first, then the coke! That shit you makin' don't even look right," Milli told his uncle, Kettle.

At forty-six years old, Kettle gave the finest young nigga a run for his money in the looks department. He kept his body muscular and lean, and his dress game couldn't be fucked with.

"I got this shit, Milli. Relax!" he said, looking over at him with a slight frown. His muscles were pouring out of the white T-shirt he wore. "You loud as shit. If somebody was in your hallway, they could hear your bitch ass. Don't get mad at me because that shawty makin' shit hot 'round Kentland."

"Fuck her."

He laughed and said, "You wildin' out, nephew."

They both laughed. Milli grabbed a beer from his refrigerator and said, "Unc, I don't know what to do wit' them peoples. Niggas 'round the way want her gone."

"So move her."

"She ain't tryin' to. She so busy worried 'bout what the fuck I'm doin'."

"Then cut her off."

"I might have to."

"She remember yet?"

"Naw. But wit' the cops bein' there every day, niggas can't pump the way they used to. And it's just a matter of time before she remembers, too. The doctors said her memory lapse is temporary."

When Milli's phone rang, he stepped to the side and answered.

"We did what you asked us to do," said the girl who threw the bottle in Ginger's window. "And Trixy stepped to her, but Ginger whipped her ass. And the cops been around again today."

Milli shook his head.

"You want us to do anything else?"

"Naw . . . let me stew on some shit for a minute. I'ma get my man to drop that money off for y'all too."

When he hung up with her, he walked back over to Kettle. "Something's gonna have to give 'round Kentland. I might have to do somethin' to Nicky I ain't want to."

Milli's drug business took care of everybody in the family. If he couldn't pump, everybody suffered.

They were still talking when Tracey Knox came home with Milli's daughter, Denise. Tracey's beautiful butter-colored skin, brown hair, and green eyes lit up the room. She stayed dipped in the finest fashions, including the fifteen hundred dollar Gucci sweat suit she was sporting at the moment and the four hundred dollar Kate Spade diaper bag which swung from her arm.

The moment Denise saw her father, her face lit up and she made her way for the kitchen.

"Ay, keep her outta here. We cookin'!" he yelled, his eyebrows pulling closely together. "The peoples from CPS already said she got that shit in her system."

Tracey dropped her four hundred dollar Kate Spade diaper bag on the floor by the kitchen entrance and caught Denise before she reached the stove.

Dressed in a cute red shirt with diamond-studded hearts and a jean skirt, Denise was just as pretty as her mother. Milli scooped Denise up into his strong arms and landed a few kisses on her face.

"Why you bein' bad as shit? Tracey told me you slapped her today."

"She told me she was my new mommy." She pointed. "And I got a mommy already."

"Oh, really," he said, giving Tracey an evil glare. Focusing back on Denise, he said, "Daddy got you a new doll. Go play wit' it. It's in your room."

When she was gone, he stepped up to his wife and said, "What the fuck you doin'? Why would you tell her some shit like that?"

"'Cause . . . I was thinkin' maybe we can raise her. That way you don't gotta take no more of Ginger's shit."

Milli sat on the sofa and Tracey said, "Baby, I know you don't wanna talk about this, but do you think the court's gonna let us keep Denise? Since Ginger actin' up again?"

"Why you always gotta ruin shit?"

"I'm not tryin' to. I just don't want you to be stressed no more."

"Fuck that. It ain't all the way right you tryin' to fuck my daughter's head up with your bullshit."

"But I'm your wife, and you don't owe Ginger shit! What's keepin' you connected to her?" she cried. "I dealt with the fact that you slept with her and got her pregnant days after we broke up, knowing we would be back together," she said, getting on her knees in front of him as he remained seated on the couch. "But I'm tired of her callin' you over there every five minutes, claiming it's about the baby. So if Denise stay wit' us, you won't have to worry."

"You mean you won't have to worry," he said, pushing her out of his way, knocking her to the floor. "Maybe if your pussy wasn't so rotten, you could have a kid of your own . . . 'cause we both know that's what this shit's really about."

"I'm sorry . . . I just—"

"You just what? The only thing you doin' 'round here is oversteppin' your boundaries. Be glad I'm wit' you and drop this shit."

Tracey backed away and sat on the sofa. She had no idea that Milli, whom she'd been married to for six years, had been with Ginger the same amount of time.

"Now, get the fuck outta my face. I gotta holla at Unc."

While she walked sadly into their bedroom, Milli walked into the kitchen with a smirk on his face.

Kettle looked at him and said, "You playin' shit real tight, nephew." He whispered, "You betta be careful."

"I been playin' shit tight forever. Tracey ain't gonna do shit but what I say," Milli said arrogantly. "And if she was gonna leave, she'd be gone by now."

"You don't think that shit gonna catch up wit' you sooner or later?"

"Naw."

Kettle laughed and Milli said, "What's funny?"

"Nephew, if you wanna be like your father, then be like your father."

"Fuck you talkin' 'bout now?"

"You don't think I see how you been carryin' shit since he was murdered? The only difference 'tween you and him is that he told his bitches 'bout each other straight up. You went too far wit' that last situation with Ginger, and it don't look like it's gonna end too good. That's why you in the shit you in now."

"That's where you wrong. My father made a mistake. Had he kept shit on a need to know basis, he'd still be alive today."

Kettle looked at Milli and felt sorry for him. He knew he adopted that same bullshit his baby brother did when he was playing females. He called it his CRAWL Theory: If a bitch was not willin' to give away her Credit, Respect, Ass, Wealth, and Life, she wasn't worth it.

Milli's father, Julius, lost his life by adopting that theory. On a hot summer day in June, his main bitch, Courtney, got tired of the other women and shot him in the face, along with herself and their two-year-old twin boys.

"Son, you got Ginger thinkin' Tracey's your cousin when she's your wife, and your wife thinkin' Ginger's your baby's mother instead of your girlfriend. You treadin' on dangerous ground."

"This why a nigga like you don't get me." He paused. "You been married to Pearl's old ass forever. You think they don't know I got somebody else on the side?" He smirked. "Fuck yeah, they do. They just don't wanna know the details, and it ain't my business to give it to 'em."

Kettle laughed and said, "You got it, nephew."

"I know I got it."

Kettle hesitated and then said, "Question, How you think shit gonna go down wit' Ginger?"

"I don't know and I don't give a fuck," he said cockily. "'Cause when this shit is all said and done, I won't care if I ever see them peoples again. Don't get me wrong, the pussy was fire, but at the end of the day, she more problems than she's worth."

What Milli didn't know was that while he spoke with his uncle in the kitchen, the Kate Spade bag lying on the floor in the doorway had the baby monitor Tracey used to keep an ear on Denise inside. It was turned on, and the other monitor was in her hand.

Gerron

Most of my shit was already packed, so movin' wasn't gonna be a problem. And I was so ready to get the fuck outta Kentland.

"I can't believe you doin' this, man! Kentland all you know, nigga," Bodie said, lookin' up at me from the worn-out beige sofa in my living room. At one point people thought we were brothers. We even had the same build, but lately he was getting thinner and it wasn't quite the same. "We ain't even hit the nigga Milli yet!"

"I already told you I'm not fuckin' wit' it. Plus, shit too hot 'round here."

"You sure it ain't got somethin' to do wit' you wantin' to fuck shawty?"

"Fuck is you talkin' 'bout?" I paused. "I might bullshit wit' her here and there, but that's it." As I was sealing the boxes in my living room, the handle of my gun pressed against my stomach, and I placed it on the glass table.

Bodie looked at it and said, "If you 'bout to leave, moe, we might as well hit the nigga. You passin' up on sure bread."

"Nigga, you ain't even hearin' me. I'm not fuckin' wit' it."

Truthfully, I didn't give a fuck if we hit Milli or not, but Bodie was a hothead, and didn't believe in just robbin' niggas and goin' on his merry fuckin' way. His trigger was loose, he ain't care, and I ain't want Ginger to get hurt.

"I'm movin' on his ass. Fuck that," he said, tryin' to test my patience.

"You do what you gotta do. You hot anyway, and I'm outta here."

Bodie separated seeds from the weed on the table with a matchbook. "I ain't hot, nigga! I'm just smart enough not to pass up on a payday."

"Smart?" I smirked. "You almost got us nicked up twice tellin' folks who we hittin' up. Had it not been for main man gettin' murdered before he found us, shit coulda got crazy."

Bodie rolled the rest of the jay and lit fire to it. When it was hard enough, he allowed the lighter to run over the tip until it turned orange. When he thought I wasn't lookin', he smirked, and I caught him out the corner of my eye. I was used to that shit, though. Ever since he started lacin' his weed with crack, I ain't trust him.

We had been robbin' niggas together for 'bout two years. Before him, I kept my work outside of Maryland. But when I got wit' Bodie, money started rollin' in 'cause he always knew when and where major drops was bein' made. Eventually I found out that he had an inside track. Turns out we was robbin' his twin brother Marvel's people, and he'd been lookin' for us both since.

"Where you movin'?" Bodie asked. "You can at least tell me that."

"Not sure, man. You just take it easy. You might not see thirty if you don't."

"You know somebody could think you was makin' a threat," he said, pullin' on the weed. "Keep tellin' a nigga he might not see thirty and shit. You might not live to move tonight."

I looked at him and said, "You trippin' hard now. Maybe you should put that shit down."

"Nigga, I'm just fuckin' wit' you! You gettin' all serious and shit. Relax!"

I was leavin' for Vegas on the first flight in the a.m. 'cause for what I did for a livin', I needed to be 'round niggas wit' lots of cash on 'em at all times. And I couldn't think of a betta place.

"So what 'bout your moms?" Bodie continued. "You know she gonna be fucked up 'bout you movin'."

I stared out in front of me for a second 'cause he was right. As grimy as this nigga was, when it came to my moms, he was different. He opened doors for her, said "yes, ma'am" this and "yes, ma'am" that. I think he took to her 'cause his mother had been mentally retarded all of her life. She could barely tie her own shoes without help and got pregnant while in the custody of a mental hospital. Her attorneys won her ten million dollars in a lawsuit, and when her twin sons Bodie and Marvel turned eighteen, they spent every last dime of their share—Bodie on gettin' high, and Marvel on a couple keys from this nigga in Brooklyn. When they couldn't get any more of her money, they both abandoned her.

"She know what it is, and I'ma be here every other week to check on her."

"I swear this movin' shit is dumb! But you do what you gotta do."

He was still runnin' his mouth when I heard commotion outside. I rushed to the window to see Ginger yellin' in a nigga's face, wit' Nicky and Stevie tryin' to pull her away.

"Fuck is wit' that chick?" Bodie asked. "I ain't neva seen a bitch that fuckin' feisty."

I could tell shit wasn't gonna end right. No sooner than I thought that did I see this bamma-ass nigga drop her.

"Oh shit!" Bodie laughed. "He dropped her bitch ass!"

"This nigga can't be for real," I said to myself. I rather a nigga pop a bitch than to hit her in the face.

I moved toward the door, and Bodie said, "I know you not 'bout to get in that shit, young! She ain't your fuckin' problem."

I paid him no attention as I rushed into the street. I caught dude just before he hit Ginger again. I pushed his bamma ass off her, knockin' him to the ground. He tried to get back up, and I dropped him with a left.

"Fuck wrong wit' you, cuz?" he yelled, jumpin' back up. He rubbed his jaw. I drew blood.

Outta nowhere, the broad Stevie caught wheels and took off runnin', leavin' her cousin Nicky and Ginger behind.

"Fuck wrong wit' me? How you look hittin' a bitch in the face? What kinda bamma-ass shit is that, nigga?"

He laughed and said, "Look at this old chival-rous-ass muthafucka!" Then he paused and said, "You must be sick for puttin' your hands on me."

I was thinkin' of droppin' him again, until he pulled his piece on me. I reached for mine, but remembered it was on the table in my house.

"You got it, young. Ain't no beef here," I said, raisin' my hands.

Ginger got up off the ground and stood behind me. Her mouth was bleedin', and I could tell she was tryin' not to look scared. I hated seein' females hurt.

"You got it, moe. Ain't no need in carryin' shit like that. Just go 'bout your business, and we gonna go 'bout ours," I told him.

"Oh, you makin' the rules now?" His eyes were rollin' around in his head, and I could tell he was tryin' to amp himself up.

"I ain't sayin' that," I said calmly. "I'm sayin' you got it, moe."

"Fuck that shit! What you holdin', nigga? You know what time it is."

"Hold up. You 'bout to rob me?" I asked, frownin'.

"Fuck you think? Since you wanna play hero, empty your pockets—quick!"

"Young, I ain't 'bout to give you no money."

I looked at his arm and saw a tattoo with the name Treasure on it. His name rings bells. We both stick-up niggas, so I know this can get ugly if I don't give him what he wants.

"You gonna empty your pockets on your own," he said, cocking his gun, "or do you want me to do it after you drop?" The streets were empty, but I knew they were watchin'.

"Fuck . . ."

"Nigga, I'm not fuckin' playin' 'round wit' you! Put that shit on the hood 'fore I unload out here!" he screamed. "Don't make the next thing you hear be the clap of my gun. All y'all!" he said, addressing the girls. "On the hood!"

Instead of puttin' the shit on the hood, I dropped my money on the ground.

"So you bein' funny huh?" he said.

"Naw, whether it's on the ground or on the hood, it's still yours."

He laughed and said, "Kick that shit over here."

I did, but it only moved a foot.

"You should've stayed your ass inside, man. Now you a few bills short." He smirked again like he just came up. This nigga was a clown.

"It's all 'bout you, homie," I told him slyly.

"Yeah, I know, Chauncey!" He laughed at his own joke. "Why y'all bitches ain't give it up yet? Put the shit on the hood, and don't try to be slick either."

"We s'pose to be friends," Nicky said.

"Don't make me ask you again," he told her.

Nicky put her money on the ground, and I saw her face redden. She looked like she was 'bout to cry.

Ginger must've grew balls, 'cause she said, "I can't believe you really 'bout to rob us."

"Bitch, give me that bracelet too," he said, pointing the barrel at her arm.

"No . . . I can't . . . I can't . . ."

He fired a bullet next to where we stood.

"Ay, Ginger, put the shit on the hood," I told her before she got us killed. If this nigga's hand shook any more, we was gonna have extra holes in our faces.

She looked at me and reluctantly dropped the money and her bracelet on the hood. I saw the stack she was carryin' and knew he came up after all. He stuffed the money in his pockets and was just about to take my shit when I heard *BOP! BOP! BOP!*

Bullets flew over our heads, and we ducked for cover.

"What the fuck!" I said.

When I looked to see where the bullets were comin' from, I saw Bodie firing at Treasure, who ducked behind his car and fired back. The girls hit the ground too and moved behind me to get out of Dodge. Bullets were flying everywhere. I wanted to run, but I needed Bodie to move a little closer to Treasure to give me cover. Then I saw that Bodie had my gun.

"Y'all a'ight?" I asked, looking at the shootout. "'Cause we gotta make a run for it."

"I'm scared," Nicky said.

"Well, we ain't got time for that shit. When I tell you to move, run toward the back of Ginger's house."

"Okay," they said.

Treasure continued to unload, but the nigga Bodie was relentless and moved closer toward him. The moment Treasure's attention was taken away from us, I grabbed my money off the ground and yelled, "Move!"

Me and Ginger dipped behind the back of her house, and Nicky ran the other way.

"Nicky!" Ginger called out.

"Fuck that bitch," I told her. "Move!"

Bullets continued to whiz through the air, but we finally made it in her backyard. We dipped inside and locked the door.

"Stay down!" I told her.

She did, and a few minutes later, I heard sirens and the shootin' stopped, followed by the sound of slammin' car doors. When I heard Bodie's engine rev up, I knew he was gone wit' my piece. I was gonna definitely have to get up wit' him before I left town that night.

I checked the window and said, "They gone. You a'ight?"

"Yeah, but that nigga got my bracelet! He took my fuckin' shit!" she cried.

"So you not happy you got your life?"

She stood up, wiped the tears off her face, and said, "What the fuck just happen?"

"I'll tell you. You started some shit again; that's what just happened."

She looked surprised and said, "So this my fault?"

"What you expect, shawty? You don't get in a nigga's face unless you ready. You lucky he ain't bust yo' ass."

"Hold up. Who you talkin' to?" she said, walking up to me.

"Yo' ass! You got me in some shit I ain't wanna be in. I was mindin' my fuckin' business when you—"

"When you got in my business!" she said, putting her hand on her chest. "I don't recall askin' your fuckin' ass to come save me. And for your fuckin' information, I would've handled that shit wit' no problem, 'cause I ain't got no problem bustin' my gun too," she said, takin' it out of her purse, which sat on the sofa. It was the new gun she told me Milli bought for her. She put it in her waist, and for some reason, the shit turned me on.

"I hate bitches who act like niggas. You can't want a nigga to protect you if you keep fakin' like you got shit. Which one is it gonna be?"

"Like I said, I could've handled it."

"Anyway, your purse was in here, so that shit was useless!"

"Well, where was your shit, Mr. Braveheart? I don't see you packin' neither. If I'm not mistaken, you was duckin' on the ground just like me."

If another nigga would've heard the way her mouth popped off, he would've walked out.

"You just betta be glad you still breathin'."

She waved her hand and said, "Was that Bodie shootin' at him?"

"I don't know what you talkin' 'bout," I said, noticing the burn on her floor from earlier. This chick stay wit' some bullshit.

"Gerron, I know you saw Bodie shootin'. He came outta your house."

"Look, some shit need to be left alone," I warned her. "For your own good." If Bodie found out she was sayin' his name, she could have problems on her hands.

When her phone rang, she ran into the kitchen and answered. I could tell by the look on her face that somethin' else was up.

Ginger

"I need to know who the fuck you are and I need to know now!"

"I can't tell you. I just wanted to say I'm sorry about what happened."

Click.

When she hung up, I rushed outside, ran halfway up my block, and banged on Shonda's door with a closed fist. I had to know who that little bitch was callin' my house. The door opened, and I walked my uninvited ass inside.

"Shonda," I said softly. Club pictures of her and Trixy were everywhere. "Shonda, we gotta talk," I whispered.

She didn't answer, but I could sense somebody was inside. When I turned the corner leading to her bedroom, I heard a panting and started to go back, but curiosity got the best of me. I never saw her with a man. Once at her bedroom door, I couldn't believe what I saw through a cracked door. Trixy was layin' on the bed with her legs wide open, while Shonda ate her pussy.

I laughed to myself, thinkin' how she had the nerve to come at me about Milli when she was a carpetmuncher. I wanted so bad to make myself known, but I knew that little tidbit of information would come in handy later.

Feelin' slightly better about my newfound secret, I was still dissatisfied about not knowing who this little girl was who decided to make my life miserable.

When I walked back into my house, Gerron was still there, and he had helped himself to a glass of my Bacardi.

"You want some?" he asked, holding the cup out. I took it from him and swallowed it all.

"Everything cool, shawty?"

"Not really," I said, lookin' into his sexy sleepy eyes. I turned away quick.

"Was that your peoples on the phone? Did she get away okay?"

"Oh . . . no. That wasn't her," I said, remembering the shootout. Too much shit was happening for me to keep up. "Let me call to see if she okay."

My call went straight to voice mail, and I was worried.

"She ain't answer," I told him, hoping he'd have an answer.

"Damn," he said, wiping his hand over his face. The sun from my window bounced off of his caramel-colored skin. For whatever reason, I was horny and knew he had to go. I could feel the seat of my panties getting slick. "Your peoples fine. You just gotta give her a minute to hit you up."

Although I was glad Gerron was there for me, it would've been nice to have Milli by my side. He was nowhere to be found and hadn't called back since our argument.

I decided to call him and give him more bad news, until Gerron said, "Well, let me bounce. I got some shit to do tonight. I'll be over there for a minute if you need me. And then I'm movin' . . . I mean . . . leavin' town."

"You movin'?" I said, more anxiously than I wanted.

He smiled and said, "Yeah, why? You upset or somethin'?"

"No . . . uh, naw. You do what you gotta do. I just didn't know."

"How would you? You don't talk to me."

"You mean *you* don't talk to me."

Silence.

"Gerron, I know you don't wanna talk about this shit, but I gotta know. Are you sure you tellin' me everything you know 'bout the night I fell? Did you hear anything else from anybody?"

"I ain't answering that shit no more. I already told you I didn't."

"Did Milli do somethin'?"

"You don't trust your man?"

"I do . . . I just—"

"Well, if you do, just drop it!" he said, walking toward my back door.

I rolled my eyes and walked with him. I didn't want him to leave, but he was on his way out—until he saw the food on the stove.

"Damn, that's all you?"

"If you askin' did I cook, the answer is yes."

"Well, it look good, but it probably taste like shit," he joked.

"I think you don't know shit about me. I got a baby and a man to cook for, and both of them like to eat, which means I can burn."

"That don't mean shit but you know how to turn a stove on."

"You wanna taste it?"

"I can."

"What do I get if it's as good as I know it will be?"

"Whatever you want," he said, lookin' into my eyes.

I cleared my throat and said, "You know what I wanna know."

"Bye," he said, moving for the door.

"Sit down, boy. I'm just fuckin' wit' you." I smiled. "Let me show you why I'm wifey material. Now, when I'm done wit' you, I don't want you tryin' to leave your girl, 'cause I'm taken."

"You ain't tellin' me shit I don't already know. Plus, I ain't got no bitch—"

I cut him an evil look 'cause I was sick of him callin' females bitches.

"I mean I ain't got no girl. You already know that shit."

"You may not have a girl, but I be seein' all them cluckers at your house. Don't forget we cool, so there ain't no reason to lie to me."

"I'm single, and I like it like that."

When he said that, I felt some kinda way.

He sat down at my table and said, "You gonna eat wit' me, right?"

Since I hadn't had anything all day, I made a plate and joined him. I wasn't worryin' about Milli comin' over early, 'cause he never came before eight o'clock at night, and it was only three.

"I can tell you was mad at me, but I appreciate you helpin' me earlier, I know a lot of people would not have done that shit," I said, drinkin' my juice and pickin' wit' my food.

"Yeah . . . me included. I don't know what came over me."

"Well, why did you help me then?" I said with an attitude.

"'Cause he hit you, and ain't no dude s'pose to be hittin' no female." I smiled. "How's your face?"

"It's cool. Just hurts a little," I said, wipin' the small scar I had almost forgotten about.

I heard raindrops rattlin' against the kitchen window. The window above the stove was partially open, and a gust of wind blew in and knocked a banana- shaped calendar magnet from the fridge onto the floor. I closed all the windows in my house. Then I realized I left the window down in my car.

"I'll be right back," I said, grabbin' my car keys from the table. "I left my car windows open."

"You want me to close 'em for you?"

"No, just give me a sec." I didn't need people seein' him in my car. It was bad enough he was in my house.

I snatched the door open and ran out my back door. A purple haze hovered over my small house, and thunderstorms lit the sky. The moment I hit the last step, one of the black heels I was wearin' got stuck in the dirt and caused me to fall flat on my face on the damp grass.

As I lifted myself off the ground, I heard someone say, "Damn, bitch! You stay fallin'!

What, you can't hold that big-ass head up?"
Trixy laughed.

"She stay gettin' shit in her face!" added Shonda.

When I stood up to see who was talkin' to me,
I saw Trixy and Shonda holdin' a red umbrella,
staring at me over my fence.

"You should know 'bout shit in faces, seein' as
though you and Shonda stay eatin' each other's
pussies."

The smile on her face was wiped clean, and
both of them hustled up the street. I was so
ready to let them know that I was on to their
little secret that I wasted a chance to ask Shonda
about that mysterious little girl who kept calling.

I spat out a few strands of grass, dusted my
clothes off, and ran to my car. Then I jumped
inside my Benz and rolled up my car windows.
I could see the open kitchen window from my
car and smiled when I saw Gerron stuffin' his
face. Then it dawned on me: If Milli for whatever
reason came home early, I would be busted.

I decided to find out where he was, so I turned
on my car, and the engine purred like a kitten.
Then I picked up the phone from the cradle and
dialed his number.

When I heard his voice, my heart sank. "Fuck
you want, Ginger?"

"Baby, can we talk? I know why you mad at me, and I know that's my fault," I said, hitting the vanilla-scented tree dangling from my mirror. "I wasn't tryin' to make you think I didn't trust you. It's just that so much shit has been happenin'—"

"Fuck this shit, Ginger. It's over."

Click.

No! It can't be over! I called him back a few times and he didn't answer. Tears snuck up on me and ran down my face. I punched my steering wheel over and over until my knuckles were sore. I lost my boyfriend, and I didn't know what to do.

I needed to be alone and decided to get rid of Gerron, so I went back to my house. Nicky approached me in my backyard. Although the rain pounded on both of us, I could still see she was angry.

"Nicky, what happened to you?" I asked, examining her body. "Are you a'ight?"

She wiped the water from her eyes and said, "You knew, didn't you? You knew that shit was gonna happen today. That's why you were actin' funny."

"Nick, let's go inside and talk about it. It's rainin' hard as shit out here."

"Did you know?"

"No—I mean yes . . . I mean, not really . . ."

"Which one is it?" she said, smoothing the wet hair from her face. "I thought we was s'pose to be friends."

"This is gonna be fucked up, but I had an idea he was gonna do somethin'. I just ain't know what. This little girl kept callin' my house and told me. I don't know who she is though."

She rolled her eyes and said, "Ginger, why you keep lyin'?"

"I'm not lyin!? I'm tellin' you all I know. Some girl called my house askin' for Shonda's daughter, Renee. She said she overheard that someone was gonna set you up."

"I don't believe you."

"Have you forgotten that I put my life on the line, lost my bracelet, and my money?"

When she looked into my back window and saw Gerron fixin' himself another unauthorized plate of food, she said, "So you fuck wit' him now?"

"You know it ain't even like that, so don't even start no shit."

When Bodie walked up on us out of nowhere, we both jumped.

"I ain't mean to fuck y'all up," he said. "Is Gerron here? I got somethin' for him."

Whenever he was in my presence, he made me nervous. "Yeah, he inside."

"You mind if I holla at him for a second?"

Since I could see them from where I stood, I said, "Go 'head."

He looked around a few times and dipped inside. The slamming of my screen door rang a few seconds before stopping.

"Wow, you got the whole crew over here now, huh?" she laughed. "First Gerron and now Bodie?"

"Nick, you my friend, but I'm startin' to get real tired of your shit."

"I bet you are." She smirked. "So tell me somethin', Ginger. How you know they ain't involved? I do recall Gerron grabbin' his money off the ground."

"I don't know 'bout Bodie, but Gerron ain't have shit to do with it.

"Please! Even Stevie saw his ass scoop his money up and run. She the one who put me onto this shit."

"Stevie?" I laughed. "You comin' at me wit' Stevie when she left your ass high and dry?"

"Whatever. All I wanna know is why the robber ain't grab Gerron's money when it was on the ground. Why he wait 'til we emptied our pockets and take our shit? Come on, Ginger. Everybody 'round here know he robs people. And if you not careful, he gonna do the same shit to you."

"Get out my backyard, Nicky."

She looked at me like she was gonna challenge me, and for the first time ever, I thought about pullin' my gun on my friend.

"Don't call me, and I won't call you," she said, lookin' behind me at Gerron standin' in the doorway.

She walked out of my backyard, and Bodie walked out the back door.

"I appreciate it, sexy," Bodie said. I ignored him.

"What he want?" I watched Bodie hop over my fence. "I never did trust his ass."

"He gave me my piece back. And stay away from him, Ginger, 'cause I don't all the way trust him either."

Gerron

When we walked into the house, her phone rang again and she answered it. I wanted her to ignore that shit, because it seemed like every time she picked up the phone, she had bad news.

"Hello?" She exhaled, floppin' on the sofa.

She looked frightened.

Here comes the bullshit.

I walked into the kitchen and poured us another drink.

"Mr. Clairmont, I still haven't heard anything about Leona. I really am sorry." She paused, taking the drink from me. She took a few modest sips before swallowing it all. "Trust me, if I hear anything, you'll be the first person I call."

When she hung up the phone, I sat next to her, and she started cryin'.

"You a'ight?" I asked.

"I don't understand why all the shit is happenin' to me! Today has to be the worst day of my life outside of the day when they took my baby. And then . . ." She sobbed harder. "And then Milli dumped me!"

"That nigga ain't gonna leave you. He just talkin' shit right now."

"How you know?"

"If he a real nigga, he'd be a fool to let you go over some dumb shit. Y'all been together too long."

"I wish I believed you, but he's been actin' different lately. And now Mr. Clairmont askin' me 'bout where his daughter is again, and me and Nicky beefin' over some bullshit." She cried harder. "I don't know what to do!"

"Shit gonna be a'ight, Ginger. You gotta take shit easy though. You takin' on too much."

Although I hated seein' females cry, I wasn't the best nigga to console 'em either. I was a gun-totin' dude from Kentland, and all I thought about twenty-four-seven was gettin' paper. But here I was feelin' like there was nothin' more I'd rather do than make her problems go away. I was s'posed to be on my way outta Maryland by now.

"I . . . I need another drink," she said, moving toward the kitchen before her body went limp to the floor and she was crying again.

I put my drink down, lifted her up, and her head fell against my chest. Her body was damp and warm from being caught in the rain. Walkin' her back over to the couch, I tried to place her down, but she gripped me tighter.

"It's gon' be a'ight, Ginger. You gotta be strong like you been," I said real slowly. I tried to place her down again, but she still ain't let me go.

"Hold me," she sobbed. "Just for a little while."

"I got you," I reassured her.

For whatever reason, her vulnerability turned me on. I was so used to shawty cussin' me out that I didn't stop to think that she might have a sensitive side. I tried my best to prevent my dick from gettin' hard, but the shit wasn't workin'. If she stayed in my arms two seconds longer, it was gonna be a wrap.

"Ginger, I ain't tryin' to disrespect you, for real, but if I don't put you down, I ain't gonna be able to help myself."

She looked up into my eyes and said, "Please . . . I don't wanna be alone right now."

It was over. I moved in for a kiss, and she kissed me back. Then I ran my tongue over her lips and gently sucked the bottom. Damn, they tasted so sweet. I think the alcohol had us on ten, and we ain't give a fuck.

"You sure 'bout this?" I asked, because I didn't want a drunk fuck.

When she didn't respond, I slipped my tongue back into her warm mouth. While our lips connected, her tears rubbed against my face. She wasn't cryin' no more.

I tried to place her down again, but this time she pulled me toward her. I threw the sofa pillows on the floor and fell between her warm legs. The handles of our guns clanked each other, and we took them out, placin' them on the floor next to the couch. Then I remembered I was in this dude's house. What if he came in here and shit got outta hand? I'd be forced to kill him when I was dead wrong.

"I'ma have to take a rain check, sweetheart," I said, lifting up.

Her eyes look sad, and she said, "So you gonna leave me like this?"

"You know I want you, but if your folks come in here, I'ma have to bust his ass."

"I told you we not together no more," she said, liftin' her shirt, freeing her titties. "And I want you to make love to me."

"So just like that, it's over?" I ain't never ask a bitch these many questions when offered the pussy, but there was somethin' 'bout Ginger I wanted, and I didn't want to start something we wouldn't finish.

"Right now, I don't even give a fuck about Milli. So what we gonna do?"

I smiled and softly sucked her nipples, one and then the other. She grabbed my head and pulled me closer to her body. I could smell her perfume.

We were all over each other, and then she disconnected.

"Stop," she said under her breath.

This chick just gave me some bullshit 'bout not givin' a fuck, and now she want me to stop? I acted like I ain't even hear that shit.

"Stop, Gerron . . . please."

I got up and put my gun in my waistband.

She adjusted her shirt and folded her hands over her breasts. "I shouldn't even be doin' this shit."

"Then why are you?"

"'Cause I'm sick of Milli playin' games wit' me! He act like he don't even care."

I stood up and said, "Well, as much as I'd love to console you, I ain't Oprah. I'm 'bout to bounce. I'll get up wit' you when I can."

"So what, you mad now?"

"Shawty, five seconds earlier we was 'bout to fuck, and now we not. You say the nigga Milli dumped your ass, and you got me suckin' all over your titties. Then you tell me to stop. You tell me if you think I'm mad or not."

"Ugggh," she said, frowning. "So what, if a bitch don't fuck you, you carry shit like that?"

"Naw, but if a bitch was 'bout to fuck me and stopped, yeah, that's how I carry it."

I moved toward the door, and she said, "I knew you was a cruddy-ass nigga."

"Call it what you want, but the one thing I don't play is games." I tried to convince my dick to go down and said, "I hope everything works out." Truthfully, I didn't.

My hand was on the doorknob when she said, "I still want you to stay."

I turned around to look at her and said, "Come on, Ginger. You fuckin' me up wit' this bullshit. I'm not 'bout to sit up in your face and pretend we twins when I just finished suckin' your titties. If all this shit ain't happen, it would be cool, 'cause that's how we got down anyway, but all this shit did happen. All I want to do right now is take a cold shower and head up the road."

I opened the back door and stepped into her backyard. I was five seconds from hopping over my fence when she said, "If you stay, it'll be worth your while. I promise."

Ginger

I don't know why, but for some reason, I felt like we connected on a deeper level. Yes, he could be mean, cocky, and straightforward, but at least I knew where he was comin' from.

He walked back toward the couch and sat down. I sat next to him and could smell Dolce & Gabbana cologne.

"I wasn't tryin' to play games. I just feel like a whore," I whispered to him.

"What's wrong wit' bein' a whore?" he joked.

"I'm serious," I said, hittin' his arm.

"Like I said, what we do between us will be between us. Me, myself . . . I love a nasty bitch—" He cleared his throat. "I mean, a chick who knows what she wants in the bedroom."

I heard what he was saying, but something else didn't sit right with me.

"Umm . . . uh, did you or Bodie have somethin' to do with what happened today, with the robbery? I know you . . . you do that kind of shit all the time."

He frowned and said, "You know what? Yeah, it's true, I rob drug dealers for their paper, but I would never turn my gun on somebody I fuck wit'. Plus, how was I involved when the nigga tried to rob me too? Come on, Ginger. You smarter than that."

"You right." I smiled, placin' his gun back on the floor. "I am."

He pulled me to him and said, "Now, get your sexy ass over here and stop worryin' 'bout the bullshit. The longer you make me wait, the badder it's gonna be when I get up in that thang."

I glanced at the door and said, "I can't wait."

He glanced at the door also and said, "That nigga ain't comin' in here, is he?"

"Naw, he said it's over, so let it be over."

He got serious with me and said, "G, I'm 'bout to move, so after we do what we do, you ain't gotta worry 'bout seein' me no more, and the nigga Milli won't ever know what happened if y'all get back together. So let's take care of each other right now and worry 'bout all that other shit later. Cool?"

No longer waitin' for my confirmation, he removed my shoes and started massagin' my feet. His hands felt warm, and his strokes were long. I've had massages before, but this took the cake. Who knew a nigga who was probably a murderer could be so compassionate? Unable to resist, I dropped my head back and let him do his thing.

"Hmmmm," I exhaled.

During the entire time Milli and I had been together, he never touched any part of my body outside of my breasts, ass, and pussy. So, I was caught off by Gerron's touch and was tempted to drift off into an erotic sleep—until he placed three of my toes into his warm mouth, his wet tongue circling each of them. At first it tickled, and I wasn't sure if I'd be able to take it, but then he applied a little pressure with his strokes. Ummm, it was just right.

"Damn, that shit feels so fuckin' good." My pussy jumped. "You must do this a lot."

"What I tell you 'bout worryin' 'bout bullshit?" He winked and continued his work.

My juices coated my panties, and suddenly I became jealous of the attention my toes were gettin'. I wondered if he could do the same thing to my pussy and if it would feel as good.

"You got some sexy-ass feet," he said, staring into my eyes. "I wonder how you taste."

He looked at me with hunger in his eyes and tugged at the bottom of the jeans I was wearin'. I assisted by raisin' my body up off the couch just a little, droppin' back down when he had both my panties and jeans off. Then he pushed my legs apart and stared into my wetness. I shivered from nervousness. I couldn't believe I was really about to fuck Gerron—my homie, my friend.

"Damn . . . it's prettier than I thought."

"Am I too wet for you?"

"How you sound?" He took one finger and pushed it deeper into my cave. My legs tensed, and he said, "Relax."

I obeyed, and he covered my clit with his warm mouth. As his finger went in and out of me, his tongue circled my clit, and I felt my body shake. If he kept it up, I was gonna cum.

"Ummm . . . and your pussy sweet." He looked at my pussy like he never saw one before, but I guess he'd never seen mine. All the talks we had on the porch at night, and this is what it came to. I guess we both knew it would happen sooner or later.

"I've fucked some chicks in my day, but I ain't never seen a bitch wit' a body as bad as yours."

Pushin' my legs farther apart, he moved in and sucked my clit again, flickerin' his tongue wildly. My body sank into the couch, and he pulled me closer to his mouth.

"Ahhh . . . Gerron . . . I . . . I wanna . . . cum so bad."

I placed my hand on the back of his head. His tongue moved from the tip of my clit to the tip my asshole. Back and forth, back and forth; he was nice and slow. I released my titties from my shirt and sucked them one at a time, something I did when I played with my pussy alone.

"Damn, you look sexy doin' that shit," he complimented, eying my work instead of his own.

"Lick this pussy, baby. Don't stop, mothafucka. You betta work that shit."

With that, he slid two fingers into my slippery wetness, and I maneuvered my waist around it. I no longer cared who he was, and for the first time ever, I would break the rules . . . all of them. If Milli wanted to act like a bitch, FUCK HIM! I was gonna do me too.

As if two fingers weren't enough, he placed three inside me, then four, and then five. Surprisingly enough, my sex-deprived pussy took them all.

I was on the verge of lettin' the rest of my wetness flow over his fingers, until he placed his mouth back on my clit and licked up more of the icing that oozed from my wet cave. His tongue felt like warm water on everything before he even fucked me. I was havin' the best sex of my life.

Gerron

The scent of her pussy was intoxicatin'—some-thin' like an aphrodisiac. Still on my knees, I removed my mouth and felt her legs tremble.

"You okay?" I asked, placin' my hand on her thighs.

"Y . . . yes, you got me feelin' so good." I had played the tongue-flickin' game long enough, and it was time to fuck.

I released myself from my pants, and she sat up and said, "I have to taste-inspect this thing first."

She got on her knees and licked the tip slowly, lookin' up at me with those cat eyes. Staring down at her pretty face ain't do nothin' but get me harder. She licked the shaft up and down, side to side, and left to right. Then she grabbed the side of my legs and pushed her mouth all the way down my dick. Damn! No gag.

"Damn, bitch! You killin' that shit, huh?"

She looked up at me and continued her deep throat skills. Her dick-suckin' skills ain't to be fucked wit'.

"I need to feel that pussy," I said.

She smiled, turned around, and got on all fours. *Oh shit! You can't be serious! Shawty's fuck game can't be this official.* Strokin' my wet dick one more time, I pushed halfway inside her pussy and felt her walls closing in on my joint.

"Damn, bitch! I shoulda been hittin' this shit a long time ago."

I pulled my dick out real quick, spread her wet pussy lips apart, and slammed into that pussy full force. She tensed up, and I pulled her back to me.

"Don't fuckin' move again! You gonna take this shit right here."

"Okay . . . okay," she moaned. "I ain't tryin' to go nowhere, baby. Just keep doin' that shit right there."

"You just keep that ass up in the air like that."

I eased out of her halfway and pushed back into that thang again. I was hard as a block of ice, and I saw her body tense up.

"You know I'm gonna break your back out for makin' me wait so long, right?"

She licked her fingers and smiled. "Tonight, this pussy all yours."

Liftin' her ass cheeks up, I pushed fully into her, and together we worked as smooth as the engine on a Bentley. She wasn't s'posed to feel this fuckin' good.

"Dammmn, girl." I pulled her closer, and she bit down on the bottom of her lip. "You tryin' to make a nigga remember this shit, ain't you?"

She grinned and bucked her hips wildly. Damnmn, she was sexy and thick in all the right places.

"Turn over on your back," I demanded.

When she did, I took her legs and put them straight up in front of me in the air. Then I closed 'em, grabbed her ankles, and banged in and out of that thang. When I felt myself cummin', I let her legs drop over my right shoulder, and decided to murder that pussy.

Smack. Smack. Smack. Smack.

"Damn, Gerron! You fuckin' the shit outta this pussy, ain't you?"

That pussy was makin' all kinds of sounds.

Slurp. Slurp. Slurp. Slurp.

"What you think . . . I was playin'?"

She bucked wilder; her titties were movin' all over the place. She held one in her hand and sucked the nipple again. I loved that shit. She was tryin' to go down as the best bitch I ever fucked in my life.

"Gerron, that's it, baby! Pound that shit! I like it rough! I'ma make you wanna fuck me again before you leave."

"Bet that," I said, biting my bottom lip.

My body shivered, and she said, "Please don't cum yet. I want this shit to last."

I heard her, but there was nothin' else I could do. She was gettin' wetter and wetter, and I was almost there. We gripped each other, and her movements became swifter and wider, while mine went harder and longer. She was rainin' on my dick, and I gripped her ass cheeks apart, dropped my head back, and it was over.

"Awwwww . . . shitttttt!"

"Just five more seconds," she begged. "Please."

I tried to think of everything in the world *but* the bad bitch up under me. But the more she begged and the more she moved, the closer I was to bustin' a nut. And then she said, "I'm cuuuuummmin'! Oh my gawd, I'm cuuuuum-mmin'."

I was cummin' too and pushed into her hard one last time, cummin' all inside her wet pussy. I fell on her warm body, and she was breathin' heavily in my ear.

"You okay?" I asked. "I ain't knock nothin' out the way, did I?"

She laughed and said, "You were great, but I think my pussy will survive." Then she wrapped her arms around me, holdin' me closer, and I felt she didn't want me to leave. We kissed. "We fuck good together."

"You got that shit right," I said.

My phone rang on the floor, and I saw it was Bodie. He was gettin' on my nerves, and it was startin' to make me uneasy.

"Look, I'm 'bout to go," I said, pulling up my pants.

"So you gonna leave me like this?"

Right before I answered, I heard keys jiggle at her door. We both whipped our heads in the direction of the sound and jumped up.

Ginger said, "Oh shit! Milli's here."

Gerron

Today was wild as shit, and I couldn't believe I let Ginger almost get me late. I was supposed to be on the road a long time ago, and if I didn't hurry up, I was gonna miss my fuckin' flight. Fuck was I thinkin' breakin' that chick's back out at her crib?

When I opened my back door, I gripped my weapon 'cause somethin' ain't feel right. Good thing Bodie brought my piece by Ginger's earlier. I had robbed so many niggas, it could be anybody.

Aimed, I walked deeper toward the living room and flipped on the light switch. When the lights came on, I saw someone sitting on my sofa, and I cocked my gun.

"Relax, nigga. It's just me," he said, squinting his eyes. "I was just takin' a nap until you got here. What time is it anyway?"

"Nigga, is you trippin'? Fuck you doin' at my crib?"

"I been here since I left that bitch's house earlier," he said, lighting a cigarette. "You can't tell me you ain't fuck that bitch now. You paid for that pussy, didn't you, playa?" he laughed.

"Bodie, what I do wit' my dick is my business." I tucked my gun into my waist. "You still ain't answer my question. Fuck you doin' at my house?"

"Shit was too hot back at my place . . . you know . . . after the shootout. So I stayed here."

"The shit happened 'round here. If anything, shit hot here."

"Relax, nigga. I'm 'bout to go anyway. Just wanted to make sure you okay."

This nigga was trippin', and I ain't never seen him like this. "Good, 'cause I'm 'bout to head up the road."

Bodie stood up and walked toward me. "So you still not gonna tell me where you goin', huh? All the jobs we pulled off, and I don't even get to know?"

I laughed, grabbed my bag from the back, and said, "You gotta go, B."

When I came back out, Bodie frowned, placed his hand heavily on my shoulder, and said, "I bet you tell that bitch where you movin'."

"Nigga, get the fuck off me!" I said, pushin' him away. He fell against the wall, dusted his shirt off, and frowned. I knew if he hadn't pawned his gun, he would've used it on me. I tapped the butt of my gun on my waist so my message could be clear.

He looked at it and said, "I can still smell her pussy on you."

"Bodie, the door!" I said, grippin' my weapon. "Don't make me say it again, 'cause I won't!"

He looked at the door, back at me, and said, "So I guess we not hittin' the nigga Milli together, huh?

Silence.

"Well, I guess I got to do it myself." He walked out the door, and I slammed it behind him.

Ginger

I never saw somebody move as quickly as Gerron. I guess years of stickin' niggas for their money paid off, 'cause by the time Milli turned the knob, Gerron was out the back door and I was in the bathroom.

"Ginger! Where the fuck you at?" Milli said, rustlin' in the living room area. "And why the fuck are pillows on the floor? And why the floor burned?"

My heart dropped. "The floor got burned from the fire. And the pillows on the floor because I was layin' on the floor watchin' TV!"

"Come out here! We gotta talk."

I wiped my pussy in the sink, and all I was thinkin' was: *Why the fuck is he even here? Didn't he dump me?* All I had on my mind was Gerron. Fuck Milli!

When I was clean and in the right frame of mind, I walked into the living room and put a fake smile on my face. But the moment I saw his face and how smooth his stance was, I wondered if I made a big mistake. There was no denying I still had feelings for him.

"Fuck wrong wit' you?" Milli asked, sittin' on the sofa. A large blue duffel bag hung from his hand. I knew it was the package for the soldiers he had workin' for him in Kentland. "And why you over there lookin' all crazy and shit?"

"Huh?"

"Huh?" he said sarcastically. He dropped the bag on the floor and rested his gun on the table. "I asked you a fuckin' question. What's wrong wit' you?"

"Nothin', baby." I walked to my purse to grab a stick of gum. "I'm surprised you here. I mean, I thought it was over."

"Whateva. You know ain't nobody leavin' you yet. But shit ain't safe for you no more. I'm movin' you out."

"Okay," I said, not feelin' like fightin'. I just had the best fuck of my life, and I wanted to savor the moment. "I'll move."

"Where's your bracelet?"

"I got robbed today."

"Was they tryin' to come for me?"

"No," I said, rollin' my eyes. He didn't even give a fuck.

"I bet that nigga Gerron was involved. I'ma have somebody smoke his ass."

"No!" I yelled louder than I wanted to. "He wasn't even home at the time."

"How the fuck you know?"

Oh shit, I fucked up. "I'm not sure. I just don't think Gerron had anything to do wit' it. He helped save me."

"You know what? Just fix my fuckin' plate while I sort some shit out. While you at it, be thinkin' 'bout five good reasons I should keep ya ass around."

How could I? I wasn't even sure if I wanted to stay around.

When I walked into the kitchen, he followed me and an evil glare spread across his face.

"Who the fuck been in my house?"

When I turned my head and saw two plates and two cups on the table, I felt like bustin' myself in the mouth.

"Nicky's greedy ass must've been over," he offered.

I felt as if a huge weight had lifted off my shoulders. "Uh, yeah . . . Nicky was here."

"Well, you coulda cleaned up. Pillows on the floor, dishes on the table . . . damn! Don't start gettin' nasty and shit."

My patience was runnin' thin with him, and then his phone rang. From where I stood, I saw Tracey's name flash on his iPhone and remembered I hadn't had a chance to ask him about Denise.

He stepped a few feet away from me and said, "What, Tracey?"

He was silent as he paced the floor. "Well, I don't know what I'm gonna do right now." He looked at me out the corner of his eye and then turned around so I couldn't read his lips. I followed him into the living room, hoping he'd give me some info about my baby.

"Well, I'ont feel like talkin' right now. You shouldn't have been tryin' to be slick by listenin' to my conversation."

"Milli . . . is that Tracey?" He threw his hand up in the air. "Can I talk to her? I wanna speak to my baby."

"Didn't you see my hand go up?" he said, covering the phone. I nodded. "Then shut the fuck up."

Directing his attention back to Tracey, he said, "I'll rap to you later."

Their conversation sounded weird, and something didn't sit right with me.

"I don't know if you know, but Denise is wit' my cousin Tracey. That was her on the phone just now," he said, sitting back in the kitchen, eating his food.

"Is everything okay? 'Cause I wanted to talk to Denise."

"Everything cool, and Denise is 'sleep right now. I'll call back tomorrow so you can speak to her. But don't worry, she good."

"But I wanna speak to her now."

"Tracey, relax! I said I'll call her for you to-morrow."

"Tracey?" I repeated. "My name is Ginger."

"You know what I meant. I get y'all names mixed up sometimes."

I didn't believe him. Why didn't I believe him?

"Is everything cool between us, Milli?"

"You gotta ask yourself that since you don't listen. You quick wit' the mouth and you got a temper. It's 'cause of you CPS took my kid."

"They sayin' she got crack in her system. Y'all cookin' around her?"

"Naw." He paused. "And what happened to your face? That nigga who robbed you hit you or somethin'?"

"Yeah."

He laughed and said, "See, that's the shit I be talkin' 'bout. Everybody not gonna let you run off at the mouth without consequences."

He didn't even ask if I was okay. What kind of boyfriend is that? I was five seconds from tellin' him how I felt when I saw a dude walk through my back door with a ski mask on. He locked the door and aimed the gun in our direction.

In a deep, distorted voice he said, "I'ma make this quick. Get me the bag over there on the floor, and I'm out."

Milli tried to move for his gun, but the robber said, "Don't fuckin' move, nigga!"

I was so scared I fumbled around and fell against the stove. When Gerron left earlier, I didn't think to lock the back door, and now I'd have to pay for it again.

"I don't even know what you talkin' 'bout, man," Milli said. "That ain't shit but clothes."

"Stop fuckin' 'round! I already know what it is."

"Fuck!" Milli said, slammin' his fist down onto the table. Food plopped off his plate and fell on the table and the floor. "Why the fuck you ain't lock the back door?"

Although the robber spoke in his fake voice, I figured it was Bodie. I never could stand that grimy-ass nigga! I was still cussing him out in my mind when I smelled his Dolce & Gabbana cologne.

"Gerron, is . . . is that you?" I hesitated, hoping it wasn't true.

Silence.

My eyes moved from the Jordans he was wearing that had sat next to my Dior heels earlier and the jeans I helped take off, to the hand, which had recently been all over my body, now holding a gun.

"Why you doin' this shit, Gerron?"

He took the mask off and said, "I'm sorry 'bout this shit, Ginger. I know you don't believe me, but I gotta do this shit."

The pain I felt in my heart hurt more than anything. "But what about . . . I mean . . . everything else?"

"All I can say is sorry," he said, not lookin' at me directly.

"Nigga, do you know what I could do to you?" Milli said, breaking the moment. "Do you have any idea on how many niggas I know?"

"Yeah, and if I gave a fuck, I wouldn't be in here." He paused. "Ginger, hand me the bag, and don't try no shit. I'll blow this nigga's head off," he said, looking at my gun.

"Fuck you, shawty!" Milli said. "Ginger, don't give this nigga shit!"

Gerron cocked his gun and fired, shootin' Milli in the arm.

"Ahhhhhh! You shot me!"

"The bag," he said, looking at him then at me.

"Ginger, give this nigga the bag," he said, holdin' his arm. "I sho' hope you leavin' town, moe, 'cause I betta never see your face 'round here again."

"Well, maybe I should take care of you right now and you won't have to."

"Gerron, please," I said softly. "Don't shoot him again. I'm gonna give you what you came for."

Milli bit his lip, and I slowly walked toward the bag. I still felt the sting of Gerron's betrayal. Then I saw the pillows on the floor, which were reminders of our love session, and I grew angry—and then my house phone rang.

I moved to answer it, and Gerron said, "Don't do that, Ginger. Bring the bag. I gotta go."

"Don't say my name outta your mouth again, nigga!" I said with the phone in my hand.

"Ginger, don't make me—"

"What? Shoot me? Go 'head, Gerron, 'cause I don't even give a fuck no more!"

Gerron looked at me and said, "Why you gotta make shit so fuckin' difficult? You knew who I was when we met."

"Yeah, but I ain't wanna believe it was true."

When the phone rang again, I decided to answer. "Hello."

"Ginger, bring me the bag, I gotta bounce!" He was frustrated, but so was I.

"Wait, or fuckin' shoot me!" I said, covering the phone with my hand.

I placed my head to the receiver, and someone said, "Can I speak to Ginger?"

"Is this Rhianna?" I asked hesitantly.

"Yes, but I'm ready to tell you who I really am now."

Despite everything that was goin' on at that moment, I still wanted to know. "Go 'head."

"My name is Melissa Rice, but everybody calls me Melli. And Stevie is my mother."

"Melissa Rice? Which one of Stevie's daughters are you?"

I saw discomfort in Milli's eyes, and I wondered why.

"Ginger, hang that shit up and give this nigga the bag," Milli interrupted. "I ain't got no time for this shit right now," he said, blood pouring outta his arm.

"I'm her middle daughter. The one you think is retarded."

Silence.

"Melissa, tell me what you gotta say. I'm busy right now."

"I want to tell you . . . I want to tell you . . . that my father is Milli."

My heart beat fast and my eyes found their way to Milli's face.

"What you mean Milli's your father?" I said loud enough for him to hear.

"He's my daddy, but I don't see him all the time, not as much as I want to anyway."

"Melli," I repeated. Sure as the breath went in and out of my body, Milli's skin looked flushed, and I knew she was right.

"Who the fuck is that on the phone? Somebody lyin' on me again? I told you to stop believin' these bitches around here."

And then I remembered, earlier in the day when I told Milli about the fight with Trixy, he said, "Why you can't walk away from the ordinary and step up when necessary? You actin' young and dumb, always believin' these bitches when they tell you I fucked them."

Either he already knew about the fight somehow, or he fucked her, because I never got the chance to tell him the details before he made that comment.

I swallowed hard and said, "I gotta go."

Milli looked uneasy, not angry like he did when he first came home. Tears filled my eyes and ran down my cheeks. All the lies, all the games, had finally caught up with him. I spent all this time bein' with a man who couldn't give a fuck about me, and the entire neighborhood knew it.

"Is Melli tellin' the truth? Are you her father?"

"Have you forgotten we gettin' robbed?"

"We ain't gettin' robbed, nigga. YOU are!" I yelled. "Now, I need to know and I need to know now, are you the father of one of Stevie's kids?"

"No," he said sternly. For some reason, I was temporarily relieved.

"I'm the father of *all* of her kids."

I stumbled back and was just about to fall against my glass table when Gerron caught me. He had the gun in one hand and my body in the other.

"You a'ight?" he asked, holdin' me up but makin' sure to keep his eye on Milli.

"Yeah . . . I'm just. I'm just . . ."

"Stupid!" Milli yelled. "Why the fuck you worried 'bout what I do wit' somebody else? Look at everything you have 'round here. Look at the whip you drivin' and the purses in your closet. You don't want for shit! Any other bitch would kill to be in your shoes."

My chest tightened. I gave up everything for him, and it was all for nothin'! I snapped, and the next thing I knew, I was wavin' wild punches in his face.

Gerron whisked me up and held on to me until I calmed down, but I smacked him in the face too. I was angry at everybody! I was angry for givin' a fuck, and I was angry for not bein' able to see Milli for the man that he was.

"Before I die, I'm gonna make sure you wish you'd never put your fuckin' hands on me! After all the shit I did for you, to keep you outta jail."

"What the fuck are you talkin' about, to keep me outta jail? You sell crack, not me!"

"I'm out," Gerron said, grabbin' the bag. "I'ma leave y'all to it."

When Gerron moved toward the door, I felt like I could barely breathe I was crying so hard.

I swallowed hard and said, "Take me wit' you!"

Both Milli and Gerron looked at me like I'd lost my mind.

"What?" Gerron said. "You don't even know where I'm goin'." But I saw in his eyes he was considering my request.

"Please . . . I can help you . . . maybe be a lookout or somethin'. But ain't shit in Kentland for me no more."

"Ginger, you need to calm down and relax. You actin' real dumb right now," said Milli.

I ignored him, took two steps closer to Gerron, and said, "I'm beggin' you to take me wit' you. I don't even care where we goin'. We connected tonight, Gerron, and I know you got feelings for me."

Silence.

"Look, I know stuff is messed up for you and your peoples, but my lifestyle ain't for you and a kid!" he said angrily. "I gotta go."

With that, he held on tight to the bag and backed out the door, with the gun aimed in our direction. When the door closed, I felt my chances of escaping go with him.

"You's a stupid bitch!" Milli laughed, standin' up. He reached for the phone. "Got a nerve to get mad wit' me 'cause of some bitches I fucked." He said "bitches" and I could only imagine how many. "There's a luxury tax when you fuck wit' rich niggas like me. You gotta recognize that shit."

In that moment, my memory came flooding back to me. I remembered being this upset and standing in this living room. It was him all along . . .

Six Months Earlier:
Carolyn pulled her Cadillac in front of her daughter's house in Kentland. They were home one day early from vacation.

"Baby, you sure you don't want to stay with me another night? I hate you leavin' so soon," Carolyn said as she parked in front of her house.

"I'm sure, Ma. I wanna surprise Milli."

Ginger's mother sighed and looked in the back seat at her granddaughter, who was sound asleep.

"So what time are you gonna pick her up on Friday?"

"I'll be there in the afternoon," Ginger said, grabbing her bag. She reached in and gave her a kiss on the cheek. "I had a good vacation with you."

Carolyn smiled and said, "Me too, baby, and I don't want y'all fighting tonight. Call me later."

When she pulled off, Ginger turned around to look at her house. The lights were off, but she could see the glow from the TV. She waved at Gerron, who was sitting on the steps smoking a jay. He jumped up and rushed toward her.

"Hey, hang out wit' me for a sec," he said anxiously.

"Not now, Gerron. I just got back in town."

"Ginger, please. Just for a minute."

"Later, Gerron," she said, going inside her house.

When she opened the door, she saw the back of the sofa in the middle of the floor. The TV was on. She smiled when she saw Milli's back raise up, the glow of the TV lighting his skin. Then she saw a woman's pink fingernails rubbing Milli's back in ecstasy.

"Damn, y'all feel good," he said.

There were eight shoes scattered everywhere.

"Milli!" she said, walking farther into the house. Milli jumped up, and so did the woman he was fucking.

She was devastated when she saw her best friend, Leona, naked and by his side.

"Oh my God. Ginger, I'm so sorry!" Leona said. "Please forgive me."

All Ginger saw was Leona and Milli, no one else.

"Fuck you doin' here wit' my man, bitch?" she screamed. Turning her attention to Milli, she said, "And what you doin' wit' my best friend?"

"It's not what you think. You been gone for a week and we missed you, so we were talkin' 'bout you, and one thing led to another," Milli said. He threw the covers over the couch and looked down again.

"And so you fucked my best friend!"

Ginger pulled the gun out of her purse and said, "Why, Leona? You were my best friend."

"I'm sooooo sorry," Leona sobbed.

"Sorry isn't good enough." She fired a bullet into Leona's head. Her body dropped on the floor with a thumping sound.

When her body fell, Nicky and Stevie, who were also there, popped up off the floor. Ginger refocused on the shoes and saw they were from four different people. Stunned, she ran outside, lost her balance, and hit her head on the concrete.

After pulling Ginger inside, Milli, Nicky, and Stevie, who were also in the house participating in the sex game for money, buried Leona's body in Virginia. Milli did not want her found with his DNA. Leona would never be seen again.

***

When I remembered what happened, I was angry all over again.

"It was you that night! You fucked my best friends . . . and I caught you."

He smirked and said, "So you finally remember, huh?"

"You fuckin' bastard! You dirty-dick bastard! Why?"

"Because I can, and you wasn't supposed to come home that night!" he yelled. "And I did you a favor! You murdered that bitch and I got rid of the body. You should be on your knees thankin' me right now!" he said, gripping his arm. "You realize how much time you would've gotten? And I got the gun you used in case you ever act up. That's why I bought you a new one."

I grabbed the new gun he was talking about and busted him five times in the chest. He fell to the floor, and more blood oozed from his body. He was a holey-ass mess.

"What you say, Milli? I'm what?" I asked, standing over top of him. "You said earlier that someone would *kill* to be in my shoes. I guess you was right."

I grabbed his phone and scrolled through his contact list. I had to get my baby. I found Tracey's number and called.

"Milli?" Tracey said anxiously. "We need to talk."

I could tell by her voice that she was fuckin' him.

"Tracey, it's Ginger."

She laughed and said, "So you finally got the guts to call me? Well, I'm glad. And just so you know, I plan to raise Denise wit' my husband."

"You fuckin' your cousin?"

"No, bitch, he lied to you and me 'bout that shit. I'm not his cousin; I'm his wife."

I realized then I didn't know shit about Milli, and I felt like shootin' him again.

"I gave Milli somethin' to hold for me close to his heart. You'll find out what later." I laughed. "I'm on my way to pick up my baby. Have her ready."

I hung up, grabbed my purse, and dug into his pockets for money. His eyes were closed, but I knew he was still alive. He'd be dead soon.

I walked outside and took all of the money out of his Range Rover. After I finished, I was up fifteen thousand dollars. There was no turning back, and I was officially on the run. His uncle Kettle was gonna kill me when he found out. Oh, well.

Before I got lost, there was one last stop I had to make.

Gerron

I knocked on the door of a run-down house up the street from my block. Bodie rented a room from this crackhead and paid her by the day. I guess they were gettin' high together.

"Who you?" a little kid asked, opening the door. He scratched at his ashy knees.

"Is Bodie here?"

"Yeah. Wait out here," he said, slamming the door in my face.

Bodie came out five minutes later, and I smelled crack in the air. I knew this nigga was gettin' high.

"What you want? I thought you was gone," he said, leaning against the doorway.

"Here," I said, throwin' the bag of dope at him. "I hit Milli. Now you ain't got no reason to fuck wit' Ginger."

He picked up the bag, opened it up, and smiled. "Damn, you really are feelin' this broad, ain't you?"

"You got what you wanted. And just so you know, me and you ain't got no more business."

"It's like that?"

I jumped in my car and rolled out.

Ginger

I banged heavily on Stevie's weak-ass wooden door, stepped back, and waited for her to come out.

"Bitch, you must be crazy knockin' on my door like that!" Kids were inside her house everywhere runnin' around, but I didn't see Melissa.

"So you fucked my man, Stevie? Is no dick off limits around you?"

She laughed and said, "So he finally told your dumb ass, huh? I didn't think he ever would." She folded her arms against her chest.

I frowned and said, "All of your kids, Stevie?"

She laughed and I grew angrier.

"Nicky knows those his kids too?"

"What you think? Are you that stupid, Ginger?"

"That's why she wanted me to dump him? So y'all could have him?"

She shrugged, and I felt flushed, embarrassed, and hurt; and then Melissa walked behind Stevie.

"Get your little nosey ass in the house, Melli! That's your problem now, always bein' sneaky, listenin' to people's conversations and shit." She slapped her so hard in the face that her skin turned red.

She looked scared, like I was going to tell on her, but I wasn't. I knew then that Stevie did not put her up to callin' me, so who did?

"You a stand-up fuckin' mother."

"You should talk." She laughed. "Where is your daughter again?"

Silence.

"So you had somethin' to do with setting your own cousin up today?"

"Settin' my cousin up?" She laughed. "Bitch, we was settin' you up! Nicky told me somebody told you. But whoever put you on to the robbery didn't hear the conversation right. He was gonna come in that bitch and rob you. We got all our money back after we met up wit' Treasure later."

"But she came to my house and acted like she was mad at me. Sayin' Gerron may be involved."

"That was all in our plan to throw your ass off. We want your ass gone, Ginger. People keep tellin' you that, but you don't listen. And Milli set the whole shit up. The fight you got in with Trixy, the shit thrown through your window, and even the robbery. Everything is his doing."

Who had I been with all this time? Half of the shit he did to me, he didn't have to do. He could've made me leave, but he kept makin' it like it was my choice. I understood he supplied Kentland with drugs, but he made it like my presence here was all right.

"Fuck Milli and fuck you and Nicky too," I said, digging in my purse for my gun.

I was about to commit murder for the third time in my life when I saw Stevie look behind me and smile. Trixy hit me with an iron baseball bat on my shoulders, and when I fell, she and Shonda kicked and punched me multiple times all over my body. I wanted to scream, but couldn't.

"Now what, bitch?" Trixy said. "I told you before the night was over you would see my ass again!"

"You ain't got so much mouth now!" Shonda said, kicking me in my stomach.

"What are you doin', Stevie?" Nicky said, rushing out of Stevie's house. "Are you trippin'?" I saw my bracelet on her arm.

As they continued to pummel my body, I was hopeful that Nicky was gonna put an end to this shit. If we were ever friends, this would prove it.

"The bitch came over here startin' shit!" Stevie said. "I ain't 'bout to let her jump in my face."

Nicky looked at me with compassion in her eyes and said, "You know what you gotta do. We can't have no more police 'round here."

Stevie smiled and said, "Y'all heard my cousin. Kill the bitch."

I felt a strike to the head, and I was out cold.

Gerron

The Next Day

Last night, when I was leavin' the neighborhood, I saw Stevie and them punishin' Ginger. I jumped out, scooped her up, and put her in my car. Stevie tried to step, and I ended up smackin' her back. I guess I ended up hittin' a female after all.

I know I shoulda taken shawty to the hospital, but too much shit was goin' on, and I ain't think she would be safe. I did all I could to take care of her, but had a feelin' she wouldn't make it. She hadn't opened her eyes since I helped her.

This morning, I found out from some people that Ginger tried to kill Milli and failed. He was in intensive care but stable. She should have shot the nigga in the head. Now he was gunnin' for her and me too.

Of course I missed my flight, so I decided we'd stay in a remote hotel in Virginia, surrounded by trees until she got better. Nobody would ever find us here. I just wanted shawty to pull through.

It was ten o'clock at night, and I was rollin' a blunt when Ginger finally opened her eyes. I put the jay down and rushed to her side.

"Where . . . where am I?" she said in a low voice, touching her head.

"You wit' me." I smiled. "How you feelin'?"

"I have a bad-ass headache." She smiled. "So you came back for me after all."

"Shawty, why you ain't shoot them peoples in the head if you were tryin' to kill him? He alive."

She sighed and said, "Damn." She paused. "I remember everything about that night. You were tryin' to stop me from goin' inside. You knew they were in there, didn't you?"

"Yeah."

"You know I can't go back, and I can never be wit' my daughter," she cried.

"That ain't true. You could turn yourself in, and maybe the charges won't be so bad."

I was talkin' bullshit and she knew it. I wanted to offer her hope.

"I committed murder, Gerron. It's over."

My phone rang. "Hello."

"Baby, can you hear me?" The sound of my mother's scared voice had me shook.

"Ma! You okay?" Silence. "Ma! What's wrong?"

"It's Bodie," she whispered. "He . . . he says he's gonna kill me unless you can give him one hundred thousand dollars."

Stevie's House

It was two in the morning when Melli snuck into her big sister Crystal's bedroom and shut the door.

"I did what you ask me to," she whispered. "I called Ginger and told her Milli was my father. Now you gotta give me my stuff."

Crystal never believed her sister would do what she dared her to, but she was wrong. Crystal hated the way Milli doted over Denise, ignoring them, and she hated the way Ginger looked down at her. A few days earlier, when she heard her mother and aunt plotting to rob Ginger, she came up with the plan to tell Ginger the truth about Milli—in the hopes of ruining Ginger's life. She wasn't concerned with getting caught, because she'd blame the whole thing on Melli.

"Let me give you your stuff."

Crystal pulled a shoebox from under her bed and handed Melli four packs of cheese sunflower seeds and a pickled sausage. Melli plopped happily on the edge of the bed and started eating.

As Melli chewed her snack, Crystal wondered, if Melli could be bribed by something so small, what would she do for something bigger? She had all intentions of finding out.

Take It to the Grave

by

Caroline McGill

Bless slowly pulled his shiny black Mercedes Benz S550 into a parking spot in front of the housing projects he resided in. He hopped out and pulled up his pants; locked the doors and activated the alarm. He made his way toward his building, #270, and proudly looked over his shoulder at his $90,000 ride—one last time. He was headed for the small project apartment he shared with his mother and little sister.

Along the way, Bless noticed Tasheema, a girl he'd been trying to bag for a couple years, walking toward him. And to his delight, she was all alone.

Bless straightened up his shoulders, and his walk changed a little bit. When they passed each other, he got bold and grabbed her hand. As usual, she played hard to get, but he saw her trying not to smile. He pressed her, like he did each time he saw her. To his pleasure, this time he made her blush.

Tasheema was a good girl, and he was attracted to that—and the fact that she wasn't easy. He liked a challenge.

"You always playin' hard to get. But trust me, ma. I'ma make you my wife, wit' ya pretty ass."

Tasheema smiled at him again, and she tried to keep it moving. But Bless was determined to get somewhere, so he wouldn't let her hand go. He looked in her eyes sincerely and decided to just be real with her.

"When you gon' let me take you out, shorty? On some for real stuff, I just like you. There's somethin' about you. Let's go out, no strings attached. We'll have a good time. You like to eat, right?"

She made a face at him and sarcastically said, "No, I hate eating. I never eat!" They both laughed.

Bless said, "Thick as you is, I know that ain't true. I can tell you be eatin' good, ma." He gave her an approving onceover.

Tasheema blushed again. For some reason she decided to take him up on his offer; probably because he had managed to make her laugh. That was something she didn't have the luxury of doing lately. She was fresh out of a horrible relationship and still quite heartbroken; so she could use some humor in her life. She once heard that the best way to get over a man was to get under a new one. She thought, *what the hell,* and told him they could make that happen.

Bless was sort of surprised that she agreed. He was used to her turning him down, but he hid his shock well. Her response sent his self-esteem soaring. Right about then, he felt like he had wings.

Bless caught himself. He regained his composure and stopped grinning so hard, and then he told her he would pick her up on Friday at around nine o'clock. She agreed, and they exchanged maths. After they were done storing each other's number in their phones, they bid each other good night and parted ways.

While he was walking away, Bless looked back at her ass. It was fat, just the way he remembered it. She turned around to see him too. She caught him sizing her up and laughed. After that, they both kept it on a hop. He glimpsed back again and noted that she'd started switching her butt a little harder.

Bless kept on up the walkway toward his building. He took the pissy-smelling elevator to the ninth floor where his apartment was. As he stepped off the elevator and walked up to his crib, he was so wrapped up in his thoughts about Tasheema, he wasn't on point. Just as he was about to stick the key in the door, he realized he had company.

Bless looked into a familiar pair of cold green eyes, and his smile faded. His stomach tightened into a huge knot. He was face to face with an old acquaintance of his. Standing before him was the last person on earth he expected to see. It was the mighty Lion, a baldheaded, light-skinned, green-eyed devil. Lion was a gargantuan 6 foot 6 inch notorious street legend who he happened to owe about a quarter million dollars. That was about a quarter million more than he had, so Bless was literally about to vomit and shit on himself.

He fought to keep his composure. Praying he didn't give off an air of fear, Bless said, "Lion! My man! What up?"

Lion wasn't in the mood to play the fake shit. He just crossed his arms and nodded, and didn't even crack a smile.

Bless's mind was racing. He wondered how a nigga who had been serving forty years' fed-time was standing in his path. He grinned and said, "Welcome home, my nigga! When you get out?"

Lion hated small talk. Still stone-faced, he ignored the question and asked one of his own. "So what you got for me, boy?"

Bless swallowed nervously and started tap-dancing around the subject. He told Lion that he had some bread, but it was a little tied up. He said he had to maneuver it around for safekeeping. The look on Lion's face said he didn't want to hear the lollygagging and bullshit.

Bless could tell he was getting short of patience, so he lied and assured him he had it. "I got you, man. Don't even worry. That's my word. Just gimme a li'l bit of time."

Lion stepped up and put his face so close to Bless's he could smell what he had for breakfast. He wasn't the type to yell, but his personality was so powerful that even his whisper came across as ferocious. The seven words he said were not to be taken lightly. He said, "You got 'til Friday, or somebody's dead."

Bless didn't even have a response for that. He knew Lion was referring to him or one of his family members. He got the picture. He knew how the game went. That was why that mothafucka had showed up at his crib—to show him he knew where he and his family lived. Damn, he had gotten himself in some deep shit.

Lion looked at the key in Bless's hand and said, "What kind of car I got now? That look like a Benz key. Let me get my keys, little nigga."

Bless opened his mouth to protest, but Lion silenced him with a look. Damn, he almost felt like crying. That car was his baby. He took better care of her than he did his own daughter; but he knew he didn't have any wins because he did that nigga dirty. That car was everything to Bless, but he didn't have a choice at the time. He wasn't strapped, and he could see from that bulge under Lion's T-shirt that he was. Reluctantly he handed over the key to his most prized possession in the world. He was sick.

Lion saw the hurt look on his face, so he smirked at him. He said, "You'll get it back when you send my fuckin' money."

Bless nodded, knowing that was virtually impossible at the time. He stood there in disbelief, and Lion continued to shake him down.

"Now, how much money I got in your pockets?"

Bless sighed and shrugged. Wow, that was some bullshit. He was getting the full court press. He dug in his pocket and handed over a small knot of bills. It was only about four hundred bucks.

Lion looked at that chump change like it was covered in monkey shit, but he took it from him. It wouldn't do much for his situation, but it was the principle. And he meant exactly what he said. If he didn't get his money somebody was dead.

He patted Bless's other pocket to make sure it was empty, and then he grabbed him by the neck. Lion leaned over and snarled in his ear, "Boy, you were like a son to me, but I'll kill you, li'l nigga." He squeezed Bless's neck until his huge biceps trembled.

Eyes bulging out of his head, Bless attempted to free himself. He couldn't breathe or speak with those mittens wrapped around his throat. Lion was a big mothafucka who had obviously been working out in the can. Bless wished he could get to his gun. He prayed that nigga wouldn't choke him to death.

Finally, Lion laughed wickedly and loosened his grip. He hit Bless on the back and said, "Get at me soon, boy. And thanks for the ride." He winked at him, and then he disappeared.

After he left, Bless went inside the house feeling like a straight herb. He locked the door and had a seat on the couch. He sat there for a minute thinking. It looked like he no longer had a vehicle to take Tasheema out on that date. And that was the least of his problems.

Bless was sick—literally. That nigga Lion really shook him down. He was glad nobody was around to witness that. He was ashamed of the way he had just allowed himself to be punked. He let that nigga just take his shit.

Deep inside, Bless knew he had it coming. He had violated and really crossed Lion, so he tried to look at the bright side. At least that man had given him the opportunity to straighten face. Lion could've just showed up gunning for him. He had to do something to get that nigga bread.

He thought back to the beginning when all the shit began.

A few years ago—when Lion was on top—Bless was a young, fatherless lad, aspiring to run with his organization. He had started out as a lookout boy and had worked his way from the ground up. Lion had liked his ambition, so he took him under his wing. Bless became sort of his young protégé. When Lion schooled him, he would just sit back and absorb everything and quietly observe the way he ran his empire. He told himself he would be thorough like him one day—if given the opportunity.

As time went on, Bless earned the position of junior executive. But before long, Lion and most of his team members were busted. After being hit with numerous secret indictments, they were carted away by the feds. It turned out that there had been an informant in the midst. They later found out it was a third level worker who was caught selling cocaine to an undercover federal officer. After he was arrested, he discovered that he wasn't at all built for the game he had chosen. He broke under the pigs' pressure when they interrogated him, and he gave up all the key players. Lion was the head honcho.

Lion had managed to bubble in the game for years because he kept the right palms greased, but that was when he was just dealing with NYPD. Playing with the feds was a whole new ballgame. They didn't take any fucking payoffs. Ironically, the dirty NYPD pigs he was paying protection money to wound up getting investigated as well.

The bigger you are, the harder you fall. So needless to say, Lion hit the ground pretty hard. The feds were meticulous. The pig bastards had done their homework and found out about everything he owned everywhere. They stripped him of all his belongings and finances until he was just about dirt poor. They seized his overseas assets as well, and froze all those accounts too.

Word quickly hit the streets that Lion and his workers were done. Rumors spread that he was facing like two hundred years, so everybody assumed that he would never see daylight again. With his back against the wall like that, even the women in his life turned on him. His wifey, Nyla, was the only chick that would've rode with him, but she was so heavily involved she was arrested too.

Lion figured he had taught Bless well, and he was about the only person on the outside he could trust, so he had instructed him to meet with an associate of his that owed him a favor. That favor was to be converted to cash and then used to retain an attorney for Lion.

Bless met with the dude, and he hit him with ten kilos of uncut cocaine. He had started getting rid of it with good intentions, but temptation was a pretty bitch that he found irresistible. Needless to say, Bless fucked up and didn't do as he was supposed to. Having all that weight had blown his mind.

He got bigheaded and decided to dead Lion on the proceeds. Bless conjured up a lie about the police running up in his spot and confiscating the work and all the money he made off it. He gave Lion the mumbo jumbo story and promised him he would make it right when he got back on his feet.

Whether or not Lion went for it, Bless wasn't really concerned. He thought he was safe because Lion was locked up. He figured that nigga was finished without the lawyer money, so he wasn't even afraid. The first thing he did was go on a shopping spree and cop a brand new Mercedes.

Now he realized how ignorant it was of him to not move his family out of the projects after he had crossed one of the most feared and respected men in the borough. If anything happened to them, it was his own fault. All the bread he ran through, he could've bought his mother a house down South or something. But due to poor money management in the past, now he couldn't even afford to relocate them across town.

Bless snapped back to reality. He realized once again that he didn't have a solution for the hole he had dug himself in. He was up shit's creek without a paddle. He needed a lifeline. The first person he thought to call was his man, Jeff. Hopefully he could assist him somehow. There was really nobody else he could turn to. Bless was known for his flamboyance, so most of the other dudes he knew were praying for his downfall.

Meanwhile, across town, Bless's closest friend, Jeff, and his girlfriend, Jill, were just ending their third round of make-up sex. The little argument they had wasn't even that serious, but Jill was pregnant and extra sensitive at the time. She took everything Jeff said to heart, so he found himself apologizing pretty often. But all the make-up sex they had been having was amazing.

Jill's legs were wrapped around Jeff while she caressed his back and shoulders. They had just climaxed together. He was still lying on top of her breathing heavily when the telephone rang.

It was as if the caller had timed their lovemaking and gave them time to finish doing the do. Jill looked at the caller ID and saw that it was Jeff's main man, Bless.

She knew he and Jeff were tight, but Bless was an asshole. He was always trying to use Jeff for something—not to mention the fact that he gave her best friend, Taj, an STD. Jill couldn't stand his conniving, cheating ass, so she purposely ignored the call. When Jeff asked her who it was, she lied and said it was her bestie, Taj, and she would call her back.

Ensconced in that warm, pregnant pussy, he was glad she said that. It felt so good he almost fell asleep in it. He rolled over and held her in his arms. For some reason, Jeff was moved to tell Jill how much he loved her and how much she meant to him. He didn't say shit like that all the time, so it came from his heart. He apologized again for hurting her feelings.

She was so emotional during her pregnancy. She started crying and told him she loved him, too, and didn't want him to leave her. Jeff laughed and told her he wasn't going anywhere.

Jill let it go, but she didn't believe he would leave her voluntarily. Bless's phone call had just left her feeling uneasy for some reason. She had the feeling he was up to no good—probably because he usually was. It seemed like every time Jeff messed with him, he got tangled up in some shit. Jill hugged her man tighter and didn't bother to voice her concerns. If she didn't say them aloud, maybe they would disappear.

Jill was a good girl. She and Jeff were from different worlds, so they had different views about survival, but they also had a love stronger than she'd ever experienced. She believed love conquered all, so she went against her mother, father, and just about all her girlfriends to be with him. And he was really trying. He had been on the right track lately, but they still referred to him as Jill's reformed thug with all the baby mamas—just because Jeff had a past and a couple of kids already.

No matter what they said, she and Jeff were a team. It was them against the world. They had been an item for three years and were recently engaged. With the child they had on the way, they were going to be the beautiful family she'd always dreamed about. Jill wasn't about to let anybody come between them.

At home, Bless was disappointed that Jeff hadn't answered the phone. He was pacing the floor and contemplating going over to his crib.

He knew the nigga was indoors that time of night. Jeff was so pussy whipped, he had basically let his girl, Jill, put him on a curfew. Or at least it seemed that way. Bless knew they were at home, but they must've been asleep. Under normal circumstances, he would've respected that, but he was in dire straits. His situation was life or death, and he didn't know what to do yet. That's why he needed Jeff's assistance.

Bless knew it was fucked up to involve Jeff in his shit because he didn't have anything to do with it. Jeff didn't even benefit from that work he stole from Lion. He was incarcerated during that time. Bless had told him what the deal was when he visited him once, and he couldn't front—back then Jeff had told him it was unwise to cross a person of Lion's caliber.

So now there he was, desperate. He had to do something. He needed Jeff's help, but he didn't want to tell him how his chickens had come home to roost. He wasn't in the mood to hear "I told you so." Bless already knew what a tangled web he had weaved. He didn't need another mothafucka to remind him.

Frustrated because he didn't have a solution, Bless got his gun. He peeked in on his mother and baby sister to make sure they were okay, and then he whispered a little prayer. Bless headed outside to get a cab. He had no idea where he was going, but he knew his problem wouldn't just solve itself.

On the elevator ride down, he prayed there weren't any nosy mothafuckas outside. He was pretty ashamed of the fact that he didn't have his whip. He usually pulled off stunting with the music bumping. He knew that car didn't make him, but he felt naked without his shit. The lyrics of that Kanye West song "Self-Conscious" ran through his mind.

There were a few people outside, so Bless nodded at dudes. He walked down to the next corner and flagged a cab. He told the driver to take him to Crown Heights, where Jeff stayed. As he rode in the taxi past the streetlights of his Brooklyn neighborhood, Bed-Stuy, the furrow in his brow got deeper and deeper. He wore a pretty grim expression, so you could definitely tell he was stressed. He was in the hole up to his eyeballs. That nigga Lion wanted his bread.

Bless was no punk. He had a lot of pride, and he was no sucker. His gun went off, and niggas knew that. He wasn't the same little Bless that nigga Lion once knew. He was known for getting busy, and he was pretty well respected in his hood. He toyed with the idea of just killing that mothafucka. Word. He should just go pop that nigga and get his shit back. He was in the back of a fucking cab! He couldn't believe it. He needed his damn car. He had an image to uphold, and his reputation was at stake.

Bless knew Lion wouldn't be easy to eliminate. He was a different type of opponent. Lion had a reputation too. He was ruthless. His government name was Richard Jamison, but he had been dubbed Richard the Lionhearted. Lion was an abbreviation of that.

Bless had heard about some of the ill fates that dudes who fucked him over faced. That was why he wasn't sure if he wanted to tango. He would never say it aloud, but Lion had him under pressure.

The more he thought about it, he knew he had to straighten that shit out. It was about honor too. That was a sucker move he had pulled, but he was young at the time. He'd never had that much money before.

Lion's return was totally unexpected. Bless was unprepared and caught off guard. Out of sheer desperation, Bless considered robbing someone. He didn't have any better ideas. As he rode down Utica Avenue, he passed a well-known, busy drug corner. There was always heavy traffic there. Them Jamaican niggas over there was getting it. It was known throughout the borough. That corner was Crack Central.

While his cab was at a red light, he watched an apparent drug and money exchange between a hustler and a fiend. Bless thought about putting the drop on them niggas. It was real enticing, but he knew chances of getting away with that on foot were slim. There was no way those dudes were out there getting money like that without being strapped. Bless didn't have a death wish. To run up on them niggas he needed an accomplice. He needed Jeff to hold him down.

The light changed, and the cabbie drove down the street. The closer Bless got to Jeff's house, the more he thought about it. There was a lot of bread on that corner, and he knew Jeff wouldn't be with it. He decided to take his chances.

Bless told the driver to let him out at the next corner. After he paid the fare, he headed back down to Utica on foot. "Some fuckin' body in trouble," he muttered. He was on the prowl.

Bless could always tell who was holding. He knew what the bank looked like. It was like a sixth sense. He formulated his plan as he walked down the dark street. When he spotted the jackpot, he would lay everything down in his path to get it.

A block and a half away, he peeped a dude walking ahead of him with a small duffel bag. He was headed toward the corner. Bless's sixth sense told him that that bag was full of loot. If he had stumbled upon a come-up while in search of one, then the cards were on his side. His heart raced with nervous anticipation.

The dude's back was to him, so he didn't see him approaching. Bless pulled out his gun and quickened his pace, anxious not to blow the opportunity. Without a second thought, he stuck his ratchet in the small of duke's back and told him to release the fucking bag.

Robbing duke wasn't easy. He didn't surrender peacefully. The nigga was unarmed, but he fought back and held on to that bag like his life depended on it. Bless wouldn't take no for an answer. He needed that money too bad. He was forced to clap that nigga.

After that bullet pierced his chest, the dude finally gave up the bag. As he lay there clutching his chest and bleeding on the concrete, Bless went through his pockets and confiscated his keys and cell phone. After that, it crossed his mind that he should finish him. He told himself another bullet would only make matters worse. He didn't want to make a stickup a homicide. The nigga was already shot. That being said, he stuck his gun in his waist and trotted in the other direction.

Bless looked over his shoulder a few times to make sure nobody was following him. As far as he could see, the coast was clear. He kept going and wished that nigga luck.

Three blocks down, Bless dipped around a corner and removed the dark T-shirt he had on. Now wearing just a wife beater and a pair of navy blue Polo sweats, he sort of appeared to be coming from the gym after a late night workout. He casually walked down to the next corner so he could find a taxi.

Bless got lucky and flagged a cab within seconds. After he settled inside and gave the driver his destination, he got down low in the back seat until they pulled up in front of his building. When he realized he was home, he smiled to himself. He had never been happier to see his projects.

Bless made a quick lick and thought that was that, but contrary to his beliefs, it was far from over. He had robbed the wrong nigga—and what he stole wasn't even money. That bag was filled with cocaine—seven whole kilos of it, and it didn't even belong to the dude he stuck. It belonged to his boss, Butch, a notorious crime lord who reigned over the streets of Brooklyn with an iron fist.

When Bless finally made it upstairs to his apartment, he deadbolted the door and then peeped out the window to make sure no one had followed him. When he was sure the coast was clear, he locked himself in his bedroom and unzipped the bag. He dumped the contents on the bed, expecting it to be filled with bread. When he realized it was full of what appeared to be taped-up packages of cocaine, his eyes almost popped out of his head. Damn, what the fuck?

Bless was so excited he was shaking. He used a small pocketknife he had in his nightstand drawer to tear a slit in one of the packages, and then he licked his finger and stuck it inside. His forefinger came out coated with a pale, powdery substance. It looked like some good shit too. Bless put it to his mouth and tasted it to be sure.

Immediately, the powder numbed his tongue. Oh shit, he thought. He knew the taste of cocaine. It was official tissue. Bless carried the open package over to the computer desk in the corner of his bedroom and poured a small pile of the coke onto the desk. He hurriedly switched on the desk lamp and closely examined his stolen booty.

Oh shit, it was Fishscale! It was love at first sight. He nearly fell back in his chair. "No moth-afuckin' way!" he yelled. He jumped up and danced a little two-step jig and thanked his lucky stars for the come-up. Fishscale cocaine! It was fucking Fishscale!

Fishscale was no ordinary coke. It was a refined and comparatively pure form of cocaine, and its description was inspired by its shiny and reflective properties. It was the highest quality cocaine you could find, usually uncut. It didn't even look like regular coke. It was flaky instead of grainy, it was sparkly instead of dull, and it was slightly yellow-grey instead of being plain white. Enough said. It was the good shit—the best. One gram equaled twelve lines.

Bless danced over to the other packages. He picked them all up and held them close to his heart. His chest swelled. He had never been in love that way before. That was the prettiest "girl" he had ever seen. He was absolutely smitten.

The best thing about the situation was the fact that the street value of his newfound fortune was worth more than he owed Lion. He could actually pay that nigga off and still profit. If he did things the right way, he would be set. That was so much work, he wouldn't even look back. He swore to himself he would never be fucked up again.

Bless knew he had to move that shit fast—at least some of it—just to get Lion's bread. He needed a quarter million by the end of the week, so he was going to need some assistance. He searched his mental rolodex and thought about his man Jeff again. He and Jeff were old cronies who at one point in time were inseparable. Former partners in crime, the two of them had run the streets together for years. They had done a ton of dirt, and neither ever said a word. Jeff was the only nigga he knew he could trust, so that was who he had to get at.

Jeff had recently taken a graceful bow out of the underworld. His sudden switch to square-dom was credited to some premonition he said his girl had—that, and the fact that she was pregnant. Bless hated to get Jeff involved in his bullshit, but he didn't know what else to do. He knew Jeff would help him if he could. And not for nothing, that nigga could use some extra bread too.

Bless started to call him again, but he didn't like playing the phone like that. He preferred to discuss business or anything else relevant in person, not on the jack. He decided to get at him the following day. He put away all the goods and rolled himself a blunt. He opted to chill that night and get some rest.

At six o'clock the next morning, Bless awakened and took a quick shower. He got dressed fast and selected a matching fitted cap. He grabbed his gun on the way out—just in case—and then he rode the elevator downstairs and got another cab.

When he got out in front of Jeff's building, he headed inside. When he reached his apartment, he rang the doorbell.

After a minute, Jeff's pregnant girlfriend, Jill, answered the door. The look on her face said he wasn't welcome.

Bless wondered what her problem was. Jill was so stuck-up; he wasn't that fond of her either. Nonetheless, he greeted her respectfully because she was his bro's wife. Jill nodded at him and pursed her lips. "How can I help you? Do you know what time it is? We were still asleep. Jeff has to get up soon to get ready for work."

Bless was displeased to hear that. He never imagined himself or Jeff getting a nine-to-five. He wondered if Jill had some type of root on that nigga or something. She made him do a complete 360. In the past, he and Jeff did crime together and time together, so his change of life had broken Bless's heart. But Bless knew Jeff was a loyal dude. If he told him he needed him, he would show up without hesitation. That was how they did.

Bless told Jill he needed her to wake Jeff up. He said it was important. She looked like she didn't want to, but she opened the door and told him to come in. She told him to have a seat and passed him the remote. She was pretty pregnant, so she wobbled down the hall to get Jeff.

Bless turned on the huge TV that was mounted on the wall and flicked the channel to BET. He watched a rerun of *The Game* while he waited on his homie to appear. A few minutes later, Jeff came out to the living room. Bless stood up and greeted him with a hearty pound. The men had a seat on the sofa, and Bless began to clown Jeff about the new gig he had.

Jeff laughed and shrugged his shoulders. "Son, it is what it is. I got a seed on the way. Those Pampers and shit cost bread, son. That shit we was doin', I can't live that life no more. Wifey got me this gig. I was fucked up."

Bless quit joking and said, "I know, son. My back been against the wall too. That's why I came." He looked around to make sure Jill wasn't within earshot and said, "Son, I got a proposition for you. I need you this one last time."

Jeff's instinct told him not to get involved. He had been through enough shit fucking with Bless. He was a changed man now. But being the good dude he was, he ignored the warning bells that went off and heard his homie out.

Bless proceeded to hit Jeff with a fabricated version of the prior night's events. "Yo, son, I found some work. This nigga was runnin' from the police and I seen him toss this bag, so I doubled backe and picked that shit up. I got like four birds, son—Fishscale." For some reason, Bless purposely understated the amount of kilos he had.

Despite his endeavors to stay clean, Jeff's interest level rose. "Fishscale? Word, son?"

Bless nodded, and then he went on to explain how Lion just came home and was on him about that quarter mil he owed him. He told Jeff he just needed him to help him get that shit off and assured him that it would be worth his while.

Jeff listened to Bless and knew the dilemma he faced was deadly. He solemnly gave him his word that he would do what he could. He knew a few people. If that shit was as good as Bless claimed, it shouldn't be hard to get rid of.

Back in the bedroom, Jill was on the telephone with her best friend, Taj, who was also Bless's former sweetheart. Taj told her she was absolutely right. She said Bless only came around when he was up to no good. She told Jill that Bless was a greasy-ass, no-good nigga. That was the reason she had stopped fucking with him.

Jill knew what a good dude Jeff was, so she hoped he didn't let Bless talk a hole in his head. They were finally on the right track, and he was trying to throw them off. The devil was a liar. They were engaged to be married, and their baby was due in just two months. She thought about going out there and asking Bless to leave, but she knew Jeff wouldn't go for that. He and Bless were like brothers.

Jeff called out of work that day, and he and Bless broke three of the kilos down into 62.5-gram and 125-gram packages, which were referred to in the dope game as "sixteenths" and "big eighths" respectively.

Jeff was a man of his word. He made a few calls, and lo and behold, they got rid of damn near three kilos that day. The next day, they made some more calls and got rid of one and a half more.

By that time, the cash they had accumulated amounted to well over three hundred thousand dollars. Bless took a quarter million out and took it straight to Lion. He got his car back, and they parted as friends—at least that's what he thought. Bless split the remaining money with Jeff, and they agreed to slow roll the last of the work. If they cut it a little more, broke it down, and sold less weight, they could make more off it.

***

Lion was glad to get his money back, but Bless' fate was sealed a long time ago. That nigga was already dead before he touched ground. Bless shot himself in the head when he crossed him. He only left him breathing that long to get back his bread.

Coincidently, he had a friend who he'd learned took a hit for seven kilos of Fishscale just days before. That nigga Bless was dead broke the other day, and then all of a sudden he shows up at his door with $250,000 cash. Lion's intuition told him that little nigga was involved in that heist somehow. It didn't take rocket science to figure that out.

Lion got his money back, so he no longer had any use for Bless. He took the liberty of making a call to his young associate, Butch—who had taken the hit—and dropped Bless's name. That would eliminate that petty nigga Bless, and also be payback to Butch, who had such respect for Lion's legend he had thrown him a half a kilo on GP so he could get right.

Lion laughed out loud about Bless's inevitable death. He wanted to kill that little nigga himself, but he knew Butch would handle it. And whether or not Bless was involved didn't even matter. He had it coming. If Butch murdered him, that would be less dirty work for him.

***

When Butch got the call he thanked Lion for the heads up. He didn't express it right then, but he was quietly enraged. After he hung up the phone, he commissioned his top two men to get out there and get that nigga Bless.

His lieutenants Phil and Loco didn't have to be told twice. They headed out with their guns to find answers. The streets talked pretty loud, especially with a little "persuasion." By sundown they had the complete names and addresses of Brian "Bless" Piedmont and his partner in crime, Jeffrey "Jeff" Staton.

Lucky for Bless, no one was at his crib when they went over there. His mom and sister were at an evening service at church, and he was out on a date with Tasheema. The goons agreed to return at a later hour, and then headed over to Jeff's crib. No one was there either, so they decided to find them niggas in the morning.

They would roll on those fools in broad daylight. That was nothing to them. Loco and Phil were both coldblooded, and neither was wrapped too tight. They loved leaving witnesses anyway.

The next day, Jeff was getting dressed to go out and meet his fiancée for lunch. He'd been so busy trying to help Bless get that shit off; he hadn't been around much the past couple of days. But he felt good because he had helped his nigga Bless raise the money to get Lion off his case. In the process, he had raised enough bread to follow his own dreams. Now he was going to start his own business instead of going to work for the white man. He felt pretty good about the nest egg he had. He couldn't wait to share the news with Jill.

Jeff felt like he was on top of the world. His swag was at a thousand. He took another look at himself in the mirror. He had to admit the color of the sky blue Polo shirt his wifey bought him worked for him. Satisfied with his reflection, he went in his bedroom to grab a brand new fitted cap that matched.

He was just about to leave the crib when the doorbell rang. Jeff went to the door and looked out the peephole. He saw a man in a brown uniform who looked like he was from UPS. He asked, "Who is it?"

"It's UPS. You got a package," a polite male voice responded. Jeff didn't think twice. Jill was always up late watching infomercials and ordering stuff. They received quite a few packages lately. UPS came there on a regular, so without a second thought, Jeff unlocked the door.

The uniformed man had his brown cap pulled down over his eyes. He nodded and pointed to a large box sitting on the floor beside him, then handed Jeff a clipboard. Jeff took it and got ready to sign for the package, but he noticed three things. One, there was another dude waiting on the side. Two, the dude who rang the bell had passed him a clipboard instead of the electronic doohickey they usually had him sign for a package. And three, there was no yellow UPS logo stitched in either of the men's shirt pockets. Jeff's animal instinct kicked in, and he sensed trouble. He was from the streets, so he knew what it was. It looked like that day the Grim Reaper had come knocking.

Without a word, he tossed the clipboard in the dude's face and quickly stepped back inside his crib. He tried to slam the door real fast, but the nigga stuck his foot in the doorway. Before Jeff knew it, there was a nickel- plated .45 pointed in his face.

Jeff was no idiot. He knew he didn't have it. He was unarmed, so he surrendered. He wondered what that was about, but deep in his heart he knew what those niggas wanted. He didn't want them in his crib, so he followed them as instructed.

The men weren't inexperienced, but they weren't professionals either, so they didn't exactly have a plan. They had just been ordered by their boss to get his shit back, so they winged it. At gunpoint, they forced Jeff up to the roof so they could demand some answers.

As they climbed the stairs to the roof, Jeff thought about Bless. It was obvious the nigga had been pulling his leg. He didn't believe he would lie like that, but he knew that unwelcomed visit somehow pertained to that work Bless "found." Jeff was no rat. Regardless of the circumstances, he wouldn't give up his homie for nothing. He didn't know anything anyway, so there was nothing for him to tell.

The dudes kept demanding the money, the coke, or Bless's whereabouts. They were violent and callous in their attempt to retrieve answers, but Jeff wouldn't say a word. He couldn't just throw his peoples to the wolves. Even in the face of death, he was loyal.

Their patience wore thin. Unhappy about his obvious lack of willingness to cooperate, they aspired to motivate him. Together, they picked him up and attempted to hang him off the side of the roof.

Jeff fought back as much as he could, but the gruesome twosome managed to get him off his feet. Before he knew it, he was dangling from the roof headfirst. They held him by his legs and tossed him around, hurling threats and obscenities at him.

Jeff wasn't fronting like he was no guerilla. Staring down at that concrete from atop a twelve-story tenement, he was scared as shit. He even considered telling them what he knew. But he knew those bastards were still going to kill him, whether he gave Bless up or not. They had taken it too far already.

As he hung there suspended in midair, his life flashed before him. Jeff thought about his family and realized how precious they were to him—his children, his pregnant girl, and his mother. He hadn't anticipated leaving them all so soon, but he prayed they would be okay. Despite his heart pounding in his chest, Jeff told himself he would not fear death.

His assailants brought him back up and said they were giving him one more opportunity to disclose the pertinent information they sought. Again, he told them he knew nothing. From the looks on their faces, Jeff knew his number was up. In a desperate attempt to break free, he kicked one of those bastards in the nuts and then tried to shake the other dude.

After a brief struggle, Jeff found himself hanging headfirst off the side of the building, again. He knew he was done, but he was determined not to go alone. He reached up and grabbed at the taller dude's shirttail. He wanted to pull that nigga down to his death alongside him.

The nigga saw what Jeff was trying to do, so he snarled, "Nigga, fuck you!" He pulled out his gun and shot him in the face. Jeff ate that bullet and held on for dear life, but he lost his grip. The goons laughed coldly and mercilessly dropped him on his head.

Meanwhile, Jill was in a cab on the way home. She was worried because she had called Jeff's cell phone and their house several times to find out why he hadn't arrived yet. They were supposed to meet downtown at her favorite restaurant, BBQ's. She'd been calling him back to back while she was in the cab, but still no answer.

When Jill pulled up in front of their building, she saw a crowd out there. There were police cars and paramedics everywhere. She wondered what happened, praying it wasn't anyone she knew. Scared, she paid her driver and got out of the cab. As she made her way through the crowd, she heard one of the nosy neighbors telling another one what happened.

"Yo, somebody threw that nigga off the roof! I seen when his body hit the ground. His fuckin' head just cracked like a real melon!"

Jill's stomach did a flip-flop. Someone had fallen from the roof! And they were still lying there on the ground. There were two men who looked like detectives standing over the body discussing something. Just before they pulled the white sheet back, Jill got close enough to get a good glimpse.

The person was bleeding profusely from the head. She didn't recognize the face because it was so swollen it was disfigured, but she saw the shirt the man was wearing. It was a sky blue Ralph Lauren Polo shirt, now splattered with blood. Minus the bloodstains, it was the same shirt she bought for Jeff the other day. The feeling in the pit of her stomach was indescribable. It was him.

Jill was so stricken with grief she was oblivious to the crowd from that point on. She elbowed her way through and tried to get to the body, but she was stopped dead in her tracks by the detectives. She tried to tell them that that was her fiancé and her child's father, but they quickly ushered her to the side. Jeff's body was placed in an ambulance and whisked away. Jill stood there powerless, watching the love of her life disappear forever. Tears streamed down her face. She was heartbroken.

***

About twenty minutes later, a hysterical Jill called Bless and "thanked" him for getting her fiancé killed. She told him she knew he had something to do with it, and said she wished he would burn in hell.

When Bless got the news, he was completely distraught. He felt horrible. Damn, Jeff was his main man. He regretted getting him involved. He would never forgive himself for that one. To save his self, he had literally thrown Jeff under a bus. His heart was heavy about it, but he had to get out of there.

Bless was no idiot. He knew he was next. He should've been dead before Jeff. That was his work. He had only dodged the bullet because he wasn't around. He took Tasheema to Atlantic City the day before.

He didn't even bother to go home and pack. Bless hopped in his car and headed for the Holland Tunnel. He knew he was making a cowardly exit, but he didn't look back. He had created a pretty hostile environment, so it was time to relocate.

A week later, Taj sat with her arm around Jill's shoulder, comforting her pregnant best friend at her time of loss. There was a woman standing

at the front of the church in the middle of a
tear-jerking solo. She was singing "Precious Lord,
Take My Hand," and Jill was crying uncontrolla-
bly. Taj's heart went out to her. Jill's fiancé, Jeff,
was in an ivory marble coffin a few feet in front of
them, and poor Jill was eight months pregnant
with their first child. She was having a boy.

Jill wasn't the only one in there crying. She
was Jeff's third baby mother. The other two sat
on the pew behind her. She and Taj sat on the
front pew with Jeff's mother, grandmother, and
two aunts. The church was pretty big, and it was
packed. Jeff was a well-loved dude. There were
so many flowers in there; it looked like a floral
shop.

But something just wasn't right. Taj had a
funny feeling. She kept on glancing around the
church nervously. Her left eye was jumping.
That meant something was going to happen. Taj
was a little superstitious because she was raised
by her superstitious, Southern grandmother.

Some folks in the South believed that your left
eye jumping meant bad luck, and the right eye
jumping was an indication of good luck. Taj tried
to be easy and relax, but her gut told her that
something was going to go down.

After the soloist was done, the preacher stood
up at the front. Reverend Bixby followed that

heartfelt solo with a sermon full of fervor. Midway through, he had half of the congregation in tears and the other half up on their feet, shouting. The reverend continued preaching and telling it like it was.

"Here lies a good man! He was a good son! A father of two, with another one on the way . . . and he will be missed. Can I get a amen? Well, now! God wanted him home. I say, God wanted this young brother home. It wasn't his time, but God knows best. Jesus! I pray for the killing to stop. It's just so senseless. Li'l children growing up with no daddies, and mothers losing their sons—it don't make no kind of sense! Lord knows, sometimes we just don't understand. God, we need you! I say, Lord, we praise you! We trust that you will make a way! Out of no way! You did it for Job! And I know you'll do it for us! I know you will!"

He removed a navy blue silk handkerchief from the breast pocket of his suit and wiped the sweat from his brow and continued.

"I heard a lot of people stand up and say how good this man was! He helped a lot of people and touched a lot of lives! See, God judge us by the things we do. He say, 'Let the works I've done speak for me.' So, to the family, I say don't worry! You see, it's all right. . . . Don't you weep no mo'! Lord, don't you mourn. Let not your hearts be troubled, 'cause Brother Jeff done gone on to another place! A better place! A place where the thunder don't roll and the rain don't pour. Good God almighty! Where troubled winds no longer blow! Glory hallelujah! I'm talkin' 'bout heaven, y'all. Do you wanna go? I say, do you wanna go? 'Cause I wanna go. And if you get there before me . . . when you get there . . . tell my mother . . . and tell my father . . . that one day . . . I'm comin' home! I said I'm comin' home! Glory be to God! Hallelujah!"

Jeff's mother threw up her hands in the air and cried out, "Rejoice! Hallelujah! Praise God! Rejoice!" Two of the church ushers dressed in white stood over her and fanned her.

Suddenly, there was a loud thud. The church doors flew open and a crew of thugs entered menacingly with big guns drawn. They were all dressed in black with matching black boots, hats, and ratchets. At the sight of the intimidating crew, parishioners began to panic and look for a way out. Everyone knew that there were slim chances of a happy ending in this situation. That posse's intent was clear. They meant business. It looked like they came to kill.

They walked down the church aisle and further intimidated everyone by ice grilling them and pointing guns at their faces. Amidst the thugs was one female, dressed in black army fatigues, black Tims, and a black hat just like the rest of them.

The last man of the bunch entered the church, and the others in the crew respectfully parted, allowing him to pass. They posted up along the aisle on both sides to make sure nobody made a move. The last man headed up to the front of the church with two men following close on his heels. His presence was that of authority. It was obvious that he was captain and the other two were his lieutenants.

The captain gave the command, and his lieutenants sprang into action. Jeff had already been shot before he was thrown from that roof, but they walked up to his casket and coldly opened fire on him again, putting a brand new set of holes in his corpse. The lieutenants, Loco and Fuck-You-Phil, had been briefed and given orders. No mercy was to be shown to anyone at Jeff's funeral, not even the preacher. Whoever didn't cooperate was to be gunned down. It was that simple.

People hovered cowardly down by the pews and witnessed the desecration of Jeff's corpse in horror. To shoot a dead man in his casket was unheard of—and in the house of the Lord? Them boys had to be out of their minds. The funeral attendees all realized that their lives were in danger. The crew of young criminals in their presence was bold and reckless.

The whole church got down searching for cover, including the preacher. Everybody ducked except for Jeff's mother. She refused to let her son's memory be disrespected that way. She had to speak up in his honor.

"My God! What have you done? What kind of people are you? Have you no hearts and no souls? My child is already dead. You all are nothing but the children of Satan! Get outta here! I rebuke you in the name of Jesus. Get outta here! My son is dead! This is his homegoing ceremony. You killed him once, and you come to shoot him again? How can he rest in peace? My God, have you no shame?" She threw both hands up to the sky like she was looking to God for answers, and shook her head helplessly.

Jeff's mother was upset and very emotional. She was a woman of God, but her son's murderers were unmoved by her display of maternal bereavement and holiness. Loco, the shorter one wearing the black Yankee fitted cap, walked right up to her and shot her in the forehead at point-blank range.

The woman fell silent and her blood splattered on Jeff's grandmother, who was seated right next to her. After witnessing her daughter's murder, the elderly woman's initial reaction was of one of protest. She called on the Lord and stood up as if there was something she could do. But her protests were powerless and in vain. Fuck-You-Phil responded with a slug to her chest. That shot knocked her back in the pew. The poor old lady clutched her chest in disbelief, clinging to her life. Two seconds later, she was dead.

The two lieutenants, Loco and Fuck-You-Phil, were a special pair. Neither of them played with a full deck. At the sight of the old woman's demise, Loco started laughing hard as hell. That was the way he had earned his street name. He was just straight loco.

Fuck-You-Phil had his moniker because his name was Phil, and he was known to have told a few dudes who begged for their lives "fuck you" before he pulled the trigger and took their heads off. Both of the lieutenants were honored to be assigned the task of shooting up Jeff's corpse, and they were delighted to take shit a step further. Fuck that nigga and his whole family.

To shoot a dead man at his funeral was the highest form of disrespect. That nigga Jeff had fucked with the wrong person's money, so Jeff had to go. The captain, Butch, was so angry about the loss he took behind that nigga, he wanted to kill him again. That was one of two reasons why he had rounded up his troops and crashed the funeral. The other reason he was there was to find Jeff's partner, Bless, to retrieve his mothafuckin' money and kill him too.

Loco had smoked a blunt laced with some powerful angel dust right before they came. He was out of his mind, and in a straight I-don't-give-a-fuck mode. He was already crazy, so dust made him insane to the twelfth degree. Loco turned to the congregation and pointed to Jeff's grandmother.

He yelled, "Yo, y'all think that's disrespectful? I'll show you mothafuckas disrespectful! Y'all wanna see disrespectful? A'ight!"

He unzipped his black fatigues and removed his flaccid penis. He waved it at the congregation with an evil smirk, and then he walked over and pissed on Jeff's corpse. Everyone gasped in horror, each half expecting God to strike him down right there for his despicable act.

After Loco relieved his bladder, he put his dick away and just stared at everyone. He yelled, "Y'all mothafuckas better act like y'all know! Who else up in here want it? Who the fuck else want it? Nobody move, nobody get shot!"

He raised his gun and fired twice up in the air. It looked like he was busting shots at God.

"TBG mothafuckas! TBG up in this bitch! Yeah, niggas!"

That was the name of their crew. TBG simply stood for The Bad Guys. Butch was the captain, and he and his team didn't give a fuck. They were pitiless. They figured shooting up the funeral was appropriate. There was already slow singing and flower bringing, so it was nothing to body a few more mothafuckas.

Jeff's mother had asked for it, and his granny was old anyway. Fuck it! Butch's heart was stone cold.

The person he had come for wasn't in sight. Bless was Jeff's partner, and he was one lucky nigga. Fortunately for him, he had been smart enough not to show up to see his best homie laid to rest. Somebody must've been praying for his ass. But he was a marked man. He could run, but he couldn't hide. Butch had already decided that his days were numbered.

After seeing that Bless wasn't there, he scanned the pews for someone he could get answers from. He zoomed in on Jill and Taj in the front. He had done his homework, so he knew who they were. They were trying to hide, but he saw them. Butch knew that bitch Jill was having a baby by Jeff, and Taj was Bless's girlfriend. He walked over and addressed them both with no nonsense.

"Where the fuck is that nigga Bless at?"

Terrified, Taj and Jill both shook their heads and shrugged. They really had no idea. The girls were petrified. After seeing them niggas shoot Jeff's mother and grandmother, they knew he would kill them without a second thought.

Butch wasn't buying it. He ordered Loco to get the girls, so they could kidnap them. Those bitches were going to give up some mothafuckin' answers. He had lost a lot of money when them niggas shot and clipped his little man for them seven kilos, and somebody was going to get his shit back.

Loco snatched Taj and Jill up out of the front pew. They were both scared to death, but Taj was more afraid for Jill because she was pregnant. Again, she told Butch they didn't know anything. Butch silenced her with a deadly look. He warned Taj that if they didn't tell him where Bless was, he would have bullets put in her, Jill, and her baby. That was the last opportunity he gave them to speak. Neither Taj nor Jill uttered a word.

Butch could see that these broads weren't going to assist him voluntarily. He was rapidly running out of patience with them. Butch was a real dangerous but quiet dude. He wasn't much of a talker, but people listened when he spoke, and those bitches weren't going to be the exception to that rule. They were going to give him the information he needed. He would make sure of that. He ordered his lieutenants to march them out of the church. There were two gray, bulletproof vans with tinted windows waiting outside.

Butch had been the last man to enter the church, but he left first. His two second in command exited the church with the girls next, and the rest of his troops moved out behind them.

On the way out, the last goon on the back of the line, named Lefty, noticed an old gray-haired man dialing on his cell phone. Lefty paused and mercilessly put a bullet in grandpa's face. He did this as a warning to the others to think twice about calling the police. After a final steely glance around the church, he exited without a word.

Outside, Taj and Jill were seated in the back of one of the vans. They were surrounded by machine gun– toting thugs. Taj glanced over at her homegirl. It was dark inside because the van windows were tinted real dark. She couldn't really see Jill, but she could feel her next to her, shaking like a leaf. Jill must've been real nervous. The last words she mumbled to Taj were, "Yo, Taj, if you know where Bless is, you need to tell these niggas."

The women were driven to what they would later learn was TBG headquarters. Inside, they were thrown into separate dark rooms and bound to chairs. They would find out soon that the rooms were for interrogation.

Butch decided that they would lean on Taj first, because he had a feeling she knew more. She had to, because to his knowledge, she was fucking Bless. At least that was the word he got. Butch figured Taj needed a little more persuasion to talk, so he locked her in a room alone and sent for his resident down bitch, Cherry. After her psycho, got-somethin'-to-prove ass got a hold of Taj, she would realize the realness of the situation.

A short time later, Taj was sitting tied up in the dark when the door opened. Her eyes squinted from the sudden light. She could make out a chick entering with two dudes behind her. Taj was approached by Cherry Coke, the self-proclaimed first lady of TBG—if a lady was what you could call her.

As soon as she came in the room, she placed her gun on Taj's temple and demanded to know where Bless was. Cherry Coke was skied up off cocaine and was mad hype. She wanted to show Butch and the rest of the team how much she repped for TBG. For those two reasons, she got real extra with Taj. She knew that bitch knew something. She was fucking that nigga.

"Taj, you funky-ass bitch! You better give that nigga Bless up, 'fore you fuck around and be the guest of honor at a funeral like the one we just left."

Taj didn't say anything. She didn't give a fuck. She wasn't talking to anybody, not even Butch. But it was hard to ignore Cherry because her breath was hot as a fire-breathing dragon's and stinking so bad it was nauseating.

Cherry Coke got fed up with Taj's silence and hauled off and smacked her across her face. She hit her like she was trying to take her head off. Afterward, she said, "Now do you hear me talkin' to you, bitch?"

Taj spat blood to her left. Cherry Coke had caught her good. She wanted to jump up and beat that cokehead bitch's ass, but she was tied up. A gun was also pointed in her face. Plus, there was an armed man in the corner of the room. Taj knew the odds were stacked against her, but she was going to get Cherry back. She would make it a point. That crack head bitch's ass was hers. Taj silently put that on her deceased mother.

Cherry Coke looked at Taj expecting to see fear, but that wasn't what she saw in her eyes. It was hatred and resistance. The bitch thought she was hard. Cherry wanted Taj to fear her. She was the first lady of TBG They were the most feared crew in all of Brooklyn, and she demanded respect. Cherry Coke slapped the shit out of Taj again.

Taj had eaten one hit. She let that bitch rock. But after that second slap, she was vexed. Her first reaction was to hock spit in Cherry's fucking face.

After Taj's spit splattered across her face, Cherry quickly wiped it off with the back of her hand. She said, "Bitch, I'ma fuckin' kill you! Do you know who the fuck I am?"

She took the gun and busted Taj upside her head. Taj's hands were tied, but she leaned back and kicked that bitch Cherry in her midsection. She wished she was free so she could beat that bitch.

Cherry doubled over in pain. After a second, she came back up with the pistol and clocked Taj in the face again. She hit her in the nose that time. Taj saw light for a minute, and excruciating pain spread across her face.

Cherry spat, "Bitch, you wanna fuckin' die today? Do somethin' else and you gon' get your death wish. I will kill you, stupid-ass bitch!" She glared at Taj. "I got somethin' for you, bitch."

She took a walkie-talkie from her hip and called for the thirstiest hounds on the team.

***

There was lots of hoopla in the streets about TBG. Just about everyone feared them, but it was safe to say that Cherry had somewhat exaggerated her position in the organization. She wasn't actually a member of TBG. She was more like their property. They kept her around for their use, like the coke whore they had turned her into. She was passed around the crew to anyone who wanted to have his way with her. Cherry was TBG property, and all the members had equal access to every hole in her body, so she was really just a whore who did all of her servicing in-house.

Cherry started out as a shorty Butch was dealing with, but he soon discovered she was weak. The day he turned her out, he had caught her stealing coke from his stash. That really pissed Butch off because he had already given her a nice fifty bag of snow to get right on. Butch realized then she had a nose like a vacuum cleaner. He had slapped her around a few times, called her names, and then poured an ounce of powder on a tray on the table. It was a real mountain of snow.

Butch grabbed Cherry by her hair and pushed her whole fucking face into the pile. He made her snort as much as she could before he let her up for air and started talking shit.

He said, "You up in here stealin' my shit? You want some more, ho?"

Then he shoved her face back down and yelled,
"You had enough yet, huh, bitch?" Since she was
such a greedy bitch, he wanted to teach her ass a
lesson.

The third time he did it, he said, "Your name is
Cherry, right? Now that shit is Cherry Coke. How
'bout that? You want more, bitch? Have some
more! You stinkin', filthy, rotten bitch!"

Cherry shook her head vigorously. She couldn't
take it. Her nose was burning so bad; she was crying. She felt like her heart was going to bust from
the rush. She wasn't an idiot. She knew snorting
that much coke could kill her. She begged Butch
to stop.

"No more, please . . . I'm so s-s-sorry!" she
squealed.

Just to show that bitch who the mothafuckin'
boss was, Butch mercilessly slammed her face
into the pile of coke one more time. He held the
back of her head so she couldn't move. Cherry
tried not to inhale, but she had no choice. She
had to breathe. That last blast was so powerful
that her tongue was numb and she couldn't even
speak anymore.

Butch yanked her hair hard and made her face
him. He looked at her with pure disgust and told
her she was nothing but a sorry-ass coke whore.
He then informed her that she owed him for all

the coke she had just snorted up. Cherry was scared and out of it. She didn't even protest.

Butch unzipped his jeans and let his dick loose. He demanded that she get down on her knees.

"Come on, bitch, and pay this bill. You in debt to me . . . Now get down and suck my joint. Hurry the fuck up!"

Cherry was high as hell, so she was out of it. A hard smack across the jaw by Butch put some sense in her head. Knowing the type of dude Butch was, she jumped down quickly and did as she was told. She could tell he would not hesitate to use that big gun he kept on his hip, so she gave that blowjob all she had. Cherry was good, so she got Butch off pretty fast.

But he wasn't finished with her. After he shot off down her throat, he summoned all of his soldiers and announced the opportunity for them to get right—all thirteen of them. Cherry was ordered to pleasure them one by one, two by two, and three by three. Butch stood watching the makeshift gangbang. He ignored her cries and protests when dudes were rough. Some of them strapped up, but some went raw, shooting their loads inside her.

A couple of hours later, he told Cherry's sore throat and pussy–having ass to take a break and a shower. When she was cleaned up, he "suggested" she do a few more lines to make herself feel better. Even though she had almost gone into cardiac arrest and overdosed barely two hours before, Cherry went for it. She got high all night, and before the sun came up, she had serviced six dudes again with no problem.

Butch wasn't stupid. He hadn't just been tricking coke for the hell of it. He knew what he was doing. His plan was to pump so much coke in her system that she would spend her days trying to reach that high again. She would probably die trying. He increased her addiction level times fifty. Butch was willing to keep her around and feed her habit, but that bitch would do as he said.

Cherry did everything he said, too, from servicing his crew regularly to even busting shots at niggas when he told her to. Cherry was gun-happy and had put many niggas who fucked up Butch's money in the wind. Niggas ran without firing back. The streets knew she was TBG property, so she was a bitch with a pass.

Cherry loved doing dirt with Butch. They only shared personal time together when he gave her one-on-one talks to go over her assignments. Cherry was so dependent on Butch and eager to please him; she never fucked up what he told her to do.

That's why she took this Taj situation very, very serious. If Butch wanted answers, he was gonna get answers. Cherry knew how to make that bitch start singing. If Taj could stand up to what she had in store for her, she was one bad bitch.

Taj was a stand-up chick, and she was from Brooklyn. BK didn't raise no rats. That was the code of the streets, and it was imbedded in her—that, and she really didn't know where Bless's conniving ass was. He had been MIA since Jeff passed, so she exercised her right to remain silent.

But there was only so much a woman could take. Taj was stripped naked and tied down horizontally with her legs open. Her wrists and ankles were bound. Cherry kept hitting her, spitting on her, and inserting foreign objects into her vagina. She fucked her with a broom, a cordless phone, a big wax candle, and she even tried to stick a sneaker in her pussy. The sneaker didn't fit, so she stuck the candle back in. Cherry even went so far as to light the end of the candle that was sticking out. The men standing around whistled like wolves. Cherry had been violated by the dudes in that house so much that it was nothing for her to violate another bitch. She was putting on a real show for the gang.

She told the fellas she was about to have some birthday cake, and that nasty bitch bent down and started eating Taj's pussy. The men went wild, and that caused her to really go in. She spread Taj's vaginal lips so that her clit popped out, and she hungrily sucked on it.

Cherry, a bisexual, was enjoying herself. Fresh meat was tasty, especially with Taj bucking in protest. Meanwhile, the candle in her pussy still burned.

Taj nearly vomited from Cherry's stink mouth on her twat. She had never been with a girl before, and the fact that it was this coke whore bitch, who she was planning on killing, really made the act a turnoff. If she could've gotten loose from the ropes she was tied in, she would've killed the bitch right then.

Cherry could see that Taj didn't approve, but she was going to make her like it. She was going to turn that bitch out. She snatched that candle out of Taj's pussy and walked around in front of her. She wrapped her arms around her thighs so she couldn't move, and shoved her face in Taj's pussy. She ate Taj out with fervor, in a way she knew was good to her. Cherry Coke looked up at Taj and said, "Say you like it, bitch! Say you like the way I'm eatin' this pussy!"

Taj was so mad, tears welled up in the corners of her eyes. She bit her lip in anger and stared at that bitch coldly. She rolled her eyes and hissed, "Fuck you, bitch! Hell no! I don't like that shit! You fuckin' nasty dyke!"

Cherry bit down as hard as she could on Taj's inner thigh. Taj yelped in pain. Cherry laughed and said, "Don't scream, bitch. You gonna like it. You gonna love it! Watch! And if you don't, I'ma blow your mothafuckin' head off."

Cherry parted Taj's pussy with two fingers, and she bent down and tongued it for a few more minutes. She slipped four fingers in and out and stuck her thumb in her asshole.

Taj just lay there with her eyes closed. There was nothing else she could do. She felt like a filthy exhibit in a freak show. The gang members surrounding them rubbed their crotches in anticipation. Some of them were literally drooling.

Cherry was concentrating on Taj's clit. To Taj's dismay, it started feeling good—real good. She tried to fight it, but she felt an eruption mounting in her groin. Taj bit her lip to keep from crying out. Against her will, she started shaking and came hard.

Cherry had eaten a few pussies in her time, and she knew when a chick was cumming. Taj's juices were flowing. She could taste them. Cherry continued to lick her clit rapidly, forcing her fist in her pussy. Taj squirmed and cried out in pain, but Cherry wouldn't stop. She fisted Taj's pussy deep. She had her whole hand inside of her.

Taj would never admit it, but she had never experienced such pleasurable pressure. Against her will, she came again. Cherry could feel her pussy walls contracting on her hand. After a few more seconds, she noisily extracted her fist from Taj's soaked tunnel.

Cherry stood up and smiled at Taj coyly. She seductively licked two of her fingers. "I told you, my little slut bitch. I knew you'd like it. Now lick your cum off my fingers and see how good you taste."

She walked over and smeared Taj's pussy juice all over her lips. Taj turned her head, but she couldn't escape the sticky film Cherry smeared on her face. Cherry wanted to eat that pussy again just to show that bitch, but the natives were restless. By now, the men were groping and pawing both of them, especially Taj.

That was where the pleasure stopped. The men pinched her nipples and roughly squeezed her breasts and jammed their filthy fingers in her ass and pussy. When she resisted, Taj was beaten and then raped repeatedly. They had their dicks all over her face and lips. One after the other, they shot semen all over her body, inside and out. Before it was over, one mothafucka even peed on her. Taj was humiliated so badly that she wanted to die.

Before Taj knew it, that bitch Cherry climbed up on the table. She stood over her and smirked. Then she squatted, putting her ass in Taj's face. Taj turned her head and fought as hard as she could, but Cherry plopped her stinking, rotten funk box right in her face. Taj spit and gasped for air.

"Get the fuck off me, you stink-pussy dyke bitch! I'ma kill you, ho! That's my word!"

Cherry grabbed her hair and said, "Bitch, you better shut the fuck up and eat this pussy. Kenny, gimme that fuckin' gat."

Kenny passed Cherry the .45. She cocked it and stuck it right to Taj's temple. She stared down at her coldly. Through clenched teeth, she said, "Bitch, I said eat. And you better do it good as I did you. You don't fuckin' stop until I get up and tell you to. You hear me?"

Against Taj's will, she was forced to lick Cherry's stinking slit. There was no way in the world she could pleasure her wholeheartedly. She just couldn't. But Cherry dug that steel gun barrel into the side of her head. Taj was afraid that crazy, coked-up bitch would make a mistake and pull the trigger, so she gave in.

"All right, get that fuckin' gun out my face, bitch! All right!"

Cherry gave her a warning look and hesitantly passed the gun to Face, another one of the goons.

"Face, do me a favor. If it don't look like I'm enjoying myself, put a bullet in this bitch's melon."

Face had a crazed look in his eyes like he would do it. Taj knew she was surrounded by stone cold murderers, and she believed he would. Cherry wrapped her fist in Taj's hair and directed her face back to the place.

Taj was afraid for her life, so she swallowed the vomit that rose in her throat and started lapping Cherry's pussy like a kitten on a bowl of milk. She tried to hold back as much as she could, but Cherry commanded her to suck on her clit.

Taj closed her eyes and tried to use her imagination. She had to pretend she was doing something else—anything else. She would've rather eaten a bowl of hyena shit than Cherry's diseased bat cave. She almost threw up again, but took a deep breath and shook it off. She placed her lips on Cherry's clit and sucked it gently, pretending it was ice cream of her favorite flavor. It was hard, though, because of the foul smell.

After a minute, she heard moaning. She guessed she was doing it right. She wanted to get it over with quick, so she started licking and sucking faster. Cherry was humping her face excitedly and moaning.

One of the dudes shouted out, "Hurry up and cum, ho! I wanna put my dick in this bitch's mouth." That drew a few laughs from the others.

Cherry looked at him defiantly and spat, "No, fuck that! Butch gave me the green light to do what I wanna do, and I wanna cum in this bitch's face. Nigga, you fuckin' up my groove. Now just shut the fuck up so I can cum."

The dude shook his head impatiently, but he didn't say another word. The sight of that girl-on-girl had him so turned-on; his dick was throbbing for release. He began unconsciously stroking his own member to please himself.

Cherry kept riding Taj's face, grinding her juices all over her nose and chin. She was taking advantage of the situation. Taj was seething underneath her, but she kept on licking the smelly pussy. She couldn't see with Cherry's ass plopped in her face, but she felt another guy mounting her. He pawed her breasts, and then he penetrated her and started stroking real deep. He was built large, which made it worse.

Taj was tied down to the table with her legs open, so she just lay there and said her millionth prayer that she didn't catch AIDS or something from those niggas.

More of the dudes wanted to participate, but there were limited holes for them to penetrate. One dude hopped up on the table, too, and stuck his dick in Cherry's mouth. She just grabbed it and started sucking it like a lollipop and kept fucking Taj's face.

Another dude yelled out, "Yo, I want that pregnant bitch!"

Cherry overheard him and said, "Word, go get that bitch! I want her out here. She gon' taste this pussy too!" She went back to sucking the dick she had in her hand.

Two of the goons, Lefty and Rell, left to get Jill. She had been sitting in the dark for too long. Jill was relieved to see light when they opened her door. The men untied her and told her to follow them. Jill didn't know where they were taking her, but she had one request.

She said, "Excuse me. I'm sorry, but I gotta pee."

The men just looked at each other. "A'ight, ma," the taller one named Lefty said. They led her to the bathroom so she could relieve her bladder.

After Jill used the bathroom, they told her to take off her clothes. She looked at them puzzled and shook her head. What the hell was wrong with them? Couldn't they see that she was pregnant?

Lefty made a face. He said, "I didn't ask you. I ain't never hit a pregnant chick before. I wanna try that pussy, so just listen to what I tell you. Don't gimme a reason, shorty." He showed her the gun in his waist.

Jill saw that he wasn't kidding. She searched the other guy's face for some sort of sympathy, but there was none there either. She didn't want these niggas to hurt her baby, so she had to do what they said. She took off her blouse, but then she hesitated.

Lefty nodded at her, encouraging her to finish undressing. Jill reluctantly removed her skirt next. The other goon, Rell, took the liberty of unfastening her bra himself. He was anxious to see those big, milk-filled jugs. When he got Jill's bra unhooked and slipped it off, his tongue hung out like a panting dog. He palmed her titties and squeezed her nipples until they stiffened in his fingertips, and then he bent down and sucked on them one by one.

Jill recoiled in disgust and tried to push him away. Rell laughed and told her they were going to a party. He and Lefty forced Jill down the hall to the room where the action was going on. Jill was nervous before they opened the door, but she was in no way prepared for what she would see next.

In the room there was a crowd of excited dudes standing around a table watching something. When the door opened, they all turned around and whistled at Jill with her filled-out pregnant hips and breasts. They all went wild like she was fresh meat.

Jill focused in on what they were watching on the table. Her jaw dropped in shock. She couldn't believe her eyes. Taj was tied up on the table, naked and spread-eagled, and there was a guy having sex with her. Worst of all, that nasty bitch Cherry Coke was sitting on Taj's face, moaning and bucking like she was cumming. The other thing Jill noticed was the crazy-looking guy with the gun pointed at Taj, forcing her to do it. Jill was afraid—very afraid. Her heart went out to her friend, and she prayed she wouldn't be subjected to the same degradation.

Jill had the feeling her prayers would go unanswered. This was evident by the seven guys groping her titties and ass. She knew they were going to rape her. They had guns. There were four visible in the room, so she knew she didn't have any wins. Just like Taj, she knew she was doomed.

Cherry hollered out in bliss as she came all over Taj's face. Taj had eaten her pussy real good, just like she ordered. The sound of Cherry yelling out in pleasure caused the guy who was stroking Taj to increase his rhythm. Now he was about to cum. He pulled out and shot all over Taj's stomach. Jill watched in horror and realized that they weren't using condoms. What the hell type of freak show was this?

Little did Jill know, most of the dudes in the gang already had sex with Taj—at least ten of them. And only half of them had bothered using a condom, even though she had begged them all to.

Cherry got up off Taj's face on legs that trembled. She slapped Taj lightly across her face and stroked her hair.

She said, "Good girl. You made mommy's pussy feel so good. Now you get a treat. You get to get your pussy licked too . . . by her."

Cherry pointed at Jill, who just stood there looking at her like she was crazy. Cherry said, "Bitch, did you hear what I just said? Get down and lick her pussy!"

Jill said, "Hell no! That's like my sister!"

Cherry said, "Bitch, I don't give a fuck if she's ya mama! I said get down there and eat that pussy. It got a sticky, sweet glaze on it for you too." Cherry smirked.

She was referring to the many different types of semen on Taj. It was like she was covered in cum punch. Jill backed up and shook her head, wide-eyed with fear. Taj pleaded with them too. She was embarrassed that Jill had seen her that way, especially with Cherry sitting on her face. But there was no way they could do each other. They were best friends and as close as sisters. She hoped that Cherry would just let it go, on the strength of Jill being pregnant.

Cherry wasn't letting anything go. She took the gun back from Face and pointed it at Jill. She smiled wickedly and walked over and placed it on her belly.

"Bitch, I said eat that pussy, or I'll blow your fuckin' baby head off! Get on your mothafuckin' knees now!"

Cherry knew what she was doing could destroy their friendship, but she was just being spiteful. If those bitches didn't start coughing up some answers about Butch's money, they wouldn't live long enough to stay friends anyway.

The dilemma Jill faced caused tears to flood her eyes. Cherry was trying to make her do some foul shit, especially with that semen all over Taj. The thought made Jill sick. She doubled over and threw up right there on the floor.

The sight of her barfing didn't stir any emotions in Cherry. She was a cold bitch with no heart. She told Jill point blank that if she vomited again, she would kill her. Then she ordered her to get over there and lick that pussy clean.

The dudes were yelling, "Do it! Eat that pussy! Do it!"

Tears streamed down Jill's face. She realized she didn't have a choice. She stood in front of Taj, who she could see was crying too. She didn't want this any more than Jill did. What type of shit were they caught up in? Those mothafuckas were sick.

Cherry Coke hit Jill upside the head with the gun to give her a final warning. She said, "Bitch, keep playin' with me! You think I won't kill your fuckin' baby?" She cocked the gun.

Jill took the hint. The knot Cherry just put on the back of her head was throbbing like crazy, and she didn't want to be subjected to any more violence. She had to worry about her unborn child. Her baby had been through enough. His father's funeral was also that day. Jill slowly bent down and took a look at Taj's vagina. Cherry Coke roughly pushed her head in it, smearing semen all over her face.

Jill vowed not to swallow that disgusting stuff. She closed her eyes and began to lick her best friend's pussy at gunpoint. Taj just lay there with her eyes closed. They both wondered how they were ever going to face each other again.

Cherry leaned down and watched Jill closely, scrutinizing her every move. She coached her and made sure she was doing it right.

"That's right, lick it. Hold that pussy open. Now suck on the clit. That's right, bitch! Suck it!"

When Cherry was finally satisfied that Jill was doing it right, she got down on her knees in front of her and parted her pussy lips. Jill looked down and saw that Cherry was preparing to eat her out. That bitch was sick. She was a straight freak.

Cherry had never eaten out a pregnant girl, so she was curious to see what flavor that milk was. She spread Jill's pussy open and stuck her tongue all the way inside. She didn't come up for air until Jill's legs started trembling. Her pussy had a distinct flavor to it. Cherry wanted more. She tongued it for a few more minutes, before she stood back up on her feet.

She noticed that Jill wasn't making Taj squirm yet, so she spread Taj's pussy lips for her and showed her how it should be done. Cherry sucked on Taj's pussy for about thirty seconds, and then she made Jill do it again the way she showed her. Jill just wanted to get it over with, so she did what Cherry said. It must've felt good to Taj because now she was breathing real heavy. This dude walked over and started rubbing his dick across her lips while he was jerking off.

Jill kept her eyes closed and kept on licking Taj the way Cherry instructed her to. Taj moaned softly a time or two, and the flavor down there suddenly changed. Jill realized she must've made Taj cum.

Cherry noticed Taj's body twitching. She liked to see that. Now it was her turn. She jumped on top of Taj and spread her legs open so that her pussy was right in Jill's face too.

Jill looked real hesitant, but Cherry pointed the gun at her head.

"Eat me, bitch! Don't worry, this shit's good for your baby. Pussy is full of vitamins and minerals. And cherries are good for you."

A few of the men laughed and tugged on their dicks. They were anxious for the opportunity to fuck Jill. They had all heard about how good pregnant pussy was.

Cherry grabbed the back of Jill's head and forced her face in her pussy. Jill gagged and choked, but Cherry wouldn't let her up for air. She traced the gun along her ear. Jill got the picture and went to work. She fought the bile that kept rising in her throat. She sucked on Cherry's clit, which caused her to moan loudly. Taj just lay there underneath Cherry while Jill licked her pussy. She was still tied up and very helpless.

Lefty watched Jill's peanut butter-colored ass up in the air while she was bent over eating Cherry out. He wanted to be the first to fuck her. He walked up behind her and slid his dick inside of her. She was already wet and slippery from Cherry eating her out, so his entry was a breeze. He palmed her titties and stroked that pussy deep.

Jill started crying again while she was raped and forced to lick Cherry's smelly box at the same time. Her name should've been Rotten Cherry, Jill was thinking, feeling like she'd lost all her dignity. All of her self-respect was gone.

More alarming, she and Taj were in a situation where they could easily be killed. These mothafuckas were crazy. They had killed Jeff's mother at his funeral, and his grandmother too. And they would kill them, too, without a second thought. This wasn't a game.

The men had a field day molesting, degrading, and sodomizing Jill the same way they had done Taj. After having an outright orgy with all three of the women, they began to disperse and retreat to their beds. Most of them were weak and sleepy from all the freaky sex they had participated in.

The horrendous torture had lasted over three hours. After it was over, Jill was escorted back to the other room and retied. They left her alone, filthy and naked.

Butch didn't have anything against Jill and Taj. His only concern was those seven kilos that Bless and that dead nigga Jeff burned him for. Those girls just messed with the wrong dudes. Those bitches still hadn't given up Bless's whereabouts, so as far as he was concerned, the team could have their way with them.

Butch ran a tight ship. Anyone who crossed him got it in the worst way. His team of goons was loyal, and they followed his orders. He treated them all well in exchange.

An hour later, Butch gave Taj another opportunity to give up her man. He had her try calling that nigga, but the calls were going straight to voice mail. Taj was desperate to save her and Jill's lives, so she looked at him earnestly and lied.

Taj convinced him that she needed to be let go so she could go set Bless up. She and Jill's lives depended on it, so she promised Butch that she would get his money.

In her heart she didn't really believe she could pull it off. She didn't even know where Bless was, but she had to do something. She hadn't seen Bless since days before Jeff was killed. They had argued like they always did, and that was that. She had thought it was a real sucker move that he decided not to attend the funeral. Now Taj wished she and Jill hadn't attended either.

After much deliberation, Butch decided to let Taj go. He didn't have many other options to get at Bless. He had already sent a team of goons to his mother's house, but the apartment was empty when they had arrived. They could tell that the occupants had vacated the premises in a hurry. They had waited hours, but no one returned. Butch guessed that nigga Bless was smart enough to get his moms out of harm's way. Butch warned Taj that if she didn't come through for him, he would be sure to kill Jill and her unborn fetus.

Taj begged him to let her take a shower. Though his eyes remained cold and expressionless, he gave her permission. He had cameras hidden in the interrogation rooms, and had seen the inhumane way in which she and her pregnant friend had been treated.

He was turned off by the display of unsafe group sex and not the least bit interested in joining in. But Butch wouldn't have participated in such festivities anyhow, because he wasn't that hard up. He was just cold. He was the type of nigga to pimp on a bitch stone cold in chilly blood. Calling him icy was a real understatement. The only reason he was allowing Taj a shower was because he couldn't stand looking at her cum-drenched body.

Taj was grateful, but she cried her heart out in the shower. She scrubbed her skin so hard; she almost took a layer off. She vowed to kill that bitch Cherry one day for violating her like that. The tears streaming down her face were immediately washed away by the much-welcomed hot shower water, but she would wear the scars from that brutal gang rape the rest of her life.

After Taj got cleaned up, Butch ordered his driver to take her home. Before releasing her, he again warned her not to try anything funny. He said he was letting her call it, but a bad choice would end in Jill and her baby's murder. Taj could tell from the steel look in eyes that he meant it.

Butch walked Taj over to the room Jill was in, and told Jill what it was. He said, "I'm letting your homegirl go so she could get my fuckin' money. She has to point me to that nigga Bless within twenty-four hours. If she doesn't, you and your baby are dead."

He grabbed Taj and hurried her along. Taj would never forget the look on Jill's face as she watched her leave. Her eyes had pleaded with her to save her and her child.

After Taj got away, she was torn. She wanted to go back and save Jill, but she knew that if she returned empty-handed they would both be dead. Taj's heart ached for her dear friend. She knew what would become of her. The thought was sad, but it was something she would have to live with. Jill was like her sister.

Hours later, after making 287 unsuccessful attempts to contact Bless, Taj sat in her bedroom crying. That nigga was not picking up, no matter what number she called him from. She tried to be strong, but knew what a fucked-up predicament she had left Jill in.

Taj had to face reality. She couldn't help retrieve Butch's money, so she couldn't go back for Jill. She had to get out of town. There was no sense in both of them being killed. Taj shook her head in disbelief. Jill's life was in danger, and there was nothing she could do.

A surge of resilience hit Taj. Fuck that. Jill was her best friend. Taj tried to formulate a plan. As she sat there pondering, she turned on the

TV and flipped to the news. The news footage she saw about the church funeral shooting of Jeff's mother, grandmother, and another elderly gentleman ended any second thoughts she had about going back for Jill.

Taj was no fool. She had to hurry up and make moves. It was only a matter of time before Butch sent his goons over to put a bullet in her head as well.

Taj packed as many clothes as she could stuff into an overnight bag and small suitcase and then hopped in her Jeep and pulled off into the night. She hated to leave, but she knew that her days were numbered if she stayed. There was nothing she could do about the guilt that was eating at her. She would be forced to take it to her grave.

The next day, it didn't take Butch long to figure out that he had been burned again. He was totally remorseless in his decision to do away with Jill's pregnant ass. Jeff had fucked him, so he would pay for generations to come. He would kill his unborn seed, and he hoped it was a boy. Butch had to send the message that he would take out nigga's namesakes if they crossed and violated him.

He glanced at his watch for the umpteenth time. Time was up. Butch mentally counted to ten. That was it. Taj hadn't called him or made any contact. That bitch must have thought he was joking or something. Did she think his threats were idle? She must have been out of her mothafuckin' mind! He mused, scratching his chin and staring out the window with his arms folded.

Anyone who had dealt wrongly with Butch knew that wasn't a good sign. The pondering, the crossed-arm stance, and the chin scratch usually meant that he was contemplating the way a person was going to die. This particular time it was Jill's fate he was sealing. He already knew she had to go, but it was just a matter of how. Butch decided to make it quick. From what he had seen on the cameras, she had been tortured enough.

Butch looked at Loco and Fuck-You-Phil and said two words, "Kill Jill." The grimy pair was delighted they were given the honors. They hurried to retrieve her.

Jill was untied and taken from the room. She began to panic because she knew where they were taking her. It became harder and harder for her to breathe with each step. Her stomach was cramping severely. She could feel her baby balling up inside of her. It was as if he sensed danger and was trying to find a corner to hide.

Jill was walked down two flights of stairs to the basement. She was pleading for her life along the way, but to no avail. Loco was heartless. He silenced her desperate pleas with a bullet to her womb.

Jill stared down at her belly in horror. She placed her hand over the gunshot wound like she was trying to stop her baby's life from draining through it. She kept praying that God was with her.

Jill had carried that fetus inside her for nearly nine months. She had developed a real connection to her son. She didn't feel her baby moving anymore, so she knew he was gone. Her eyes watered up at the thought. Her heart was broken.

Jill looked in the eyes of her baby's killer, fearless at that point. There was nothing worse they could do to her. She used what she knew were the last few precious seconds of her life to pray for her soul to get into heaven with her baby's, and then she spit in his face.

Loco just wiped the spit off with his sleeve and laughed coldly, and then he squeezed his hammer. He nailed Jill in the forehead, right between the eyes. Her lifeless, naked body slumped to the floor. After she dropped, Loco returned the rude gesture and spit on her.

They stuffed her body into a heavy-duty black construction bag, and then she was taken to a dark alley. Her naked corpse was dumped in a garbage dumpster.

A short time later, a miracle happened in that dumpster. It was as if an angel flew over Jill. She could actually feel the breeze from the flapping of wings. God had smiled down on her, and by His grace, she was still alive. But Jill was fighting for her life. She had taken a bullet in her forehead.

Luckily, it wasn't long before she was discovered by sanitation workers during their routine early morning garbage pickup. They immediately notified the paramedics. Jill arrived at the hospital naked, battered, and covered in crusty, dried semen. Her heartbeat was extremely faint. She was weak, but she was holding on.

The dead fetus was removed from her belly through a caesarean incision, and then Jill lay unconscious for eleven days. When she finally regained consciousness, she could remember her traumatic ordeal like it was yesterday.

When the authorities questioned Jill, she just played dumb and acted like she didn't know who the perpetrators were. She didn't give anybody up because she didn't plan on going to court to testify against them. She didn't want to face TBG. Not that way. She wanted them to believe she was really dead. That way, when she initiated her revenge on them for killing her unborn child, they wouldn't know where the heat was coming from.

While Jill lay in the hospital healing, she thought about Taj a lot. Her best friend had left her for dead. And that bitch was part of the reason her baby was murdered. The thought was enough to make Jill want to kill Taj too. Their paths would eventually cross again, and when they did, there would be hell to pay.

But the way they had both suffered at the hands of TBG would bind them forever. No amount of therapy would erase those scars. The things she and Taj had been subjected to and forced to do to each other, Jill would never tell a soul. That was something she would pray about for years to come. She would never forget. She would wear the scars forever, but the memories she would take to her grave.

Smooth As Silk

by

J.M. Benjamin

Chapter 1

"Yooo!" was the cheer that could be heard coming from one of the craps tables at the Bally's Casino in Atlantic City, New Jersey. The body-infested gamblers surrounding the oval-shaped table roared in unison as the numbers five and six appeared on the two ice cube– sized dice for the tenth time within the past fifteen minutes that evening since Rasheed Phillups aka Big Sheed had been rolling them. Those amongst the fortunate who had placed bets on the number eleven, which paid thirty-to-one or fifteen-to-one odds—depending what bet they had made—collected their payouts with smiles. Other men and women from all over the globe—young and old—of all shapes, sizes, and colors excitedly and thankfully egged Big Sheed on while exchanging high fives around the table as he continued to contribute to their winnings with each roll. Some of them were more grateful than others. They were the ones who had lost every dime they had come to the casino with and nearly all of what the nearest ATM would allow them to withdraw for the day. They were the ones that had just about given up all hope of at least winning back a portion of what they had so rapidly squandered—if not being able to break even for the night.

Now here it was—moments ago, the young, six foot one inch, bronze-complexioned, well-dressed man, looking like someone straight out of *GQ,* with a beautiful deep-chocolate woman in tow, who had matched him in height and could have easily been mistaken for a model herself, emerged on the scene with a hot hand and had been saving the day since. Twenty minutes prior, Big Sheed appeared out of nowhere, approached the table, pulled out his Seven Stars Total Rewards Card—which meant he was a high-roller and considered to be amongst the elite of gamblers who frequented the casino and any other casinos under the Harrah's umbrella—along with a stack of one hundred dollar bills wrapped with a ten thousand dollar bank wrapper, and confidently tossed it onto the table and asked for change.

Five minutes later, Big Sheed received the dice after the elderly Caucasian man beside him crapped out instead of rolling his intended point.

Big Sheed raised what was to be his fourth glass of
Rémy VSOP—containing a double shot—threw it
back, then chased it with a Corona and lime, and
then chose the two dice he felt would make him
some money for the evening. Having had the dice
for what seemed like an eternity, Big Sheed not
only had his initial ten thousand dollars in casino
chips in front of him, he also had an additional
thirty thousand–plus profit in chips thanks to
what he considered to be his latest lucky charm.

"Press my six and eight hard—five hundred
each." He tossed two purple chips on the table to
increase his bets on the numbers he most favored.
Ever since he started coming down to AC from
Plainfield—where he was from—he'd been hooked
on the numbers: double three and double four
that paid nine-to-one odds if they were rolled.
Those numbers had contributed to his financial
rise and fall over the years since he had climbed
the criminal ladder in the drug game. On many
nights he had jumped in his ride and hopped on
the parkway with his entire stash consisting of
just enough money to purchase two ounces of
coke—which back then valued at five hundred a
pop—and within an hour and ten minutes he'd
exit the AC Expressway at thirty-eight, placing
him at a craps table in fifteen minutes. Within
three hours he'd make enough paper to purchase

a quarter kilo. Then there were those nights when he had made his way up to buying a whole kilo of cocaine when the prices ranged from eighteen to twenty-one grand, and he was seeing more money than he knew what to do with. He would often take both his profit and re-up money down to the gambling casino and lose it all within an hour's time. But that was long ago, when he was in his twenties and didn't have the coke connect he had now. Although his wins and loses still fluctuated, Big Sheed generally came out on top; and tonight he was proving that as the dice continued to work in his favor.

He now had fifteen hundred on the hard six and the same on the hard eight. In addition, he had five hundred dollars on the numbers five and nine as he placed bets; and six hundred dollars on the easy six and eight.

"No more bets," the stickman called out as he pushed the dice in front of Big Sheed.

"Drinks, cocktails," the waitress announced in passing.

"Yeah, right here, sweetheart." Big Sheed waved her over as the stickman pulled the dice back.

"Yes, sir?" the waitress smiled.

"Yeah, lemme get another double shot of Rémy and Corona with a lime, please," he ordered.

Normally, other gamblers would be murmuring derogatory comments and sighing in frustration when someone held up the flow of the game and momentum of the table, but not so much as a peep was made against Big Sheed. Instead, everyone surrounding the table waited, keeping their thoughts and comments to themselves.

"Anything for the lady?" she politely asked.

"Just water," Silk answered.

"And a Grey Goose and cranberry," Big Sheed added for her.

"Okay, here's your water. I'll be right back with your drinks," she replied before leaving the table.

"I don't know why you're try'na get me drunk," Silk said playfully.

"You know why." Big Sheed matched her tone. The stickman and male gamblers within range all smiled in envy.

"I don't have to be drunk for that," she shot back in a seductive tone.

"Here, blow on these." Big Sheed grinned. He then held the dice up to Silk's lips, careful not to violate the casino's strict policy by moving the dice away from the table. The last thing he wanted was to be accused of being one of those who made failed attempts in switching casino dice and have his high roller privileges revoked.

Silk puckered her lips and seductively blew onto the dice. Big Sheed then leaned in and embraced Silk's luscious lips. He was into lips and Silk's were full sized. The lip gloss she wore illuminated her lips and turned Big Sheed on. The thought of where Silk's lips would be later and how they would make him feel excited Sheed and boosted his confidence even more. A mixture of envious and lust-filled eyes zeroed in on the intimate exchange. Big Sheed loved the attention he and Silk were receiving and the fact that he was responsible for all the happy faces and smiles around the table with stacks of chips in front of them.

Even the on-lookers cheered him, wishing they were amongst the lucky ones that benefitted from his time on the dice. Big Sheed knew that if he rolled the number four, pandemonium would break loose at the table, and that's exactly what he wanted. With that intention, Big Sheed released the dice.

"Nine," the stickman called out as the dice came to a halt. Everyone who had placed bets on number nine were paid, including Big Sheed, whose payout was seven hundred dollars.

"Press my five and nine up a hundred and up my six and eight inside, ninety each." He increased his inside bets. The stickman took four black hundred-dollar chips and gave Big Sheed three blacks and four red five-dollar chips then pressed his bets.

The stickman on the right, in the middle of the table, scooped up the dice then pushed them back in Big Sheed's direction to roll again.

"Ma'am, no cell phones at the table." The stickman directed his words to Silk, who was text messaging, while pulling the dice back toward him.

"Oh, I'm sorry," she replied apologetically before putting away her BlackBerry Curve.

"She didn't know, my dude." Big Sheed immediately came to her defense. "Here, put the dealers on hard six and eight." He then tossed two black chips, valued at a hundred dollars each, to place bets for the table workers. "And a hundred on the six and eight hard—for my baby," he added, pulling Silk closer in to him.

"Thank you, sir," they all chimed together.

Silk smiled and rubbed the lower part of Big Sheed's back.

"Now, let's get this money," he barked as he released the dice onto the table. One of the dice immediately stopped on the number three, while the other hopped off the table.

"Damn, that was my hard six," he cursed under his breath, convinced the die that flew off the table would have been another three. Although he was not superstitious, there were certain things about gambling Big Sheed believed in, and a die flying off the table while one remained on a number that could potentially be a number he bet on was one of them.

"Same die, Mr. Phillips?" the pit boss asked.

"It don't matter," Big Sheed answered, but the table felt different.

"Same dice, same dice," they all sang in unison.

Big Sheed changed his mind and chuckled. "Give the people what they want."

The pit boss was handed the die that was retrieved from the floor. After examining it, he allowed the stickman to place it with the other die remaining on the table.

Big Sheed scooped up the dice. "I feel it, babe." He turned to Silk.

"I feel it too," she cooed, inconspicuously rubbing the front of his linen pants.

Big Sheed cut his eyes over at her. It took all his will power to maintain his composure despite Silk's soft hand on his semi-hardness getting him aroused. Big Sheed had to tell himself right now it was about money. As a gambler, he knew he had to stay focused. He slightly slid to the left to derail Silk's distractive hand.

"Later," he said in a low tone. The waitress then returned with their drinks.

"Here you go, sir. And for you, ma'am."

"Thank you. Here you go." Big Sheed tipped the waitress the four five-dollar chips he had in front of him. He then threw the double shot straight back, chased it with a swig of Corona, then shot the dice. Again, the first number he saw was the number three, but the other dice was hidden behind a stack of chips. He waited for the dealer to call out the point. The dealer peered behind the stack of chips, looked at the pit boss then Big Sheed, and yelled, "Six—the hard way. Six hard."

"I told you," Big Sheed roared as he turned and pulled Silk in tightly. His words could be heard throughout the entire casino. Between his excitement and the other gamblers at the table, one would have thought a million dollars had just been won. Other gamblers and game workers were distracted by the commotion and drew their attention to the table where Big Sheed was located. Those who had benefitted from the double three number Big Sheed had just rolled offered their appreciation by way of gestures and a wave of hands as the dealers from both ends of the table began paying everyone who had bet on both the easy and hard six.

"Nine hundred dollars for the lady." The stick-man tapped his stick in front of Silk.

The dealer closest to her grabbed hold of a stack of black chips, made two piles consisting of four and five, then re-stacked them and slid them over to Silk.

"That goes to him." Silk refused, pushing the stack of chips back to Big Sheed.

"Nah, that's yours, baby," Big Sheed replied.

"Just take the money, please," Silk insisted.

Big Sheed did not press the issue; instead, he snatched up the nine hundred dollars in chips.

After the pit boss, stickman, and dealer all tallied up the payout for Big Sheed's bet, the stickman banged the stick in front of Big Sheed, while the pit boss began to slide different color stacks of chips over to the dealer. The dealer began paying Big Sheed his winnings for the hard six and then announced loudly, "Hard six money—thirteen thousand five hundred."

A thunderous clap by an appreciative and congratulatory gambler followed.

Orange chips valued at a thousand dollars each, along with purple and black, were pushed in Big Sheed's direction. He smoothly picked them up and placed them in the now filled chip holder section in front of him.

"Thank you for the bet." One of the dealers nodded to Big Sheed, pleased by the nine hundred dollars the hard six paid out for him and his colleagues.

"Dice out," the stickman called. "No more bets," he added as Big Sheed grabbed up the dice again.

Big Sheed tossed the dice onto the table. As the dice were released, something didn't feel right to him. He felt the roll was not his normal throw. As one dice stopped short of the back wall, the other dice hid itself behind a stack of chips again. Instantly, the dealer on the opposite side of the table confirmed what Big Sheed had already felt.

"Seven out!" he called out.

"Aggh." The betters gathered around the table all made a sound of disappointment as the dealers began raking in thousands of dollars of chips on the craps table.

"Helluva roll," an elderly Caucasian man announced before clapping. His comment was matched by others who joined him in applause. Even the table dealers, stickman, and pit boss clapped for the twenty-minute rolling spree Big Sheed had displayed at the table.

The stickman poured the bowl of dice onto the table and pushed them over to the next shooter. Just as Big Sheed was about to place a bet, Silk leaned in and whispered in his ear, "You promised me we'd go to the 40/40 and then work on round two." She licked his inner earlobe with her tongue, then planted a light kiss on the outer one before backing away.

Big Sheed's manhood stiffened. He knew if he moved right now, everyone with eyes would see all that he was working with poking through his linen pants.

"Color me up," Big Sheed announced, placing all of his chips on the table. He knew it was best to quit while he was ahead, especially since he knew he was capable of losing it all.

Besides, after all the excitement and hard work on the dice, he felt he deserved to have some fun. He was already nice from the six double shots of Rémy and three Coronas he'd had, so he knew once he and Silk went to the 40/40 Club and grabbed a bottle, he'd be ready to give her a strong second round off the cognac dick.

"Sixty-eight thousand, five hundred seventy-five." The pit boss informed Big Sheed of the winning.

You could hear the murmur and comments from the admirers as Big Sheed confiscated the stack from the table, consisting of grey five thousand-dollar chips.

"For the dealers." Big Sheed tipped the table two hundred seventy-five dollars before he and Silk exited the table.

After cashing out at the cashier window and refusing a security escort, Big Sheed made his way to his hotel suite with Silk in tow. Silk wrapped her arms around Big Sheed's waist and rested her head on his massive chest. Between the shot of Grey Goose and cranberry, which was her third, and the time she stood watching Big Sheed gamble, she was somewhat drained.

Sensing it, Big Sheed said, "I'ma just drop this paper off up in the room and then we out, unless you wanna stay in," he asked Silk while waiting for the elevator.

"No, I'm okay." She lifted her head and looked into his eyes. "I still want to go."

"Okay." He paused. "Damn, you're beautiful," he complimented, kissing Silk on the forehead.

Silk blushed. "You're not too bad yourself."

"You're funny." He laughed. He knew he wasn't the most handsome brother, but felt he compensated in other ways like personality, finances, and most importantly—in the bedroom. Silk sat on the living room sofa while Big Sheed gathered the ten thousand stacks of money on the table. Once he was done, he turned and walked over to her with a stack of bills in hand. "Here, put this in your pocket," he said, handing Silk ten hundred dollar bills he counted out from the stack.

"Nah, I'm good, baby," she declined politely.

"I didn't ask if you were you good. I said take this. You're always good when you're with me, love," he insisted. "Besides, you won this." He reminded her of the hard six money she refused.

Silk smiled. She knew they'd be there going back and forth and never make it to the club if she didn't accept the money. She took the thousand dollars from Big Sheed and placed it in her clutch.

"Now let's go party." Big Sheed extended his hand.

The summer eve's cool breeze instantly hugged Big Sheed's linen attire and Silk's sundress as they exited the escalator and made their way out the front entrance of Bally's Casino, heading for Jay-Z's hot spot.

"Taxi, sir?" the man with a Middle Eastern accent boomed from out of the partially rolled down window of the yellow taxicab parked in front of the casino.

"Thanks, Habeebee, but we good," Big Sheed declined, adding a little mocking to his reply.

Silk nudged him in the side and smiled. "Baby, don't do that. That's disrespectful," she said disapprovingly.

Big Sheed knew she was right. Normally he wouldn't have made fun of the man, but the liquor had him in a humorous mood.

"You're right, love," he said, trying to keep a straight face.

"Thank you." She smiled even though she could see he was trying not to laugh.

"The least we could do is patronize him," she continued, "since you were mean to him."

Big Sheed shook his head and revealed a slight grin. He had no objection to what he assumed Silk meant. He stuck his hand in his linen pants pocket to retrieve a peace offering, only to be stopped.

"I meant let him take us to the club, silly." She chuckled.

"I think you had too much to drink," Silk concluded.

"Nah, I'm good, ma," Big Sheed shot back in his smoothest tone.

"If you say so, daddy." Silk took him by the hand and guided him to the taxi and opened the backdoor. Big Sheed willfully climbed in as she followed.

"Where to?" the taxi driver asked.

"The 40/40 Club, Hab—" Big Sheed caught himself. He could feel Silk's eyes on him.

"You know where that is?" Big Sheed asked, trying to be more serious.

"Yes, sir," the taxi driver answered.

"Where you from, my dude?" Big Sheed questioned, making small talk.

"Pakistan, sir."

"That's what's up. Are you Muslim?"

"Yes, I am," was the taxi driver response.

"Salami as salaikum," Big Sheed slurred, trying to offer the greeting of peace to the taxi driver in his best Arabic impersonation; although he himself was not Muslim. The taxi driver did not respond. Instead, he turned up his radio, which was playing music in Arabic, and drove the taxi.

"Baby, leave him alone and let him drive," Silk spoke up. "You're distracting him."

"I'm not messing with him. How am I distracting him?" Big Sheed wanted to know.

"The same way I'ma distract you," Silk replied, sliding her hand between Big Sheed's inner thighs. Big Sheed could see the devilish look in her eyes. The sight aroused him. His dick instantly began to throb as she caressed him through his linen pants.

"Ma, you wildin'," Sheed whispered, getting turned on more each second. Big Sheed's eyes shifted back and forth from the front seat of the taxi to Silk, as she unzipped his linen pants and stroked him with her petite hand.

"Damn, love, that shit feels good," he moaned.

Silk looked at him and smiled. "You like that?" she cooed.

"Yeah, definitely." He matched her tone.

"Well then, you're gonna love this."

All in one motion Silk pulled Big Sheed's dick out and wrapped her lips around him. Big Sheed was caught completely by surprise and off guard. He was, without a doubt, down for some freaky shit when it came to his sexual preference, but he had never been in a situation like the one he was in now. His eyes shifted back to the taxi driver, who seemed to not be paying any mind as to what was taking place in the backseat of his vehicle. All Big Sheed could see was the back of the taxi driver's kufi swaying to the foreign sounds coming from the car's stereo system.

As Silk took him deeper into her mouth Big Sheed couldn't help but savor the moment. He placed his hand on top of her head and threw his own head back, enjoying the ride. By now, Silk had his linen pants unfastened and belt unbuckled, fully exposing his sexual jewel. He could feel himself building up with each lick, suck, and slurp Silk performed in her dick assault.

"Yeah, right there," Big Sheed hissed, not caring if the taxi driver was watching or not.

Between the alcohol and the oral pleasure Silk was providing him, Big Sheed's head was spinning like a Ferris wheel. He was, in fact, so engrossed in what was taking place that he had lost track of time, which is why he didn't realize he and Silk had been traveling in the taxi longer than it would usually take to reach their destination.

It wasn't until the music had lowered, the taxi had come to a sudden stop, and he heard a man's voice that Big Sheed's eyes popped open. His eyes grew wider when he saw what stared back at him. Although his vision was slightly blurry from the alcohol and his eyes being closed for a lengthy period of time, there was no mistaking the sight of the silencer's barrel of the gun pointing in his face. A look of confusion appeared across Big Sheed's face, and it became evident that he had literally been caught with his pants down.

"I said, 'Are you enjoying yourself?'" the taxi driver repeated.

By now, Silk was sitting upright and sat back next to Big Sheed.

"What the fuck is this shit?" Big Sheed blurted out, not wanting to believe the obvious. His outburst caused him to receive a wakeup call. Big Sheed screamed in agony as the bullet from the silencer-equipped weapon tore into his kneecap and shattered the bone separating the connecting joints.

"The next one will separate your soul from your body if you don't be quiet," the taxi driver warned.

"Fuck you, you big-beard bin-Laden terrorist muthafucka," Big Sheed cursed.

"Nooo!" Silk cried out just before the taxi driver was able to pull the trigger. Her cry caused him to pause.

"Please, what do you want?" Silk asked.

Before the taxi driver could answer, Big Sheed interjected. "Fuck that. I'm not—aagh!" His words were interrupted by a bullet to the right shoulder.

"It's because of the lady you are still alive," the taxi driver informed Big Sheed after delivering the second shot.

"Sheed, be quiet—please!" Silk begged.

"Yes, Sheed, if you want the both of you to make it out of here alive, you will listen to her," the taxi driver retorted.

The pain the two shots inflicted on Big Sheed was enough to sober him up. Under the influence, he had been known for making irrational and egotistical decisions, but when he was sober, he was a rational individual. The last thing he wanted was to die in the back of a taxicab with his pants down and his dick out over what he believed to be a few dollars. Furthermore, he felt that Silk did not deserve to go out like that either, especially when she didn't have anything to do with it.

Big Sheed weighed the pros and cons of the present situation and made a decision.

"What the fuck do you want?" he barked.

"Everything!" the taxi driver shouted. "My allies have been following you. We have been watching you, Rasheed Phillups, son of Nancy Bowers and Shawn Phillups, father of Rasheed Phillups, Jr."

The mention of his parents and child sent a fearful chill down Rasheed's spine. Other than himself, those were the only people in the world Rasheed loved. The fact that they knew his loved ones existed made Rasheed vulnerable. Big Sheed took a deep breath then sighed. He knew all the money he possessed was replaceable, but his family wasn't. He knew it was best not to play with the man behind the gun.

"I only got about ten Gs on me, but another fifty-something back at the hotel." He paused for a brief second. "And I got one hundred and fifty more in the trunk of my car," he added.

"Give me your hotel key and room number and do it slowly or I kill the girl," the taxi driver stated. Big Sheed did as he was told.

It had been a long time since he had been robbed at gunpoint, or any way, for that matter. The last time someone made the fatal mistake of choosing him as their potential come-up, they found themselves slumped and dumped in the Weequahic Park Lake out in Newark where they were from. It only cost him five thousand dollars after putting the word out to find the culprits, but Big Sheed knew it would take far more than that to find out who was behind this one. He was already envisioning going broke to seek revenge on the taxi driver and whoever else was behind this robbery.

"Suite thirty-seven forty-three," Big Sheed told him, handing him the room key.

"Very good. Now, what is the combination to the safe?" the taxi driver asked.

"Safe?" Confused, Big Sheed replied, "I don't have no money in the room safe. That's everything," he added.

For the first time, the Pakistani taxi driver chuckled. His laugh was sinister.

"Please do not play on my intelligence," the taxi driver then snapped, revealing a second silencer weapon through the open window. "I'm going to ask you one more time and one time only, and then I will kill the girl. Then you, then your son, and father, and save your mother for last after my associates and I rape her repeatedly. Now! What is the combination to your wall safe at ten twenty-seven Gresham Road in Plainfield?"

If he wasn't convinced before, he was now. He was dealing with some professionals. He wondered if it had anything to do with his connect. He knew how the Colombian cartel got down and thought he may have been targeted for his connection with one of the drug families. Either way, he knew it was in his best interest to comply.

"Zero-three, zero-seven, zero-eight," he chanted through clenched teeth.

Big Sheed grilled the taxi driver as he gave him a rock hard stare. The more he looked at him, the more the taxi driver's eyes seemed familiar. His thoughts were immediately interrupted by the bullets that exited the chamber of the taxi driver's gun and slammed into his skull. His hard stare was instantly replaced with a blank one.

Silk sat there motionless. The taxi driver drew both weapons on her.

"As for you, my sweet African American queen, I would like for you to do to me what you were just doing to your ex-lover," the taxi driver requested.

Silk continued to sit there a few seconds longer.

"Get those fuckin' things outta my face," she spat with venom. "And stop talkin' to me with that stupid-ass accent," she added with attitude. "I told you I hate how you sound when you be talkin' like that."

The taxi driver laughed. "Come on, babe. I had to make it sound good or the nigga would've caught on," he said in his own defense as he peeled off the fake beard he wore. "Tell me I didn't sound like Manny and 'em at Hubblee Bubblee and Red Tower."

That drew a laugh from Silk. "Yeah, you did. I didn't think I was gonna be able to keep my composure. You were good, baby." Silk praised her partner in crime.

"All them years in the feds around my Arabic-speaking Muslim brothers rubbed off on me."

"I see. I think that's the best I've ever seen you. Denzel ain't got nothin' on you," she joked.

"How about you, Halle Berry? Talkin' about, 'Nooo, Sheed, be quiet, please.' And earlier where the nigga called me Habeebee, you like, 'Baby, don't do that. That's disrespectful,'" he mocked as he broke into laughter.

"Shut up, boy." She smiled.

"Didn't I tell you, though, babe? I knew the nigga had it," her partner said, amped. "And I can tell by the expression on your face when he said it that you didn't know he had paper in the whip."

"I'm not even going to lie. I didn't," Silk confessed.

"I can imagine what he got in that safe. We gotta get back to the Field and up in that piece."

"Yeah, but right now we gotta get up out of here and up in that hotel room," Silk stated matter-of-factly.

"No doubt. Let me throw this nigga in the trunk with the taxi driver first and then we out."

Chapter 2

As usual, Atlantic City was operating on full throttle. Even at the wee hours of 2:15 a.m. the flow of traffic on Pennsylvania Avenue was heavy. Despite having two dead bodies in the trunk of the taxi he had car-jacked, Jaheem Gamble aka Smooth sat cool, calm, and collected just a block up from the Bally's Casino—or so it appeared on the surface. On the inside, his patience was wearing thin as he waited for his partner Silk to return with the fruit of their previous labor, realizing that nearly twenty minutes had passed since she had gone in the casino.

For over a month, Smooth had thought out and put together the latest caper they had just moments ago pulled off; and now to see it executed the way he had envisioned pleased him. Normally, it wouldn't have taken him so long to come up with a job and carry it out, but the fact that he grew up with and knew their last victim's family gave him mixed emotions about choosing who he had. He and Big Sheed had a history that dated back to second grade when Big Sheed was just little dirty Sheed.

The two had met outside a house on Orchard Street while their mothers and Big Sheed's father drank and played tonk, pitty-pat, and bid whist for hours. Although Smooth was from the New Projects on the Second Street side and Big Sheed was from the Old Projects on the Third Street side, the two befriended one another and often played together in the open field and tennis court on the side Big Sheed was from, before it was transformed into a park. They had remained friends up until junior high, when Big Sheed went off to Hubbard Middle School, while Smooth and those who lived in the Second Street Housing Projects had to attend Maxson Middle School on the other end of the city. By the time they were ready to attend Plainfield High School, Smooth had dropped out and took on the streets as a full-time job and educator around the low-income housing apartments, while Big Sheed embraced football and did the part-time hustle gig on the other side of the tracks where he resided.

A year later, they found themselves on the opposite of the battlefield after a war erupted over which side could sell what drug and for how much. In the midst of others from both sides getting hurt, whenever the two crossed paths during that time, they always stood down on the strength of their history. Two years later, when Smooth's mother passed away from cancer, Big Sheed, along with his parents, attended the services. It wasn't until ten years later, after Smooth was released from federal prison on drugs and gun charges, that the two had run into each other again. It was then Smooth had recognized the change in his childhood friend.

The respect the two once had for one another had diminished. Their encounter and conversation left Smooth with a bad taste in his mouth and a feeling that Big Sheed was trying to belittle him due to his newfound wealth and status in their city. That day, Smooth made a decision to stand clear of his childhood friend and vowed that if they ever crossed paths again, it would be on different terms.

That was five years ago. Since then, Smooth had also climbed the criminal ladder through drug selling and gambling, and added the robbing and murder game to his street résumé. During that time, he met Silk. He stared into the rearview mirror at himself and let out a light chuckle. His eyes were bloodshot from the seventy-two hours straight he had been up making sure his plan had been carried out properly, and his adrenaline was in overdrive from the rush he received from the caper and the high he felt from the coke he had been sniffing since he had jumped on Parkway South and headed toward Atlantic City.

He licked his thumb then began wiping the outer lining of his nostrils, noticing the slight dried-up residue of the white powdered substance on his nose. Seeing the drug still lingering caused him to let out a light chuckle. It made him think about him and Silk's first encounter. He found it to be ironic that the very same place they had just pulled off their caper was in fact the same place the two of them had met. He couldn't help but shake his head. Smooth pulled out a folded-up twenty-dollar bill from out of his shirt pocket. He opened the bill and scooped up a miniature mountain of the drug with his pinky nail and held it up to his right nostril. The cocaine instantly traveled straight to his brain as he turned back the pages of time to where the chapter of their relationship began.

Smooth lay stretched out on the plush king-sized bed with hands folded behind his head and a blank expression on his face. He stared up at the ceiling at nothing in particular while the young, dark-skinned version of Kim Kardashian gave him her best fellatio performance. He had given the Snickers bar–complexioned girl three crisp hundred-dollar bills to help take his mind off of what had just happened downstairs in the casino. Judging by the way she was handling his tool Smooth knew she intended to do more than just perform oral on him for the next hour. Normally, he would have been all into what was taking place and thought that some good head by a bad-ass chick would help and do the trick, but he was wrong. Smooth could not bring himself to enjoy or show any real interest in what she was doing to him. Meanwhile, in her mind, she figured once she started working her real magic she'd be able to take his mind off what had him in the daze he was now in. Confident she had picked a winner, she felt if she played her cards right, then the next time he frequented the Atlantic City area he'd remember her.

Normally she didn't deal with or do business with black men because of all of the stories she had heard and the few past experiences she had over the years. Sad but true, the average black man she encountered was extremely cheap and always tried to run game when it came to what they wanted. They always expected more for less, when other races spent big, tipped bigger, and were always satisfied customers.

There was something different about the guy who she met, moments ago, downstairs in the lobby's bar. He not only seemed to be a man who was no stranger to money and had plenty of it, but he also smelled like it. She had noticed the expensive-smelling fragrance he wore before he'd taken a seat next to her.

The scent was masculine yet subtle and had a freshness about it that was breathtaking. When she turned in the direction of the smell that drew her attention away from her Grey Goose and cranberry juice concoction, she saw the handsome man. Having been attracted to dark men over light as a teen, she couldn't help but admire his deep, smooth chocolate skin tone and dark brown, almond-shaped eyes that were complimented by his thick eyebrows. His clean-shaved bald head glistened from the casino's lights like a crystal ball that held the future inside. His neatly trimmed goatee was razor sharp, outlining his full-sized lips.

What stood out and impressed her most was the well-manicured hand that placed the Seven Stars Card on the bar's counter. It was not so much the card that grabbed her attention, but his hand. Being the clean and neat freak she was, she appreciated a well-groomed man, not to mention one in shape, and she believed him to be just so.

Unable to notice the twenty-five thousand—dollar Cartier watch he sported, she could see his muscles chiseled and sculpted in his forearm, and the nice-sized biceps and triceps that made up his arms protruding through the short-sleeved polo shirt. Her first thought was that he may have been a professional football player, but she immediately excused the theory as she studied him more.

She had been around enough people of all walks of life in her line of work to have acquired a good sense of character and one's occupation. Something told her that if he were any type of professional, it pertained to the streets. A professional drug dealer or even gambler came to mind. She had been so focused on her analogy and evaluation of him that she hadn't realized he caught her staring. He said something to her, but she didn't notice until he had to repeat himself.

"Huh?" she asked, wide-eyed and dumbfounded.

"I said, do you like what you see?"

Embarrassed, she flashed him a smile. "Oh, I'm sorry," she replied apologetically.

"Is that your answer?" He grinned.

"To what?" A confused look appeared on her face.

He shook his head and maintained his grin that revealed a deep right dimple. "This'll be the third time asking." He paused. "Do you like what you see?"

She cleared her throat and answered, "Yes."

Her response came out childlike. She felt like a school girl being confronted by an elementary crush. She didn't know why, but something about him made her nervous. Maybe it was his baritone voice that commanded attention, or the way he held eye contact with her while he spoke, as if he could see right through her. To her, he seemed to be someone who was used to getting his way, and that turned her on, but at the same time he intimidated her. The next words he spoke confirmed that he'd known from the time he sat next to her why she was sitting at the bar alone.

"Me too," he replied, then added, "So what are we going to do about it?"

The ball was in her court now, she thought. He was talking her language. This was what she did for a living for the past four and a half years of her twenty-two years of living, and she had become pretty good at it. To many, she would be considered a prostitute, hooker, or high-priced whore, but to her, she was a saleswoman or hustler.

"You tell me, baby. What do you wanna do?" she cooed in her most seductive tone as she leaned in closer so only he could hear. Within the past three years, after relocating from her hometown of Staten Island to Atlantic City to work the strip, boardwalk, and casinos, she had been escorted out, asked to leave the premises, and even jailed for what she was doing now. The last thing she wanted, after a non-profitable evening at one-something in the morning, was to catch a soliciting charge. Besides, above all, she enjoyed working the Bally's Casino floor and didn't want to jeopardize or mess that up; especially since she had been banned from most of the others—from the Borgata and Trump on down to the Taj Mahal and Caesars.

As if he had read her mind, he said, "Come on." He retrieved his total rewards card, placed a twenty on the counter as a tip for a drink he never touched, then stood and walked off. Normally she would've discussed particulars and payment before agreeing to go anywhere with anyone, but the almost six foot tall man had forced her to change her game plan and make a sudden decision.

She checked the time. It was approaching midnight, and still she had no luck in the lobby. What the hell, she thought. Feeling his tip covered the both of their ordered drinks, she rose and followed.

As they made their way to the elevator, the nervous feeling she had resurfaced. She knew it had nothing to do with fear, but rather intimidation, and she couldn't understand why she felt so powerless around him. Even his stride was one of an individual of confidence and strength. As she trailed behind him, she attempted to gather her thoughts.

She wondered how she was going to go about approaching the money matter and run down her rates to him. It was true she was attracted to him, but she had been attracted to others in the past, so there were no exceptions. Regardless of how she felt, everyone had paid one way or another, so she knew she was not getting on the elevator with him until payment arrangements were discussed. Just as they reached the elevator, her mind was made up. She was all too ready to spring into action and settle the business of price and payment, but when he stopped and smoothly spun around, what she saw silenced her.

"This should cover your time for the next hour," he offered. Smooth slipped three crisp hundred-dollar bills he had fanned out into the palm of her hand. Her eyes told him he had given her more than enough for her borrowed time.

Now they were in his two-bedroom suite and she was earning her money. As she deep-throated his length with expertise, all Smooth could think about was how he felt like an idiot, while she wondered how much he had actually lost down in the casino. In her years of working the floors, she had learned the many different facial expressions of the biggest to smallest of winners and losers, and was convinced his face was one amongst the big losers.

Smooth stared down at her oddly as she gently stroked his manhood and massaged its helmet with her lips. Feeling his eyes on her, she peered up at him sexily, but to no avail. Her gesture went un-noticed as he shifted his gaze back up at the ceiling. She couldn't believe the emotionless demeanor he was displaying. Since age fifteen, her dick-sucking skills had made the strongest of the strong weak in the knees. She had been proposed to and offered elaborate shopping sprees and lavish trips to anyplace in the world all because of her head game.

It was because of the reputation of her lips and tongue feeling as smooth as silk by many men that she had gotten her street moniker, so she was confident in her skills. But she believed her name was earned due to what she had between her inner thighs. She knew not all men were into getting head or enjoyed it the same, so she chalked it up as her mouth not being irresistible to all she came in contact with. She decided to change her approach, knowing there were other ways to please a man.

Smooth continued to beat himself up mentally behind his loss. He was almost oblivious to the girl he had paid to be in his presence. That is, until he felt warmth gripping around his dick. The feeling of being inside her drew Smooth's attention to the girl. He couldn't recall when she had undressed, but suddenly he knew she existed. It was as though he was seeing her for the first time. He grabbed hold of her petite waist and repositioned her on top of him as she caressed her Hershey's Kisses–shaped breasts while licking her erect nipples.

"Um," Smooth heard her purr as she swayed her hips in a wavy motion.

"I knew this pussy would do the trick," she cooed with a seductive facial expression.

Smooth let out a light chuckle at her words as he grabbed hold of her hips firmer and matched her movement.

"You like this pussy, baby?" she asked, placing her hands on his chest.

Smooth responded with a head nod.

"This pussy feel like silk, don't it?" she leaned in closer and whispered in Smooth's ear.

"Better," he moaned. His hands were now palming her ass while spreading her cheeks.

Smooth began to thrust upward, wanting her to feel all of his length.

"You gonna make me cum," she admitted as he continued to hit her spot.

"That's what I want," he shot back. As he spoke he could feel her body shudder and her juices dripping on him.

"Um, yes," she said, pleased. "Your turn," were her next words. She removed Smooth's hands from her ass, lay flat on his chest, and then arched her back. She used her legs to spread his, and then commenced to going to work.

At that moment, the only thing on Smooth's mind now was how her ass was clapping while she sexed him. She had managed to take his mind off his present predicament and focus on something else. He lay there while she rode his dick.

She rose up off his chest and increased her pace. Smooth could feel himself building up. Her pussy was so wet and hot; he felt as if he were sexing her raw. By now, her body was erect and her hands were back on Smooth's chest. Her pace was now rabbit-like. Smooth's body began to tingle and his legs stiffened. He grabbed hold of her waist and began bouncing her on top of him. His actions created another orgasm for her and caused them to explode together. Despite the coolness from the air conditioner in the room, they were both dripping with perspiration and out of breath.

"Damn, you serious," Smooth was the first to say.

"So are you," she replied, climbing off him.

"You want a water?" she then asked.

"Yeah," Smooth replied, admiring her nakedness as she sashayed over to the table. Her ass was picture perfect, he thought.

"So, what's your name, ma?" Smooth asked, realizing he had never bothered to ask before.

"They call me Silk," she replied, handing him a bottled water.

"And yours, darling?" she retorted.

"Smooth."

She smiled. "Yeah, I can see that." Silk plopped in the chair closest to the king-sized bed with legs gaping open and took a sip of her water.

Smooth returned her smile. He took a quick scan of her. Minus what appeared to be an old scar near the mid part of her waist, her body was intact. He couldn't find a stretch mark or ounce of fat on her. Although he considered himself to be a ladies' man and wasn't into buying sex, he was glad he had made the decision to pick Silk up and bring her back to his room. After the loss he had taken downstairs, she was just what the doctor ordered.

"How old are you?" Smooth asked.

"How old you want me to be, baby?" was her response. Her voice and look were childlike. Smooth knew she had misread her question.

"Nah, ma, I ain't no perve or nothing. And I'm definitely not into that role-playin' shit. I was just askin' 'cause ya body mad tight."

Silk blushed. His compliment seemed genuine to her. Normally customers had paid her just to talk, and most of the time it was to talk dirty to them while they masturbated or performed oral on her. It had been a long time since she had actually held a normal conversation, especially after sex. By now she would've been freshening herself up, out the door, and on to the next; but something about Smooth delayed her from doing her norm.

"Thanks. You're not bad yourself." She returned the compliment. "Looks-wise and in the bed," she added.

"That's what's up." He laughed lightly.

For a brief moment, silence lingered in the air. They both stole glances at one another, sipping on their bottled water, then stared at nothing in particular around the suite. Each was lost in their own thoughts, cautious and careful of their next words spoken, worried about what the other may think. Silk was the first to break the silence.

"So how much did you lose?"

Her question caught Smooth by surprise. "How you know I lost?" was his nonchalant reply.

"Well, how much did you win?" She switched up, knowing she was right the first time.

"You got a slick tongue, you know that?" Smooth remarked dryly.

"Sharp is more like it, baby, but I apologize if I'm askin' too much. I'm not a talker like that anyway," Silk offered, feeling she had overstepped her bounds. She looked at her wrist for a watch that wasn't there, checking for the time. She stood up and began looking for her clothes.

She was sure she had been in the room for over an hour and her performance was satisfying, so it was time to go. She couldn't believe how caught up in the moment she had gotten, but Smooth's words had brought her back to reality.

Smooth realized his dry tone had put her on edge as he watched her scramble to find her belongings. "Ma, you good. You don't have to leave," Smooth told her.

"No, I really do," she shot back. "Do you mind if I use your bathroom?" she then asked, already heading toward it.

"Nah, I don't mind."

After a couple of minutes, Silk came out of the bathroom in her lace thong, fastening her bra. She retrieved her hairbrush out of her big Coach bag and stroked her hair to the back then took the hair tie out of her mouth and wrapped it in a bun.

"Okay, sweetheart, see you around. I gotta go." She waved and smiled, making her way to the door.

"But I don't want you to go, though," Smooth announced. His words were strong. They were enough to get her to stop in her tracks. She braced herself for the game she felt he was about to come at her with. She put her hands on her hips and turned to face him.

"And why is that?" She gave him attitude.

Smooth grinned. He cleared his throat and then placed his hands behind his head the way he had when she was going down on him.

"I'm sayin'." He paused. "After damn near losing about a hundred stacks in an hour on that fuckin' craps table, I was just beginning to shake that shit off with you being here," Smooth openly and honestly admitted. He had just about lost all of the hundred thousand dollars he had to his name, besides the five thousand he had unintentionally left in his glove compartment. Had it not been for him retrieving his gun to place it in his lap while he drove home, he would have never known it was in there.

The discovery of the money and the fact that his mind was made up to go home caused him to weigh his options. Rather return to the table and risk contributing to his losing streak for the night, he decided to contact his host, reserve a suite, have a few drinks, then take it down for the evening and start fresh in the morning. His plans were altered when he saw Silk sitting at the bar. Now he was down to his last forty-seven hundred dollars after paying her.

Silk couldn't believe her ears. Although she was a hustler, she was not a gambler, at least not when it came to her money, so the amount Smooth had lost surprised her. She knew people gambled and lost thousands. Even millions, but she seldom came across guys who looked as young as Smooth gambling and losing the way he had.

"Wow," she managed to let out. She had an idea he had lost, but had he not told her, she would have never imagined him losing as much. His eyes nor his demeanor gave off that impression. Although she felt for him, she was impressed by how he was handling the situation.

"It's cool," he said. "I'll get it back," he added matter-of-factly.

Silk noticed his eyes glowed as he spoke. His statement turned her on. It made her want to stay, not because she believed he would get the money back, but because he believed he would.

She had never met a man with so much belief in himself before. His words were spoken with confidence, as opposed to the arrogance so many other men with money had whose paths she had crossed. Smooth reminded her of herself. She thought about all the times she had started out her day with no money in her pockets, but was confident that before the day was out she would not go hungry or go to sleep broke.

Her brief trip down memory lane was cut short by the raspy sound of Smooth's voice.

"So, are you gonna chill with a brother for a li'l bit longer?" he asked.

Silk removed her hands from her hips and slid them down to her side.

"I'll stay for a few," she replied, taking a quick glance at her watch for a second time, as if she had somewhere else to be.

A pleased look appeared on Smooth's face.

Silk made her way back over to the king-sized bed and sat on the edge.

"So what's your story?" Smooth asked.

Silk let out a deep sigh and smiled. "Well," she began.

For the next thirty minutes, Smooth listened attentively as Silk shared with him how she'd been through hell and back. When she was done, Smooth revealed a great deal of what life was like for him coming up and how he'd gotten to where he was at that very moment. Over an hour had gone by now. Smooth knew he had held her up longer than his money had paid for, and he was sure it was time for her to go, but he was still not ready for her to leave.

"How much will it cost me to have you chill with me for the rest of the night?" he asked out of nowhere.

Silk chuckled. "Are you serious?"

"Dead ass," Smooth replied with a straight face.

Silk stared at him for a moment then checked the time. It was after two in the morning. She knew this was the time the casinos would be jumping with tricks. She also knew it was the time where she had to settle for less because this was the time when the "bargain hoes" as she called them, would be out turning tricks for a hundred or lower. She thought for a second.

"Give me five and you got me until the sun comes up," she presented, knowing she had taken it light on him. Normally she would shoot for a thousand, but she actually liked Smooth's company.

Smooth reached for his pants and pulled out a stack of bills. He counted out five one hundred–dollar bills and gave them to Silk. He put his money back in his pocket and retrieved a small plastic baggie from the other one. "Get dressed," he stated just before opening up the plastic baggie containing his nose candy.

Silk gave him a puzzled look, but her eyes sparkled from the sight of the baggie. She was confused by his statement, but interested in what he had in his possession. She watched as he dumped the white powder onto the back of his hand.

In an instant, the powder vanished. Smooth wiped his nose then wiped the residue from the back of his hand on his teeth. He saw Silk standing there watching him intensely. He recognized her look immediately.

"You want some?"

"What is it, boy or girl?" she asked, wanting to know whether the drug was coke or heroin. She only used coke and nothing else.

"Straight raw, baby," Smooth announced, informing her that it was in fact her drug of choice.

Silk lit up like the Christmas tree in Rockefeller Center. She had gone all day without getting high after not being able to score any good product from her normal supplier. Now here it was, she had walked right into some.

Silk moved in closer and held out her fist. Smooth poured a small mountain onto the back of her hand. Wasting no time, Silk devoured the drug. Instantly she realized the potency of the drug. Her entire left side became numb and it was as if her brain had been frozen. She shook her head and blinked a few times while wiping her nose as Smooth had done. She then rubbed the residue on her teeth with her pointer finger. "Thank you," she said. "I needed that."

Smooth smiled. "No problem." He knew the feeling all too well. It was a feeling he'd been getting since the first time he started using coke socially six years ago.

"So where are we going?" she asked, slipping back into her outfit.

"I wanna take you downstairs to the table," Smooth told her. Ever since their talk, something in his mind was telling him he could win with Silk by his side. He was a firm believer in following his gut instincts, and that's exactly what he intended to do.

"You sure you're ready to go back down there?" she genuinely asked.

"Definitely," was his response.

"I'm with you then, sweetheart."

Within minutes, the two of them were standing around a craps table and Smooth had thrown four thousand dollars in hundreds onto the table. Within forty-five minutes, Smooth was smiling from ear to ear and the two of them were returning to his room with all that he had lost and then some.

Smooth's reminiscing time was interrupted by a knock on the passenger side window just as he was about to revisit how Silk had sprinkled coke around the helmet of his dick and sucked and sexed him until the sun came up. When he looked over, he saw Silk standing there with her arms stretched out. He hit the unlock button on the side panel.

"Damn, nigga. What, you were daydreaming?" she said as she hopped in the car.

"Something like that." He smiled. He noticed how full her pocketbook looked.

"I got it all," she said as if to read his mind.

"That's what the fuck I'm talkin' about. Now let's go get the rest of that shit."

Smooth cautiously pulled off and headed for the Atlantic City Expressway.

Chapter 3

"Smooth, come to bed." Silk yawned as she rubbed her right eye. She had awakened and rolled over only to find that Smooth was not lying next to her. "It's almost one o'clock." She glanced at the clock on the kitchen wall. She herself had taken it down a little after ten p.m. after she grew tired of watching Smooth prepare the drugs.

"You can finish this later. You need to take you a power nap." Silk lugged her way over to Smooth and began massaging his broad shoulders. She could feel the tenseness they'd possessed. She knew how hard he had been running—they had been running—which was why she was not surprised at how tight they were.

"You need to get some rest, baby, or you ain't gonna be no good for your trip." She continued to try to reason with Smooth. Ever since he'd gotten the call from his peoples in North Carolina, who had placed an order for ten kilos and specified that they needed them like yesterday, Smooth had been working like a slave to complete the order.

"I'm good." Smooth leaned forward, never looking up or back at Silk. His slight change in movement was enough to release Silk's grip. She sucked her teeth with attitude, but it went unnoticed by Smooth. He was too busy and too focused on the reading of the balance beam scale he was using to weigh up another portion of the product he had just finished converting from powdered cocaine to rock.

"I'm a muthafuckin' chemist," Smooth chimed, seeing the rock substance read the same exact 250 grams the others he'd cooked up previously had weighed.

Silk shook her head and smiled. She knew Smooth was like a kid in a candy store or like a proud father whenever he accomplished something he set out to do when it came to drugs or any criminal behavior. She was used to seeing him like this, especially when he was on a mission.

Before she had gone off to bed, Smooth had one kilo brick of coke busted open and four stacked up. Now, there was only one partial brick of raw coke remaining, while the others had been stretched and transformed into rock.

"How many you used this time to make the quarters?" she asked him, wondering how many extra grams of coke he had stretched out of the four and a half kilos he'd cut already.

Since she had been around Smooth, she had learned so much about drugs. Prior to him, all she knew was where to buy it and how to use it and enjoy it. Now, she knew how to determine good from bad coke, break it down, cut it, cook and re-cook it, stretch, weigh, and bag it up—thanks to Smooth.

"This batch I got from them jokers down in Florida is some strong shit," he started out saying. "Basically, I've been getting seven-fifty off of every three-fifty." He glowed as he spoke.

"Damn," Silk said in disbelief.

"Exactly," Smooth retorted.

"Baby, you sure that's not overdoing it?" Silk then asked. She knew normally it would take Smooth at least a hundred and fifty grams more, along with the baking soda, to bring back an additional two hundred and fifty grams, just to ensure that the product was potent enough for the hustlers who copped from him at wholesale cost to break it down and repackage it for the users or small-time hustlers in the streets.

Smooth disregarded her question. "This gonna put us over the top," he said instead, thinking about the two hundred eighty grand he looked to make on his trip to North Carolina.

Ever since they had gotten away with their Atlantic City caper and found the three hundred plus grand and eight bricks of coke back at Big Sheed's house in Plainfield, he and Silk had been stacking their paper. Now, almost four months later, they had nearly three quarters of a million dollars in cash, compliments of Big Sheed.

The thought of being a millionaire excited Smooth. Due to his extracurricular habit of gambling, the closest he'd ever come was being a half-millionaire, but after he returned to New Jersey from the South, he knew he'd officially be a million dollar man. Smooth was so engrossed with the thought that he hadn't heard a word Silk had said.

"Smooth?" She called his name for the second time.

"Huh?" He snapped out of his trance.

"You didn't hear shit I said," she stated. "I said, and then what?" she repeated.

"Whatchu mean, and then what?"

"Like I said . . ." She paused. "And then what?" She pulled his chair out from under the table from behind, just enough for her to fit, and then straddled him.

"Boo," she started, "we can't keep doing this shit forever. Right now we damn near got more money than we know what to do with. Hell, I ain't never seen the type of money you've exposed me to, and I've been around the block a few times and back. You showed me so much love from day one and had my back no matter what. I'll never forget that." She cleared her throat before she continued as Smooth sat and listened.

"I knew when I first met you there was something about you, Smooth." Her words caused Smooth to raise an eyebrow and flash a half grin.

"I never thought I could trust a man the way I trust you." Her tone came out somewhat shaky. Smooth noticed the creases of her eyes beginning to fill with liquid.

"Yo, what's good? What are you talkin' about?" he asked, puzzled. She was making him feel a little uneasy.

"If you listen, you'll hear what's good and what I'm talking about," Silk replied. The tone of her voice now became evident to Smooth, and he did not like what he was hearing.

"Yo, you buggin'. Get up." Smooth made an attempt to remove Silk from his lap, but she wrapped her legs around the chair's legs to prevent him from doing so.

"No, I'm not. Just listen to me for a minute." Her pitch heightened. Silk clasped Smooth's face with both hands. "Just listen to me," she repeated.

Smooth's face scowled. "What the fuck's wrong with you? You high or somethin'? Get off of me." Smooth pulled his face back and grabbed hold of Silk's wrists. He then used his lower body strength to push the kitchen chair further back, raise up, and break hold of Silk's lock.

Silk caught her balance just in time not to hit the floor. "Why are you acting like that?" she exclaimed.

"You the one buggin' and shit, talkin' all crazy," Smooth rebutted.

"How am I talking crazy, Smooth? Huh? Tell me." Her voice had become stronger as she spoke. "All I'm saying is we've been lucky and let's get out while we still can. What's the point of having all this fucking money if we can't enjoy it. Let's enjoy it, Smooth. Let's enjoy life."

Smooth found humor in her demeanor. They had had disagreements and minor fights over some of the dumbest and most irrelevant things, especially when they were both coked up, and Smooth had never taken her seriously even when she was trying to be, so this was just another one of those cases to him. He couldn't help but snicker.

"I'm not laughing. I'm for real," Silk chimed. "Let's get the fuck out of beat-ass Plainfield and travel, just me and you. Let's do some adventurous and wild shit like go to Vegas, get drunk and high, and wake up married," she rambled.

Smooth shook his head. "Ma, you are fuckin' trippin', word up. You talkin' and actin' like one of them silly-ass broads who be catchin' feelings or somethin','" he teased.

He could have never known how his words had stung Silk, which is why he could not have predicted her reaction to them.

"Muthafucka, whatchu mean I'm actin' like I caught feelings? I—" She paused briefly, until she couldn't hold her tongue any longer. She closed her eyes and let the words spill out. "I'm in love with your dumb ass!" she cried out. Her heart could not withstand the pressure any more. The feelings had been balled up in her chest like a tied knot for over a year now. Revealing her true feelings was as though a thousand pounds had been lifted from Silk's heart. She let her words linger in the air.

"Whoa!" Smooth threw his hands up in the air. "You definitely gots to be trippin' off somethin' now, ma." He chuckled. "What you do, pop a e-pill or somethin'?" Smooth was convinced Silk had to be high off of something other than their choice of drug. There were times when the two of them were high out of their minds, floating on cloud nine, and not once had he ever heard her express any feelings toward him, let alone speak the *L*-word. He was sure something had her talking what he believed to be nonsense.

"Fuck you, Smooth!" she screamed. She was unable to prevent the tears that appeared out of nowhere. This was the first time since she was a little girl that Silk had shed any tears or showed any emotions, especially in front of, or over, a man. She became angry with herself for showing what she felt to be her vulnerability and weakness.

Her tears were enough to make Smooth realize he had misread her behavior, but rather than be sympathetic toward the situation, he chose a different approach.

"You can't be serious," he retorted. "I know you not fo' real, ma." He sighed.

"How the fuck we get to this? Huh?" he stated rather than asking. "All this time we been gettin' it in, gettin' this paper, ridin' on some Bonnie and Clyde shit, livin' the life, comin' and goin' as we please, and *now* you comin' out the woodworks with some love shit. That's crazy, yo," Smooth pointed out in disbelief as he shook his head.

Silk was about to speak, but Smooth continued before she got the chance.

"From day one, this shit was business. That's what it's always been about. Look how we met. I believe if shit ain't broke then don't try to fix it, and shit was good the way it is. Or at least that's what I thought. But you on some new shit." Smooth frowned. "Besides . . ." he said then paused. "Come on, ma. You think if you was my wifey I'd let you be out here suckin' and fuckin' dudes the way you do? Psst! You can't believe that. There's no way in hell," he went on. "You do you and I do me—that works for us. No strings attached, feel me? I mean, you my bitch and all, but all that other shit is extra. I could nev—"

He never got to finish his sentence. The smack came from out of nowhere and dazed him. Before he was able to fully recover from it, Silk was clawing at his face. The first set of scratches brought him back to the present.

"Bitch!" He caught hold of her wrists just before she could deliver another set of tiger claws. In one instant he flung her across the room. The living room coffee table broke her fall as the glass shattered from her body weight. Smooth examined his bruises with his hand. The blood on his fingers confirmed she had dug deep. The whelts were already beginning to swell. The unexpected smack had forced him to taste his own blood.

"I should break your fuckin' neck," Smooth barked as he watched Silk attempt to recover from the fall. He could see her mouth was outlined with blood, while traces of an opened gash trickled down her forehead onto her face.

"Fuck you!" she yelled hysterically. "I hate you! I fuckin' hate you." Silk was now in a blind rage. She stormed out of the living room.

"Yeah, get the fuck outta here," Smooth's voice echoed into the other room.

Within seconds Silk returned. "I don't want shit else to do with you. I never want to see you again, you ungrateful muthafucka," she calmly spoke, regaining her composure somewhat. "And I don't want shit from you. Keep all that shit 'cause that's all you care about." Silk made her way to the front door of their home.

Smooth did not respond. Instead, he ignored her. As far as he was concerned, there was nothing else to say that he hadn't already.

The sound of the slamming door shook the walls of the two-bedroom condo. Smooth didn't think twice about not going after her. Instead he sat in front of the kitchen table. He picked up the quill and took two strong, quick pulls of the small mountain of coke he had laying off to the side of the table.

"That's okay. You'll be back. Two Quaaludes and you'll love me again," he mimicked in his best *Scarface* impersonation then took another hit of the drug.

Chapter 4

"Who dis?" Smooth answered aggressively, the irritation revealing itself in his tone by the disturbance of his cell phone. The ringing of his BlackBerry had been loud enough to wake him from his sleep. His voice was both groggy and raspy.

"Nicca, wake yo' bitch ass up," the caller's voice boomed.

The words instantly got Smooth's attention.

"Who the fuck is this?" He shot up in his bed and became fully alert.

"Don't worry about who this is. Just shut the fuck up and listen."

"Fuck you!" Smooth roared into the phone just before disconnecting the call.

Three seconds later the call from the blocked number filled the air once again.

"Look mu—" Smooth's words were overpowered by the unidentified caller.

"No, you look, pussy. Hang up again and yo' bitch dead!"

"What?" Smooth exclaimed.

"Oh, now it's what? Nicca, you heard me. We got yo' bitch," the caller announced.

Smooth let out a chuckle. He knew there was some type of mistake. "Yo, my dude, you got the wrong muthafuckin' number, homie."

"Nah, I got the right one, nicca. And I ain't ya mu'fuckin' homie, Smooth."

"Yo, who the fuck is this?" Smooth asked, seeing that the call was intended for him.

"Nicca, ask another mu'fuckin' question and we gon' kill this dumb bitch!" Something about the way the caller had put emphasis on his words sparked something within Smooth.

And then, as if he had just discovered America, it dawned on him. Silk was not home. He had almost forgotten what had transpired earlier. He glanced over at the clock. It was three a.m., just three hours before he was scheduled to get on the road to make his trip. Smooth shook his head. There was no doubt in his mind that the "bitch" the caller was referring to was none other than Silk. He couldn't believe this was happening. His blood pressure shot up from warm to volcanic.

"What the fuck you want?" he snapped. He was growing tiresome of the games being played over the phone by the caller.

"Now you talkin'." The caller sound pleased. "I want everything!"

"Ha!" Smooth laughed.

"Yeah, mu'fucka, laugh," the caller snarled. "But you got thirty minutes from the time I hang this fuckin' phone up to bring *every* mu'fuckin' thing to where I tell you, or else you can follow the map I put in your condo's mailbox to collect pieces of this bitch's body."

Smooth listened attentively as the caller explained his options, hoping to recognize the voice, but to no avail. He was sure the caller had Silk, but still he made one attempt to be one hundred percent sure.

"You keep talkin' about my bitch, but you ain't givin' me no proof that we talkin' 'bout the same person."

"Ha!" It was the caller's turn to laugh. "Yo, you's a slick-ass nicca, you know dat?" the caller slyly remarked. "If I ain't need yo' shit, I could fuck with you, 'cause I can tell you don't give a fuck. You gonna try yo' head. But you right. Hold on."

Smooth could tell the caller had moved the phone away from his ear and lowered it down to his side. "Yo, bring that bitch in here."

Seconds later he heard, "Bitch, say somethin'," and then he received his confirmation.

"Hello, Smoo—" was all he heard.

"A'ight, bitch, that's enough," the caller ended. "You satisfied, nicca? You know your bitch voice."

Smooth's mind was speeding a hundred miles a minute. He knew he had to make a decision and make it quick. Although he had a falling out with Silk, still she was his people. This didn't have anything to do with loving or not loving her or how he felt about her; this was about loyalty. Smooth weighed the pros and cons, and the scale always weighed the same—in Silk's favor.

When he met her, he was down to his last, and she had contributed in a major way to him getting back on his feet. He weighed up the fact that she had rode with him to hell and back and never left his side since they'd met. And most of all, he weighed up the most important fact that if the shoe were on the other foot, she'd give it all up for him.

With those being his thoughts, Smooth made his decisions knowing that after this was all over, he would be able to get it all back and then some with the help of Silk. Besides, now that he had come down off his high, his conscience began to kick in about the way he had handled things with her earlier that morning.

"Where the fuck you want me to meet you?"

"Listen to you, still try'na keep it gangsta," the caller said in a mocking tone. "You New Projects jokers kill me." He laughed lightly.

Both men could hear the other breathing as silence filled the air. "Nigga, you know the ole horse trail in Edison?" the caller then asked.

Smooth thought for a moment, but his thoughts were interrupted.

"Mu'fucka, you know where that shit at!" the caller boomed. "Take Stelton Road and make that right before you get down to White Castle's. It's on the fuckin' right."

"I know where it is," Smooth retorted dryly, remembering the abandoned trail.

"I knew you did, you slick-ass nicca," the caller said through clenched teeth. "You got thirty minutes to grab all that shit up and get that shit to me or she a dead bitch and you a dead-ass nigga. And don't try no funny shit, and try to be no fuckin' hero," he then commanded.

"Nigga, how the fuck I know you ain't gonna slump her and then me when I get there?" Smooth barked. He had long ago grown tired of the whole ordeal.

"You don't, mu'fucka!" the caller shot back. "That's a mu'fuckin chance you just gonna have to take. A half an hour, bitch!" The phone went dead.

"Mu'fucka!" Smooth cursed, frustrated. The deck was indeed stacked against him and the odds were definitely not in his favor, he thought.

It hadn't dawned on him until he had just said it that there was a possibility the kidnappers would take everything he and Silk possessed and still kill them both. Furthermore, he had no way of knowing if they had killed Silk as soon as they hung up and were waiting to kill him next. The money, he knew, he could get back and then some, but his life was something else. Smooth was no stranger to danger, but he was also no dummy.

With those thoughts on his mind, Smooth decided that if he was going to go out like this and play their game, then he was going to add some of his own rules and go *all* out.

He glanced at his Bulova and hurried to the bedroom. There, he snatched two pillowcases off the bed pillows, then removed the floor panel and began shoving the stacks of fifty thousand-dollar bundles into them. Initially, he intended to comply with the assailants for the sake of his partner in crime and let them have everything. Now, he was bagging everything up for a different reason. Smooth knew that when he walked out of his condo, he would not be returning under any circumstances. After this, he was leaving New Jersey. As bad as he hated to admit it, Silk was right, and he promised himself he would tell her—but first he had to save her.

Once he was done, he made his way to the bedroom closet and grabbed his Kevlar from the back of it, threw it on, and strapped it up. He lugged the pillowcases to the living room and propped them up against the wall. He removed the black and white framed picture of Malcolm X and Muhammad Ali together to reveal a wall safe. He emptied the bricks of coke he had packaged up earlier out of the safe and dumped them in the duffel bag he intended to put them in before taking his North Carolina trip. He then retrieved his two P89 handguns and snatched up the two extra clips he had sitting in the safe. Just as he made his way to the front door, he remembered the twelve-gauge he had in the hallway closest. Five minutes later, Smooth was in his 2008 Yukon with all of his street earnings and enough heart and fire power to protect it.

Chapter 5

Smooth killed the engine of his SUV. *It's showtime,* he thought as he pulled out his infamous dollar bill. He took two big snorts of the drug, snatched up his weapons, and then hopped out of his truck. He tucked one of his P89s in front of him, the other in the back, and shoved the 12-gauge down the side of his right leg.

After traveling past the old horse trail and finding a secluded parking spot just up the street, he doubled back and headed toward the trail. Smooth crossed the road in order to be on the same side as the trail. It was nearly pitch dark on this particular path. He was thankful for the abundance of tree-filled and dark roads. It made it easy for him to blend in with the darkness being dressed in all black.

As he approached the land where the trail was located, he noticed how he could barely see the farm that sat off toward the back—nearly three hundred feet away from the road—due to nightfall setting in. Smooth took the 12-gauge out of his pants leg in order to climb the old worn-out wooden fence that surrounded the place.

He cautiously made his way through the knee-high grass toward the abandoned farm, ready for whatever. As he drew near, he checked the time. Only twenty-two minutes had passed since the caller had hung up on him. Smooth intended to utilize the eight minutes of battery life remaining on his cell.

The closer he got to the farm, the steadier he became. He told himself this wasn't any different then any other situation or predicament he had made it out of. Smooth shrugged his shoulders up and down repeatedly to loosen himself up. *This is nuthin', you do this shit for a livin'. These mu'fuckas picked the wrong dude to fuck with,* thought Smooth.

His pep talk was disrupted by a crackling sound. At first he couldn't pinpoint where the sound was coming from, but the second sound, which was a familiar tune, gave him confirmation.

"Y'all been eatin' long enough now, stop bein' greedy. . . . Keep it real, partna, give to the needy. Ribs is touchin', so don't make me wait. Fuck around and I'ma bite you and snatch the plate. . . . I can get—"

"Shut the fuck up." Smooth's tone was low but strong. The cold steel of his gun was pressed against the unidentified man's temple. It was the words of one of rapper DMX's songs that allowed him to get the drop on one of the would-be kidnappers. He literally caught him with his pants down.

The man cursed himself. Without having to see, he knew who had caught him slipping. Although he was strapped, there was no doubt in his mind that if he made a move for his weapon, he'd be killed where he stood. So instead, he stood there with his dick in his hand, hoping someone came to his rescue.

"How many niggas in there?" Smooth asked, careful to keep his voice down.

"In where?" the would-be robber answered.

"Wrong answer, mu'fucka. Last chance," Smooth told him. He grabbed the would-be robber by the shoulder and spun him around. "Now, how many nig—" Smooth's eyes grew cold as he recognized the face of the kidnapper. He didn't bother to finish the sentence. He knew there was no need. The identity of the man was more than enough information for him.

POW! The bullet tore into the man's face at point blank range, ending his young life instantly. Wasting no time, Smooth rushed to the stable.

***

"Riq, what the fuck was that?" the leader of the crew asked his younger brother.

Riq shrugged his shoulders. "Sound like a fuckin' gunshot."

The leader of the crew held his wrist up and glanced at his Seiko. He saw there was only five minutes remaining of the time he told Smooth to come to the horse trail. Something told him it was a bad idea for him to appoint his young homie the job of lookout man. Against his better judgment, he brought him along and gave him the position only because he was the type to shoot first and ask questions later.

"Yo, go check on that silly-ass nigga Blaze," he instructed.

"On it." Riq drew his Glock and cocked it back, then made his way out of the abandoned horse stable.

"I hope that's not your mu'fuckin' boy try'na play super save-a-ho." The leader looked over at Silk, who was duct-taped to a chair and gagged.

"I bet that's that nigga!" the leader spat.

No sooner than he thought it, his words were confirmed.

Luckily for him, he spotted Smooth before Smooth had spotted him. Had it not been for Smooth using his little brother as a human shield, he would have already pumped a half dozen shots into him.

The leader of the crew let out a loud chuckle. "You never cease to amaze me!" he bellowed. "I fucks with this nicca," the leader added as he made his way behind Silk.

"Whaddup, Troub?" Smooth said, calling the leader by his street moniker.

"What's poppin'?" Troub replied with his Blood gang greeting.

"Fuck this slob, bro. Eat this nigga!" Riq called out, despite having a gun pressed against his dome.

"Relax, li'l bro. You good," Troub said calmly, but on the inside he was boiling. It was apparent to him that the gunshot they heard had found its way into Blaze. Judging by the blood leaking out of his brother's mouth and the fact that he was in Smooth's custody, he was no match for Smooth.

Troub could not believe how a foolproof plan had turned disastrous in a matter of minutes. He had a headache that had Excedrin written all over it, but he maintained his composure. "I told you I had your bitch." He smiled as he ran his 40-caliber down alongside Silk's face.

"And now I got ya punk-ass brother and slumped ya dumb-ass man. Now what?" Smooth said with confidence, feeling that he had gained some leverage.

"Now what, huh?" Troub laughed. "Let me tell you now what. You let my mu'fuckin' brother go and I let your bitch go. You cough that paper up and I don't send every Shine homie from east to west at yo' ass, smell me?" Troub threatened.

It was Smooth's turn to laugh. "Nah, I don't like them terms. Tell me something better, mu'fucka." Smooth matched his tone.

Troub shook his head. "What's wrong with this nigga?" he bent down and said into Silk's ear. Then he stood back up, grabbed a fistful of Silk's hair, and pressed the nose of his 40-caliber on top of her head.

"How 'bout I push this bitch wig back then!" Troub roared.

"An eye for an eye then, nigga!" Smooth shot back, pressing his gun harder against Riq's temple—but Riq had other plans.

"Agh!" Smooth scowled. The blow came from out of nowhere. Smooth released the hold he had on Riq and grabbed his side with his free hand as he screamed in agony. There was no way Smooth could have anticipated the concealed knife that Riq had been inching out of his front pocket as Smooth and his brother went back and forth with their word play. Now free, Riq spun around with the intent of finishing what he had started only to be met with a spiraling bullet that was wildly released from the barrel of Smooth's P89.

By the time the first shot ripped through his left cheek, the second one was already finding a resting place. The third consecutive shot was the one that slammed into his chest plate and knocked him to the ground. Everything happened so fast, Troub didn't have time to react. It seemed as if everything was fast forward, while he was moving in slow motion. It wasn't until he felt the breeze of a bullet whizzing past his head, followed by another one ripping through the flesh of his right shoulder, that he realized he was also under attack and snapped out of his *Matrix* state.

The impact of the bullet wound to the shoulder caused Troub's gun to fly across the room as he hit the floor. Despite the puncture wound he endured, Smooth was in combatant mode. Seeing Riq fall, he wasted no time redirecting his assault on Troub. He knew he was losing a lot of blood, but between the coke he had sniffed and his adrenaline pumping, he felt invincible.

Smooth struggled to stand. He fell against the barn's door and caught himself just in time before he fell back down. He applied pressure to the stab wound. "Man the fuck up!" he said to himself aloud.

He looked over to where Silk was strapped down and noticed Troub on the ground. He hadn't even realized he hit Troub. It never crossed his mind until just then that when he was shooting in the direction of Troub, he could have mistakenly shot Silk. All that mattered was that he hadn't. Smooth took a deep breath then released himself from the wall and sluggishly made his way over to Silk.

"You good, ma?" he asked, freeing her mouth from the gag.

"I am now," she replied. Smooth could hear the fear in her tone despite her response.

"You knew I wasn't gonna leave you for dead," Smooth said proudly.

Silk's heart melted. It was the first time she had ever heard or seen Smooth display some type of emotion or love for her. She revealed a half smile.

"No, you didn't leave me for dead," she repeated. Smooth noticed how her eyes had softened.

"Later for that. Let me find something to cut you loose, but first let me handle this." He turned his attention toward Troub, who had found the strength to roll over onto his stomach and was trying to squirm his way over to where his gun had landed.

"What the fuck you think you doin'?" Smooth's tone switched back to raw. He rolled Troub's body over to face him.

"Yeah, you punk-ass nigga. You ain't shit without a gun in ya mu'fuckin' hand," Smooth antagonized. "Ain't no fun when the rabbit got the gun, huh, nigga?"

"You think you won?" Troub managed to chuckle. "Nigga, this shit is bigger than me. You don't know—"

Troub's next words were silenced by the bullet that shattered his two front teeth, ripped through his tonsils, and exited the back of his head.

"You lose, pussy!" Smooth spat.

Smooth dragged himself over to where Riq lay. He picked up the bloody knife that had him in the condition he was in and made his way back over to Silk. Once he freed her, Silk flew into his arms and rested her head on his chest.

"Whoa, ma!" He caressed the back of her head. "You good now. It's over," he assured her.

Tears began to spill out of Silk's eyes and onto Smooth's shirt. He could hear her sniffling.

"Come on, babe. Suck that shit up. We good." Smooth released her.

"I'm good," Silk said, wiping her face.

"That's what I'm talkin' about. That's my girl. Now, let's get the fuck outta here," Smooth suggested.

Silk nodded her head in agreement. She slid her arm around Smooth's waist and guided him as the two of them made their exit.

The Aftermath

Silk's eyes burned fiercely as the brightness of the sun beamed through the front windshield of the SUV. She had been driving aimlessly for the past six hours, nodding occasionally on the interstate. Between all she had been through back in Jersey and then jumping on the road, she was exhausted. She looked over at Smooth, who was fast asleep in the passenger's seat, and sighed. She couldn't believe he had risked it all, including his life, to save hers. Just the thought of his actions caused tears to moisten the creases of her eyes.

When the situation had first unfolded, never in a millions years would she have thought that Smooth would consider agreeing to the demands the three Bloods had presented. When she heard Smooth had agreed to the terms, she had mixed emotions. Both fear and joy overcame her. Fear of the outcome, but joyful that he had cared enough to consider. She couldn't help but shake her head. Her emotions had nearly gotten the man she loved killed.

The night she stormed out, she had no intentions of returning. All she had wanted to do was to get as far away as possible from Smooth. She felt that he had hurt her deeply without any remorse. She drove around the city of Plainfield without any particular destination and found herself riding through the Bricks. How ironic, she thought, as she rode through the very same housing projects Big Sheed was from. As she floated down Liberty Street, she heard a voice *yo*'ing her down. For the life of her, she did not know why she stopped, but she did. She saw a short, light-skinned brother with dreadlocks wrapped up in a red bandanna. She clenched her baby 9 mm as he approached her car.

When he asked her to roll down the window, she could have easily pulled off, but instead she did as he requested. His first words had thrown her back. "Yo, didn't you used to fuck with the homie Big Sheed?" Before she could have conjured up a lie, his second statement eased her. "Man, fuck that nigga anyway. He gone. I wanna know what's real with you."

Before she knew it, she and Troub were engrossed in a deep conversation, which found them in his crib, then eventually in his bed, with Silk telling him about all the money and drugs she knew Smooth had. She never thought she would have followed her plan all the way through, but at the end of the day, she was grateful for the final outcome.

She couldn't help but smile. Smooth opened his eyes and yawned.

"Whatchu smilin' about?" he asked.

Silk's heart nearly leaped out of her chest, but she played it cool.

"You."

"What about me?" Smooth questioned, not convinced.

"Glad you're alive," is what she answered. But her thought was how she had managed to survive and get away as smooth as silk.

"That's what's up." Smooth grinned then closed his eyes.

Nothing to Lose

by

Boston George

"Please drive this motherfucker!" Monica yelled from the back seat as she held Abel's head in her lap.

"Is it bad?" Abel asked, looking up in her eyes.

Monica looked out the window as she replied. "It's not that bad. You going to be fine," she lied. Abel's whole blue mechanic jump suit was now red from the amount of blood he spilled. "Please drive faster. We have to get him to the hospital," Monica yelled as she saw Abel's eyes start to roll in the back of his head.

"A hospital?" Kane echoed as he snatched his clown mask off his face and looked at Monica through the rearview, zipping through highway lanes like a NASCAR driver. "We can't take him to a hospital," he told Monica, while looking at her like she was crazy.

"If we don't get him to a hospital he's going to die!" Monica yelled. "He's your brother for God's sake!"

Monica knew if she wanted to get Abel to the hospital, she was going to have to make a move. She quickly reached down in her mechanic jump suit and removed her 9 mm. "Take me to the hospital right motherfucking now!" she demanded as she pressed the barrel to the side of Kane's head. She had heard stories of how grimy and low-down Kane was, but right now she was witnessing it firsthand.

Kane and Abel got their nicknames from their own mother. Ever since they were kids, Kane was always doing dirty, grimy shit. Abel did the right thing most of the time. One day she sat both of them down and read them a story out of the Bible about two brothers. From then on, Kane and Abel were the brothers' new names.

"Bitch, you gon' pull a gun out on me?" Kane growled as he quickly stomped on the brakes, causing Monica to come crashing to the front of the vehicle. Immediately Kane grabbed the gun, trying to pry it from Monica's hand. As the two fought for the gun, it accidentally discharged. *POW!*

Kane violently elbowed Monica in her face as he snatched the gun from her hand. "Dumb-ass bitch!" He opened the door and kicked Monica out of the truck, then pulled off, leaving her lying there, bleeding on the concrete.

5 Days Earlier . . .

"Why you gotta go and pick him up?" Monica asked from the passenger seat.

"'Cause he's my brother," Abel replied, keeping his eyes on the road. He knew a lot of people didn't like his brother, but no matter what, Kane was still his brother, and in Abel's eyes, family always came first.

"He just gon' be back in jail next week anyway," Monica said half jokingly as they pulled up in front of the prison.

After a forty-five-minute wait, Abel and Monica saw a group of inmates being released. Immediately, Abel spotted his brother out of the pack.

"I see you, my nigga!" Kane yelled, sounding extra ignorant, with a smile on his face as he walked up to the car. The two brothers gave each other dap followed by a hug.

"I see you been in there getting your workout on," Abel said, touching his older brother's muscles.

"You know I had to keep my weight up, just in case one of them clowns tried to stunt on me in there," Kane said, looking inside the car. "Who that smutt?"

"Watch your mouth," Abel said, throwing a phantom punch at his brother. "That's my baby right there, Monica," he said, tapping on the glass.

Monica stepped out of the car looking extra sexy to Kane, especially since he hadn't seen a woman besides the lady C.O.s in years.

"Hey, it's nice to meet you. I've heard so much about you," Monica said, extending her hand.

"The pleasure is all mines," Kane said, looking in Monica's eyes as he raised her hand up to his lips and kissed the back of her hand gently.

"So I hope you plan on getting a job," Abel said as he quickly got in between the two. "Mommy already got a few interviews lined up for you."

"Man, fuck a job. I'm ready to make some real money," Kane huffed as he hopped in the back seat.

"Listen, I ain't gon' let you have Mommy crying like last time," Abel said as he pulled off. "You gon' do right this time. Mommy been talking about you coming home for the past two weeks non-stop."

"All right, all right, all right," Kane huffed, already tired of hearing his little brother's mouth.

Ever since they were little, Abel was always the "good kid" in his mother's eyes, the one son that could do no wrong. But the master plan that Kane had up his sleeve would sure change the way his mother and the rest of the family looked at him forever.

"I'ma make the whole family proud."

"That's what I'm talking about," Abel said with a smile as he pulled up in the empty parking spot in front of his mother's building. He couldn't wait to see the look on his mother's face when his brother walked through the front door.

"Ay," Abel said, looking at his brother as the trio entered the building. "Try to be nice to Mommy's boyfriend."

Kane sucked his teeth. "She still with that bitch-ass nigga Darrel?"

"Yes," Abel told him as he pressed the button for the twelfth floor in the elevator. "Darrel is a cool dude. You just never gave him a chance."

"Fuck him," Kane said, waving him off. "Only reason I ain't kill him yet was 'cause of Mommy."

"Would you two please cool it?" Monica said. "Y'all been going at it for the whole ride."

Abel shook his head as he walked down the hall to his mother's apartment. He took a deep breath as he raised his arm and knocked on the door. "Here, you go in first," Abel said, moving out of the way so that Kane was standing in front of the door.

Seconds later, Ms. Linda answered the door with an excited look on her face. "Oh my God!" she screamed as she hugged Kane tightly and dragged him inside the house. "My baby is home!" She continued to rant.

As soon as Kane stepped inside the house, a packed living room yelled "Surprise!"

Kane smiled from ear to ear. "Thank you, thank you." He smiled even harder when he saw his little sister Cindy come and give him a hug.

"Glad you made it home safe," Cindy said, kissing her brother on the cheek. "I want you to meet my new boyfriend, Black."

"What's up?" Kane said as he shook Black's hand. Just from taking one look at Cindy's new boyfriend, he could tell that he was a drug dealer. "You take care of my sister, a'ight?" he said as he walked through the living room and said hello to all the other guests.

"Look at my baby looking all buff," Ms. Linda bragged with a huge smile on her face. "I'm so glad he's finally home."

"Let's just hope he can stay home this time for longer than a week," Darrel said, seeming to appear out of nowhere. "Glad you home," he said, extending his hand for a handshake.

Kane looked at Darrel until he finally put his hand down. "Maybe if you stopped living off of my moms and got out here and got your own money, then you would see how hard it is to get a job," Kane said, looking at Darrel like he was pathetic. "Especially when you have a record."

"You may not like me, but you damn sure will respect me in *my* house," Darrel said, setting his cup down like he was ready to get busy.

"Don't y'all dare start," Ms. Linda said, quickly jumping in front of the two. She already knew how they felt about one another, and a fight between them was the last thing she wanted to happen, especially in her house.

"I'm cool," Kane said, throwing his hands up in surrender. As soon his mother moved out of the way, Kane was already in motion. He stole on Darrel, dropping him with one punch just off impact alone. Kane quickly hopped on top of Darrel and rained blow after blow on the older man's exposed face.

Once the fight popped off, the whole house immediately went into a frenzy. Abel and a few other people in the house quickly hopped on Kane and dragged him up off of Darrel. He was one bloody mess.

"Fuck is wrong with you?" Abel yelled as he finally pushed Kane out of the house and into the hallway. "You ain't been in the house for five minutes and you already fucking shit up."

"Fuck that old nigga," Kane said as he walked down the hallway and disappeared in the stairwell.

All Abel could do was shake his head as he walked back inside the house. His mother was crying, Darrel was lying on the floor bleeding, and the whole surprise was ruined. Something had told him that this surprise was going to be a bad idea, but since his mother was so excited, he'd decided to go along with it.

"You all right?" Abel asked his mother, who sat on the couch crying.

"That boy just can't do right to save his own life," Ms. Linda cried. She had hoped that this time when Kane came home from jail he would be different, but instead he had come out even worse than when he went in. "Please go and try to talk some sense into your brother, 'cause I don't want to see him get killed out here on these streets," Ms. Linda said as tears ran freely down her face.

"I got you," Abel said as he and Monica stood up. "You all right?" he asked, looking down at Darrel.

"Please," Darrel said, waving him off. "Your brother hit like a bitch," he lied. The truth was his face felt like a few bones had been cracked or maybe even broken. Abel knew that was just Darrel's pride talking, from how his jaw sagged down on his face.

"Come on. Let's go try to find this nigga," Abel said, as he exited the house with Monica.

When Abel and Monica made it downstairs, they saw Kane sitting on the bench in front of the building, smoking a cigarette.

"What is wrong with you?" Abel asked, snatching Kane's cigarette from his hand. "Do you know how hard Mommy worked to set that up for you?"

"Fuck all them fake people up there," Kane huffed. "I can't stand being around fake motherfuckers."

"You keep on acting like this and you going to be right back in jail," Abel said, shaking his head. He knew his brother was a loose cannon, but now it seemed like he had gotten even worse. Jail had only turned Kane into more of an animal.

"Yo, I need you to take me downtown real quick," Kane said, standing to his feet. He had only been out of jail for a few hours, and already he didn't feel like he fit in.

"What you need to go downtown for?" Abel asked curiously.

"I'll tell you when we get in the car," Kane said as he walked off toward the car. They saw an ambulance pull up, followed by a cop car.

"Okay, now where we going?" Abel asked once they were inside the car.

"That motel down by Sixty-fifth Street," Kane replied.

"The one where all the dope fiends be?" Monica asked with her face crumpled up.

Once Abel heard where his brother wanted to take him, he knew that trouble wouldn't be too far behind. "What you need to go down there for?"

"Business," Kane said flatly. He didn't want to get into details, because he knew his brother would start acting like a punk.

"I ain't taking you nowhere until you tell me what's going on," Abel said, cutting off the car.

Kane sighed loudly. "Listen," he began, "me and my homie who I was locked up with up came up with this plan to rob a bank."

"Rob a bank!" Abel echoed, looking at Kane like he was crazy. "You a stupid motherfucker!"

"We got four people working on the inside. No way we can get caught," Kane said. "In and out in less than two minutes."

Abel started up the car. "If you want to throw your life away then go right ahead. I don't even care anymore," he said as he headed downtown to the motel. Abel was tired of trying to save his brother from himself. If he wanted to go out and rob a bank, then that was on him. If Kane didn't care about his life, then so be it.

Abel pulled up to the motel and placed the car in park. "Go throw your whole life away," Abel said.

"Let me use your cell phone real quick," Kane said with his hand out. He took the phone and quickly dialed a number that he read from a crumpled up piece of paper that he pulled from his pocket.

"Wassup? This Kane. What room y'all in? Okay. Be there in a sec," Kane said, snapping the phone shut and handing it back to his brother. "You sure you don't want a piece of the action?"

"Get out," Abel said, not even bothering to look at his brother. He couldn't believe his brother was stupid enough to go out and try to rob a bank. He knew his mother had taught him better than that, because they both had the same mother.

Abel got ready to pull off, until Monica stopped him. "You don't want to make sure he makes it inside first?"

Abel sucked his teeth as he watched Kane knock on one of the doors.

Kane stood in front of the door, waiting for someone to answer it. He could hear feet shuffling inside the room from behind the door. Seconds later, a man with a full beard and sunglasses answered the door with a .38 in his hand.

"Who the fuck are you?" he growled, his breath smelling like a mixture of alcohol and cigarettes.

"Kane," he replied. "Snoop sent me. I was locked up with him. I just got out today."

The man with the beard stuck his head out the door and saw Abel's car sitting there. "Who the fuck is that?" he asked suspiciously.

"That's just my brother and his girlfriend," Kane told him.

"Tell them to come inside for a second," the bearded man said.

Kane walk back over to the car. "Yo, my man wanna meet you two," he said as he stuck his head in the passenger side window.

"Nah, we leaving," Abel said. "We don't want nothing to do with nothing you got going on," he said as he started up the car.

When the bearded man saw the car start up, he ran up on Kane from behind and placed the .38 to the back of his head. "Cut the car off now!" he yelled.

Abel quickly did as he was told. Abel and Monica slowly got out of the car.

"Get in the room!" the bearded man commanded and then watched the couple do as they were told. Once inside the room, the bearded man slammed the door and locked it. Inside the room, another man with short dreadlocks stood holding an M5 machine gun.

"What is this all about?" Kane barked. "I'm here to do a job."

"We told you to come alone," the man with the short dreads said as he quickly patted down the trio.

"I just got out of jail a few hours ago. I needed a ride," Kane said. "Which one of y'all is Styles?" The bearded man raised his hand. "So you must be Jimmy," Kane said, looking at the man with the dreads.

"Listen," Abel said, "me and my girl have nothing to do with this. If y'all want to go on a suicide mission, that's y'all's business," he said as he tried to leave.

"Fuck you think you going?" Styles said as he blocked the exit.

"C'mon," Abel pleaded. "Let me and my girl go, please . . . Please."

"Sorry, but I can't do that," Styles said. "Y'all know too much for me just to let y'all go."

"Nah, you don't understand," Kane said, jumping in the conversation. "My little brother don't got nothing to do with this. He a school nigga. He don't know nothing about the stree—" A punch to Kane's mouth interrupted his sentence.

"Shut the fuck up!" Styles barked. "If you didn't want them in this shit, then you shouldn't have brought them in the first place."

Kane touched his lip, and his hand came back bloody.

"What you want me to do with these two?" Jimmy said, looking at Styles quizzically. "I say we kill 'em"

"Kill us!" Monica snapped. "We didn't even do shit."

"Two choices," Styles said, turning to face Abel. "Either I kill you and your girl right now . . . or you and your girl have to come on the job with us. Choice is yours. What's it gonna be?"

Abel hesitated before speaking. He knew nothing good could come from either choice. He looked at Monica, who had a scared look on her face. Abel knew he should never have given Kane a ride in the first place.

"I guess we gon' have to go on the job with y'all" Abel said, feeling backed into a corner.

"Good," Styles said. "The more eyes we have on the job the better."

"If anything happens to my brother, I promise it's going to be me and you," Kane said, looking Styles in his eyes.

Styles didn't reply. He just stared at Kane, his face remaining unmoved.

"Okay, let's get down to business," Jimmy said, reminding everybody that he was still in the room.

"Fuck all the small talk," Kane huffed. "When is the job and what's the plan?"

Styles and Jimmy broke out laughing. "We have to know we can trust y'all first."

Abel's eyes glazed over in anger, but he kept his voice neutral. "What do we have to do?" Whatever it was, Abel knew it wasn't going to be good. When you do dirt, you usually get dirt back in return.

"It's this big-ass card game going down at The Plaza Hotel in about a hour," Styles said with a smirk on his face. "A bunch of Chinese mother-fuckers go there every month just to gamble, but tonight they not gonna know what hit 'em."

"So you want us to rob a card game tonight?" Abel asked.

Styles chuckled again before he replied, "Of course not." He paused. "I want y'all to *help us* rob the card game," Styles said as he grabbed a bag full of guns from under the bed. "And don't get any ideas, 'cause if anything happens to me or my partner, y'all can say good-bye to your mother," Styles said, pulling out a picture of Ms. Linda from his back pocket and handing it to Abel. "We just protecting ourselves. Y'all do y'all part and we'll do ours."

Abel took the picture then turned and looked at Kane with fire in his eyes. Not only did Kane get him and Monica caught up in some shit, but he also got their mother in the middle of his shit too.

"I didn't know it was gonna be like this," Kane said in a concerned tone. Deep down he wanted to kill the two men for holding his family hostage, but he knew if he did try to make a move, his whole family would have to pay for it with their lives.

"Just shut up," Monica said with a disgusted look on her face. She couldn't believe what was happening right now, all because they decided to give Kane a ride to the sleazy motel.

"So what is it that you need for us to do?" Abel asked as he grabbed a 9 mm from the bag and examined it closely.

"I need you two," Styles said, pointing at Abel and Monica, "to just stay in the car and keep it running. I don't give a fuck what happens. That motherfucking car better be there when we come downstairs." Styles' voice was soft, but Abel didn't miss the order beneath the surface. "While they outside in the car," he said, turning to face Kane and Jimmy, "we gon' go up in there and go rob these Chinese motherfuckers blind." He grabbed a shotgun with a pistol's grip on the handle.

Styles then reached inside the bag and re-moved three masks. He tossed two to Kane and Jimmy and kept one for himself. The mask looked like a brown paper bag with holes for the eyes and mouth, but the material wasn't paper; it was cloth.

"Fuck it. Let's go get this paper," Kane said, grabbing two .45s from the bag.

"I told you you shouldn't have volunteered to pick him up today," Monica whispered to Abel.

"I'm sorry, baby. I wish I would have listened to you," Abel said, blaming only himself for the situation that they were in. All he had to do was say no to his older brother, something that he hadn't been able to do since they were kids.

"Come on. It's time to go," Styles said, looking at his watch. "Them Chinese niggas should be just now getting there."

"I promise I'll get y'all out of this somehow," Kane whispered as they all exited the raggedy motel.

The Plaza Hotel

Abel pulled up in front of the hotel and placed the stolen van in park. "Y'all niggas hurry up. Don't be in there playing."

"You just make sure this van is here when we get back!" Styles said as he hopped out of the van with Jimmy and Kane and headed inside the hotel.

Abel looked over at Monica and noticed that her leg was shaking. "You all right?" he asked.

"No, I'm scared," Monica admitted. "What happens if this doesn't work out how it's supposed to?"

"Everything will be fine," Abel assured her. "All we have to do is stick together and we'll be fine."

"Fuck that. I say we just leave and say fuck it," Monica suggested. She just knew that if she and Abel didn't get killed, they were going straight to jail, and she didn't like the sound of either option.

"We can't do that," Abel said. He wanted to just say fuck it and leave, but the first thing that came to his mind was his mother. "They know where my mother lives."

"Damn." Monica sucked her teeth. She so badly wanted to leave, but there was no way she was going to leave her man hanging like that.

"All we have to do is—" Abel's words got caught in his throat when he noticed an officer walking up on the van. His eyes quickly went down to the screwdriver sticking out of the ignition.

"Hey, you can't park here!" the officer shouted. "Keep it moving!"

"Fuck!" Abel mumbled. "Sorry, officer" he said as he pulled off.

Inside the hotel, Styles walked right up to the woman who stood behind the counter with a huge smile on her face.

"Hi. May I help you?" she asked in a friendly voice.

"Yes," Styles said, looking the woman dead in her eyes. "I need a room next to the action." He licked his lips.

"Not a problem," the woman replied as she handed him a key. "That will be four hundred dollars."

Styles reached down in his pocket and peeled off four hundred-dollar bills and handed them to the desk clerk. "Have a nice day," he said with a wink as he and his partners walked over to the elevator.

Once the elevator door closed, Kane started up. "If one of them Chinese niggas even look at me funny, I'm popping off," he said, sounding ignorant as usual.

"Shut the fuck up!" Jimmy said, nodding toward the camera that rested in the upper corner of the elevator.

Once the elevator finally came to a stop, the trio quickly stepped off one by one. Styles immediately turned his back to the camera at the end of the hall as the men put on their masks. Styles removed his shotgun from the duffle bag then handed the bag to Jimmy, who removed his M5 machine gun. Kane removed his two .45s from the small of his back.

Once Styles saw that everyone was ready, he quickly slid the key card in the slot. As soon as the lock on the door turned green, Styles pushed his way inside. "Let me see those motherfucking hands!" Styles yelled as the trio barged inside the room.

In front of Styles stood a Chinese man with a dumb look on his face, like he didn't understand English. Styles viciously hit him across the face with the nose of the shotgun, dropping him instantly.

"Get on the floor!" Kane yelled then watched the Chinese men do as they were told.

"Do you fools even know who you're robbing?" one of the Chinese men said in a calm voice. "I'm Charlie Young Fat," he said with authority.

Kane walked up and punched the Chinese man in his face. "I don't give a fuck about no Charlie Young Fat!"

"We don't care who you are. All we want is the money," Styles said as he removed all the gambling money from the table and put it into the duffle bag. Styles had the hustler's eye, so just by looking at the table he could tell that there was around $200,000 on the table, if not more.

"You can take the money, but there will be consequences behind this," Charlie Young Fat said in an even tone.

"Shut up before you make me mad!" Styles said, shooting the Chinese man an evil look.

"Those masks can't protect you," Charlie Young Fat said with a smirk on his face. Seconds later he felt a fist smash into his face. Blood flew from his lips and dotted the floor.

"Say something else," Styles said, hoping the Chinese man was feeling brave; but Charlie Young Fat decided to just keep quiet. "That's what the fuck I thought," Styles said as he removed a roll of duct tape from his back pocket.

After Styles taped each man's hands behind their backs, Jimmy and Kane quickly searched every man's pockets, removing all money and jewelry.

"Y'all niggas ready?" Styles asked, looking over at Kane and Jimmy. Once they gave him the head nod, they all quickly exited the room, heading straight to the stairs. In the stairwell, all three men quickly removed their masks and tossed them, along with their guns, in the duffle bag.

"Damn, my gun won't fit," Styles huffed.

"Fuck it. Throw that shit away," Jimmy said, looking back and forth over his shoulder.

"Fuck outta here. I ain't throwing my shit away," Styles said, looking at Jimmy like he was insane.

"Well, nigga, you better do something," Kane huffed.

"Fuck it." Styles sucked his teeth, but he left his shotgun in the stairwell as he ran down the steps.

When the trio made it down to the lobby, each man walked at a normal pace, trying not to draw any attention to themselves. Styles winked at the desk clerk as they exited the hotel.

"What the fuck?" Styles cursed when he didn't see the getaway van waiting out front. "Where the fuck are they?" he growled, looking over at Kane.

"How the fuck am I supposed to know?" Kane replied. "I was upstairs with y'all."

"Fuck that," Jimmy said as he walked off. "Y'all can argue all y'all want. I'm outta here."

As the trio walked down the street, all Styles could think about was how he was going to brutally murder Kane and his mother for Abel and Monica abandoning them like that.

As they continued to walk down the street, a van pulled up on the side of them. "Get in!" Abel said, coming to a sharp stop.

"You don't know how close you just came to almost getting all of us killed," Kane said as they all hopped back in the van.

"Y'all thought I bailed out on y'all?" Abel asked, glancing at them from the rearview mirror.

"You just don't know," Styles said with a smile on his face, but a few seconds ago, wasn't shit funny.

Are You Serious?

Back at the room, Styles paced back and forth with a cigarette dangling from his mouth, while Jimmy sat on the bed, counting the money. Even though the job went smoothly, Styles still wasn't sure he could trust Abel and Monica. Their hands were still too clean.

"One more job and you two are free to go," Styles said.

"One more job?" Kane repeated. "This some bullshit. I thought we was supposed to be robbing a bank."

"That's not going down until the end of the week," Styles said quickly. "But I can't just let your brother and his girlfriend go that easy. One more job and they are free to go."

Abel didn't say a word. He just looked over at Monica and shook his head in disgust. This was definitely a day that neither one would soon forget.

"I'm a man of my word," Styles said, looking at Abel. "One more job and y'all are free to go."

"What do we have to do this time?" Abel asked, knowing it was going to be something crazy.

"I'll explain everything to you tomorrow," Styles told him as he continued to pace the small room. The .38 on his waist was visible to the entire room.

"Two hundred thirty thousand," Jimmy said with a smile on his face. "Here," he said, tossing Styles his cut. "That's a hundred." He kept a hundred for himself, and tossed the remainder over to Kane. "That's thirty thousand, ten a piece. Split that up."

Kane nodded his head as he handed both Abel and Monica their share of the money. At first Abel wasn't going to accept the money, but after giving it some thought, he figured why not take the money, especially since he had risked his freedom for it.

"I'm hungry," Monica said, looking at Styles. She hadn't eaten anything since earlier in the day. "Can we order something?"

"No!" Styles replied. He didn't want anybody coming to the room. He turned to Jimmy. "I need you to make a store run."

"I got you," Jimmy replied as he grabbed the 9 mm from the dresser and stuck it down in the small of his back. He took everyone's order and quickly exited the room.

"You sure you going to let my brother and his girlfriend leave after this next job?" Kane asked as he helped himself to a glass of Grey Goose that rested on top of the dresser.

"That's what I said, right?" Styles snapped. "I don't know why you even brought them here in the first place."

"Like I told you the first time," Kane said, "I needed a ride. How else was I supposed to get here?"

Styles looked over at Abel. "You can thank your idiot brother for y'all being here."

Kane was about to reply, but Styles quickly put one finger up, hushing him. "You hear that?" Styles asked as everyone in the room got quiet. Loud voices yelling in the next room could be heard, followed by loud banging against the wall.

"Somebody in there getting fucked up." Kane laughed out loud. Seconds later, the fight got even more intense; then a woman's screams could be heard coming through the cheap walls.

"That don't make no sense," Monica said, shaking her head. "I don't even understand why y'all would even meet up in a sleazy place like this."

"Needed a place that was low key and under the radar," Styles said. "And besides, they don't ask for ID here."

"Man, fuck all that," Kane interrupted. "This nigga need to hurry up with the food," he said, peeking out the window.

"Y'all hold it down," Styles said as he went in the bathroom to take a shit.

"I'm about to take a nap," Monica said as she lay back on the bed. "Wake me up when the food get here."

Before Abel could reply, the trio heard a loud knock at the door.

Kane pulled out his .45 as he eased his way to the door. "Who is it?"

No answer came back.

Kane cracked the door, and on the other side stood a nice-looking young girl, standing butt naked and covering her breasts with her hands.

"Please help me," the naked woman begged. "Can I please come in? He's going to kill me!" she yelled in a strong whisper.

Kane didn't hear anything the woman said. The only thing he knew was that the girl who stood before him was butt naked. "Yeah, come right on in," Kane said, hungrily eyeing the woman's body as she entered the room.

"So what's your name?" Kane said in his mack daddy voice, eyeing the young woman's curves.

"Please don't let him get me," the woman said with a terrified look on her face as she backed up against the wall.

"Baby, don't be afraid," Kane said in a smooth voice. "I ain't gon' let nobody hurt you."

Monica quickly hopped up and snatched the sheet off the bed and covered the woman's body. "Are you okay?" Monica asked.

"No. He's trying to kill me," the woman said, looking around nervously. "He's going to find me."

"Nobody is going to find you, baby," Kane said, moving closer toward the woman. This was the first naked woman he had seen in the past five years, and she had his rod standing at attention.

"Yo, what the fuck is going on out here?" Styles snapped, anger showing in his voice. "And who the fuck is this?" he asked, looking at the woman who had a sheet wrapped around her body.

"I don't know," Kane said. "I just found a bitch naked outside the door and told her to come in."

"Motherfucker!" Styles growled, getting all up in Kane's face. "We got over two hundred thousand dollars and a bag full of weapons in here and you invite a total stranger up in here?" he asked in disbelief.

"But she was naked," Kane said, not understanding what the big deal was.

Styles sighed loudly. "Get her the fuck up outta here—now!"

"So you want to throw a naked woman—" Kane held on to the rest of his sentence when they heard another loud knock at the door.

Kane was getting ready to head to the door, but Styles quickly stopped him. "I'll get it," he said as he walked to the door and snatched it open. On the other side stood a Spanish man with long braids flowing down his back. He wore a wife beater and his arms were full of tattoos.

"What's up?" Styles said, looking at the Spanish man.

"I believe some of my property might be in your room," the Spanish man said in an even tone. He tried to peek inside the room as much as he could.

"I don't have nothing in this room that belongs to you. I'm sorry," Styles said politely as he went to close the door. The Spanish man quickly stuck his boot in the door before Styles could close it all the way.

"I don't think you understand," the Spanish man said calmly. "I'm not leaving without my property."

"Yo," Styles said. "Didn't I just tell you ain't no property up in here?" Just as Styles got ready to punch the Spanish man his face, the Spanish man quickly removed a 9 mm from behind his back.

"I ain't leaving without my property!" he yelled as he shoved his way through the door.

Immediately Styles grabbed the gun and he and the Spanish man tussled and fought over the gun. Kane pulled out his .45, but didn't pull the trigger because he didn't have a clean shot. As the two men continued to fight over the gun, the gun went off by mistake—four times. *POW! POW! POW! POW!*

Seconds later Jimmy charged through the door. "Yo, what's going on up in here?" he said just as a stray bullet pierced through his neck, dropping him instantly. Once Jimmy hit the floor, the naked woman and Monica started screaming.

"Fuck this," Abel said as he hopped off the bed and jumped on the Spanish man's back and put him in a sleeper hold. Within seconds Styles took the gun from the Spanish man's hand.

"Don't kill me, please," the Spanish man begged. "All I wanted was my property," he stated, panic all in his voice.

Styles didn't say a word. He slowly raised his arm and fired two shots into the Spanish man's head. Abel and Monica watched in horror as the life drained from Jimmy's body onto the dirty carpet.

"This is bad," Abel said over and over. He paced the room back and forth.

"Come help me get him out the doorway," Styles said. He and Kane picked up Jimmy's dead body and laid him on the bed. "Now help me get this Spanish nigga in the tub."

Abel and Monica watched as Styles and Kane struggle with the Spanish man's lifeless body.

"Nah, nah, I'm out," Abel said as he stood to his feet. "Y'all just going to have to kill me." Abel had seen enough. If they didn't kill him or Monica, they were probably going to have to spend the rest of their lives in jail, and Abel wasn't having that. "Get your shit, baby," he said, looking over at Monica.

"I wouldn't do that if I was you," Styles said, removing the .38 from his waistband and pointing it at Abel. He didn't want to shoot Abel, but if he had to, he definitely would—and he would not think twice about it.

"Do what you gotta do," Abel snarled. His eyes had turned a cold, freezing, jet black. "I've already did everything you've asked of me."

"Abel, chill. We all in this together now," Kane said. He knew for sure that Styles would shoot him and not lose a bit of sleep over it.

Abel turned and looked at his brother. "Fuck you!" he said as he headed for the front door.

"Don't do it!" Styles warned, still aiming the .38 at Abel.

"Fuck y'all," Abel said as he grabbed the door knob and cracked the door open, only to quickly close it. "The cops are right outside!" he announced in a strong whisper.

Styles ran over to the window and peeked out. He saw two cop cars outside, four cops in total, all looking around with their flashlights. "Fuck!" he cursed as he reached down in his bag, removed his mask, and slid it on his face.

Kane quickly followed his lead. "Fuck that. I ain't going back to jail," he said as he tossed Abel a mask along with one of his .45s. Kane threw his mask on and picked up Jimmy's M5.

"What about me?" Monica asked. "I don't have a mask."

KNOCK! KNOCK! KNOCK!

"Police! Open up!" a voice on the other side of the door demanded.

Styles gripped his shotgun and stepped over in the corner of the room, where everyone else stood. "Answer it," he whispered.

Monica swallowed hard as she walk over to the door.

BANG! BANG! BANG!

"Police!"

"Yes?" Monica said as she cracked the door. Immediately the officers were shining their bright flashlights in her face.

"Ma'am, we got a call about a shooting around this area. You know anything about that?" the officer asked.

"Nah, I don't know nothing about no shooting," Monica replied, playing it cool.

"So you didn't hear any shots?" the officer asked.

"Nah, I was in here sleep," Monica said with a light chuckle.

The officer looked at her suspiciously. "So the gunshots didn't wake you up? Are you in here alone?"

"No, I'm sorry, I sleep hard, and yes, I am in here alone," Monica said politely.

"Mind if we come in and take a look around?" the officer asked, taking a step forward.

"Not unless you have a warrant," Monica told him. She might not have been from the hood, but she knew the procedure.

The officer stared her down. He wanted so badly to push his way inside the room, but he knew if he did that and there was nothing inside the room, that would be his ass.

Just as the officers were about to leave, they heard a noise from inside the room. The naked woman sneezed from being wrapped up in only a sheet in the New York winter.

The officer looked at Monica with a serious look on his face. "I thought you said you were in there alone," he said as he pulled his 9 mm from his holster and pushed his way inside the room.

As soon as he stepped foot in the room, he was looking down the barrel of Styles' shotgun. Styles made eye contact with the officer from behind his mask as he pulled the trigger.

BOOOOOOM! The pellets from the shotgun blew the officer's head clean off his shoulders, and a few pellets hit the officer that stood next to him. The other two officers quickly returned fire inside the room, not caring who they hit.

Kane ran toward the front door and with a sweep of his arm, he sprayed the two remaining cops with bullets, turning the motel room into a bloody mess.

"Come on! We gotta go!" Styles announced as he turned and aimed his shotgun at the naked woman.

"Please don't. I have three kids at home," she pleaded.

"Let her go," Abel said from the sidelines. "She's already been through enough."

Styles pulled the trigger on the shotgun and watched the naked woman's body hit the floor then skid out into the doorway. "Let's go," Styles said as he grabbed the bag that was full of money and slid it over his shoulder.

"We going straight to jail." Abel panicked as he and Monica hopped in the back of the stolen van. Kane slid in the front seat, and Styles quickly pulled away from the curb.

"Are you two out of your mind?" Abel yelled from the back seat. "We going to be wanted by every cop in the city by morning time."

"Fuck was we supposed to do?" Kane asked. "Just let them take us to jail?"

"Don't even waste your breath," Monica said to Abel. She knew the two of them were nothing but heartless monsters, so trying to reason with them wouldn't do any good.

"Where are we going now?" Abel asked.

Styles didn't reply. Instead, he pulled over on an empty block and placed the van in park then calmly slid out and walked over to the side. Styles opened up the passenger door and roughly snatched Kane out of the van. Before Kane even got a chance to say anything, Styles had already punched him in his face. He got on top of Kane and punched him in his exposed face over and over again, until his arm got tired.

Abel and Monica slid out of the van. "Come on, that's enough," Abel said as they stood around watching Styles pound away on Kane.

"I've been working with Jimmy for eight years," Styles growled as he punched Kane one more time. "And now just 'cause you wanted to let a naked woman in our room, my best friend is no longer here!" he huffed as he stood up and kicked Kane in his ribs. "You ain't did nothing but fuck up since you got out."

Once Styles stopped hitting on Kane, Abel quickly walked over. "Let's go get a drink or something," he suggested.

"I swear if it wasn't for you . . ." Styles paused. "I would have had him and your mother murdered."

"Thank you. I appreciate that," Abel said. He definitely knew how Styles felt because right about now, Abel was ready to kill his own brother. Not only did Kane get Abel caught up in his bullshit, he also had his mother caught up in the drama, all on his first day out of jail.

"You all right?" Monica asked, handing Kane a tissue. She didn't like Kane, but she felt sorry for him after watching him get his ass whipped.

"The only reason I ain't killed that bitch yet is 'cause of my mother," Kane said through clenched teeth. The more he tasted his own blood, the more he wanted to murder Styles.

"You must have saved Snoop's life while you was in jail," Styles said as he walked back over toward Kane. "'Cause there's no way he would have put a dumb ass like you down on the team with us. From here on out, just shut the fuck up and stay the fuck out my way!" Styles told him as he hopped back behind the wheel of the van.

In & Out

The rest of the ride was a completely silent one. Everyone seemed to be caught up in their own thoughts.

Abel sat in the back, while Monica slept on his chest. It had been a long day, and Abel was just happy that it was over—or at least he thought it was.

Styles pulled into the parking lot of the strip club.

"What are we doing here?" Abel asked, not understanding why they would go to a strip club when every cop in the city was looking for them.

Styles didn't reply. He just dug in his duffle bag, counted out five thousand dollars, and handed it to Kane. "Here. Y'all two split that," Styles said. "Might as well have some fun," he said, digging into his bag again and removing four thick stacks from the bag. He stuffed them down into his pocket. "Come on."

As soon as they entered the strip club, the bass beat immediately slapped them in the face as

Gucci Mane pumped through the speakers. Styles made his way over to the bar, where he ordered a bottle of Grey Goose.

"So what's the new plan?" Kane asked, not able to concentrate with all the naked women floating around.

"The plan is for you to have some fun," Styles said, patting him on the back. "Go in one of them back rooms and get yourself together. Then maybe you'll be a little more focused."

"Yeah, I think that's what I need," Kane said, rubbing his hands together as he watched all the sexy strippers strut around.

Styles poured Kane a drink and handed it to him. "Go get right," he said as he watched Kane walk into the crowd.

"What's good? You don't see nothing you like?" Styles asked Abel while Monica was standing right there.

"Nah, I'm good," Abel said. "Besides, we could use the money," he said, putting his half of the five thousand dollars in his pocket.

Styles shrugged his shoulders and took a swig from his bottle. He bobbed his head to the music, until a white woman walked up to him and hugged him tightly.

"What's good, ma?" Styles said with a smile. In front of him stood the desk clerk from The Plaza Hotel.

"I'm happy y'all made it out of there alive," Beverly said, accepting the drink that Styles had handed her.

"I appreciate what you did for me back there," Styles whispered in Beverly's ear. He handed her the stacks of money that he had stuffed in his pocket.

Beverly quickly slipped the money in her pocketbook and kissed Styles on the cheek. "See you around," Beverly said with a wink as she left the club.

"I want to go home," Monica said in a naggy, whining voice. She didn't understand why she and Abel had to stay when they didn't have anything to do with anything.

Monica walked over to Styles. "Why are you holding us hostage?" she asked.

"I don't know what you talking about," Styles replied, not even looking at Monica.

"Can me and Abel please go home? Please?" Monica begged. "I swear we won't say shit to anybody about what happened."

"I can't do that," Styles said, taking another swig from his bottle. "I have too much to lose," he told her. "All y'all have to do is be cool and I'll let y'all go . . . my word."

"But at the rate we're going, if we don't get killed, then we'll be spending the rest of our lives in jail, and I don't think that's fair."

"Listen," Styles said, turning to face Monica. "Thanks to Kane, I'm short a man for our big job at the end of the week, so I need y'all for that job. Once that's over, y'all are free to go."

"But what happens if something goes wrong on the job?" Abel asked, jumping into the conversation.

"Nothing is or can go wrong," Styles said with a smile. "I got four people on the inside working with us to make sure everything goes according to plan, an escape route, and a backup escape route. Any other questions?" Styles smiled. "You think I would walk into a bank and just rob it and hope I get away?"

"Well, shit." Abel chuckled. "You working with my brother, so ain't no telling."

Styles laughed loudly. "I didn't and still don't want to work with your brother. The problem is we needed another man for the job, and my man Snoop, who's locked up, highly recommended your brother. . . . I don't know why, but he did."

"So you positive can't nothing go wrong?" Abel asked, still not sure if he could believe or trust the man.

"Positive," Styles told him. "And I'll give you a piece of the action for your patience. That way y'all can leave and live good and never worry about coming back."

Abel accepted the drink that Styles handed him, and then he really sat back and thought about his options. He really didn't have any. It was either make a run for it and risk getting his mother murdered in the process, or he could just do this one job, get paid, and later on forget that this whole thing ever happened. "Fuck it. I'm down," he said then shook hands with Styles.

Kane sat over in the cut, looking around as a stripper's head bobbed up and down between his legs. "Damn, baby," he groaned as he looked down and watched the stripper do her best to make him cum faster than a speeding bullet. Kane placed his hand on the back of the stripper's head as he exploded.

"Damn!" Kane cursed as he handed the stripper two hundred-dollar bills. "You got a number?"

As the stripper wrote down her number, Kane looked over and saw Styles and Abel shaking hands. "What the fuck are they up to?" he said out loud to no one in particular.

"You better call me, too, daddy. I'm not playing," the stripper said as she strutted off, her ass switching from side to side with each step she took.

"Fuck them niggas," Kane huffed as he waved them off and continued to flirt with the strippers.

Styles took another swig from his bottle as he watched a sexy green-eyed stripper headed his way. "Damn," he said under his breath.

"Hey, daddy," the stripper named Green Eyes sang happily as she posted up in front of Styles.

"I hope you got some good news for me," Styles said, openly looking over the sexy woman's body. Styles and Green Eyes had been seeing each other for about two years off and on, but their relationship wouldn't and couldn't go to the next level because Styles was married.

"Actually, I do have some good news for you," Green Eyes said, looking Styles in his eyes. The last time the two were together, they had an argument over Styles' wife. She was still actually mad at him, but when it came to getting money, Green Eyes put her feeling to the side.

"What you got for me?" Styles asked, taking another swig from his sip. He could see the hurt look in the green eyes of the woman that stood before him, but he did his best to ignore it.

"You see that tall guy over there?" Green Eyes said, nodding her head to signal to Styles on which way to look.

"The tall guy with the braids?" Styles asked just to make sure they were talking about the same person.

"Yeah, him."

"What's the scoop?" Styles asked.

"I been chilling with him for the past couple of days at his house," Green Eyes began. "And—"

"You fucked him?" Styles cut her off.

"No, I didn't fuck him," Green Eyes told him. "Now, like I was saying, I been hanging out with him for the past few days, and I know for sure he got about sixty thousand in cash in his house, and maybe even a few pounds of weed."

"Sixty thousand?" Styles repeated. "What's your cut?"

"Twenty thousand," Green Eyes answered quickly.

"Damn, that's a lot," Styles said with a smile.

"Fuck you," Green Eyes said, returning his smile. "As much shit as you put me through, you owe me. I'll text you the address in a few, and make sure you don't rough me up too bad, baby." Green Eyes winked as she walked off.

Styles watched her ass jiggle and switch as her heels stabbed the floor, until she stopped in front of the tall man with the braids. Even though Styles was married, he still didn't want Green Eyes talking to other men. In his eyes, she belonged to him.

Styles sat back and watched how Green Eyes interacted with the tall guy. The more he watched, the angrier he became.

"You all right, man?" Abel asked, noticing the mean look on Styles' face.

"I'm good," Styles said, cracking a light smile. "I'ma need you to put in a little work tonight."

"No problem," Abel said, finally getting with the program. He figured since he had to go along anyway, he might as well get paid for it and use the money for something good. "As long as it's a clean getaway, I'm down."

Styles smiled. "It's always a clean getaway when dealing with me. Like I told you earlier, jail is not an option," Styles said as he kept his eyes on Green Eyes' every move.

He watched as she seductively bent over in front of the tall man with braids and spread her ass cheeks open. Styles put his bottle back up to his lips, and only a drop came out. "Damn, I finished this shit already?" he said out loud then ordered another bottle of Grey Goose.

"Where your brother at?" Styles asked as he watched Green Eyes and the tall guy exit the club.

"He right over there." Abel pointed to where Kane stood whispering in a stripper's ear.

"Do me a favor," Styles said as he read the text message that just came to his phone. "Let him know we rolling out in the next thirty minutes."

He watched Abel walk over to get his brother. Styles looked over at Monica, who had a worried look on her face. "Here, have a drink and loosen up."

"I am loose," Monica replied, declining the drink. "I just don't see a good ending coming from this."

"I got everything under control." Styles laughed. "You don't trust me?"

"I don't know you," Monica replied as she kept a close eye on Abel.

"I understand," Styles said with a smile. "The great thing about this is once this shit is over at the end of the week, we never have to see each other again—but until then, we work together as a team," he said, holding out his hand.

"Deal," Monica said as the two shook hands.

Once Kane and Abel returned to the bar, it was time to go.

"Damn, it's time to leave already?" Kane huffed. "I was just about to have a stripper sandwich."

"You're disgusting." Monica rolled her eyes as they all exited the club. Outside, Styles walked over to the van and removed all of his belongings. He walked over toward an all black Yukon truck and broke into it.

"Y'all niggas come on," he said as he quickly started up the truck and peeled out of the parking lot.

As Styles drove, he received another text message.

WE'RE ALONE. LET'S GET THIS MONEY!

Styles smiled as he headed toward the address that Green Eyes had texted him. Twenty minutes later, Styles pulled up a block away from the place.

"Okay, y'all listen up," Styles said, getting everyone's attention. "You," he said, looking at Monica. "I need you to get behind this wheel and keep this motherfucker running."

Monica nodded her head as she hopped out of the back seat and hopped up in the driver seat. Styles, Abel, and Kane stood around the back of the truck.

"Everything is all set up already," Styles said as he slid his mask over his face. "Me and you," he said, looking at Abel, "we going to take care of this tall motherfucker. You—" Styles said, looking over at Kane. "There's going to be a woman inside the house." He paused. "She's on our team. I need you to rough her up a little bit, but don't hurt her. I repeat, *do not* hurt her. It's all an act. She might try and resist a little, but just go with it, all right?"

"Damn, I heard you the first time." Kane sucked his teeth. "You talking to me like I'm retarded or something," he huffed as he slid his mask over his face.

When the trio reached the front door, Styles turned the door knob and saw that the front door was open just like Green Eyes said it would be. Styles eased his way inside the house, with his shotgun held in a two-handed grip. He heard movement coming from upstairs. He quietly led the way up the steps.

Once his foot hit the top of the steps, Styles couldn't believe what he was seeing. Green Eyes was lying on the bed with her legs wide open, while the tall guy's face was buried in between them.

"What the fuck is going on up in here?" Styles barked as he hit the tall guy across the face with his shotgun and then aimed it at the man's head. "If you even breathe the wrong way, I'ma blow your motherfucking head off!" Styles growled, meaning every word. He couldn't believe what his eyes just saw.

Abel quickly removed the roll of duct tape that he had in his pocket and tied the tall guy's hands behind his back.

"Where's the money at?" Styles asked.

"What money?" the tall guy asked, faking ignorance.

Styles removed the .38 from his waistband and fired a shot at the tall guy's leg.

"AHHHH!" The tall guy yelled. He went to grab his leg, but he couldn't because his hands were taped together. "It's in the closet in the safe. The key is on the dresser." He yelled out in pain.

"Hold him down," Styles said as he went inside the closet looking for the safe.

Kane looked down at the tall guy and started laughing. When Green Eyes saw Kane start laughing, she made her move. She knew if she didn't do something believable that the tall guy would automatically think she had set him up.

As soon as she was sure Kane wasn't paying attention, Green Eyes jumped off the bed and landed on Kane's back. She wrapped her arms around his neck, making it seem like she was trying to choke him. "Leave us alone!" Green Eyes repeated over and over again as she hung on to Kane's neck.

"Bitch!" Kane snarled as he bent down and flung Green Eyes over his shoulder and down to the floor like a rag doll. He then hopped on top of the woman and began rearranging her face with his .45.

Styles ran out of the closet to see what all the commotion was. When he saw Kane on top of Green Eyes, hitting her in her beautiful face with his gun, he snapped.

"What the fuck is you doing?" Styles yelled as he pushed Kane off of Green Eyes. He looked down and immediately felt sorry for Green Eyes when he saw the amount of pain she was in.

"I need a ambulance," Green Eyes slurred through a mouth full of blood.

Styles grabbed Kane by his shirt and rushed him until his back hit the wall. "What the fuck is wrong with you?" he huffed. He had Kane jacked up against the wall.

"Bitch tried to kill me!" Kane lied.

"Bullshit" Styles yelled as he jammed his .38 into Kane's stomach.

"I swear," Kane pleaded. "Ask him. He saw the whole thing," he said, nodding toward Abel.

Styles quickly turned and looked at Abel. "What happened?"

Abel looked at Kane, then back at Styles. "She tried to kill him," he lied to save his brother's life. "I saw the whole thing."

"Fuck!" Styles cursed as he walked over and shot the tall guy in the head. He knew Kane was lying because Styles, Green Eyes, and Jimmy had been through the same routine over thirty times, and not once had Green Eyes done some shit like try to kill Jimmy.

Styles opened up the safe and quickly emptied the money into his bag. "Come on, let's go," he said as he lifted Green Eyes up and carried her downstairs and out of the house.

"Get us to a hospital!" Styles ordered once everyone was back in the truck.

"What the fuck happened back there?" Monica asked as she cruised down the highway headed toward the hospital.

"Just drive," Styles told her. He was pissed. He couldn't believe he held Green Eyes in his arms, heading toward the hospital. On top of that, she was naked. This wasn't how the plan was supposed to go.

Ten minutes later, Monica pulled up in front of the hospital. Styles quickly opened up his door, still wearing his mask. He laid Green Eyes' naked body right there on the concrete. Random people who were standing around the entrance screamed and yelled for help as they watched the masked man laying the bloody naked woman on the ground.

Once Styles got back inside the truck, Monica quickly pulled off.

Laying Low

"Right here is good," Styles said from the back seat. That was the only thing he had said since they had dropped Green Eyes off at the hospital.

Monica pulled over to the side of the road and placed the truck in park. "Now what?"

"Now we walk," Styles said, finally removing the mask from his face. His house was only a few blocks away. "Make sure y'all get all y'all shit out of this truck," he said as he walked straight up to Kane.

"Damn, you still stressing over that bitch?" Kane said with a "you can't be serious" look on his face.

Styles sighed loudly before exploding in motion. He caught Kane in the jaw with a hard blow. "Motherfucker!" Styles growled. "I told you she was on our team!"

"Chill!" Abel said as he and Monica tried to get Styles up off of Kane. "That's enough!"

After about three minutes Abel and Monica finally separated the two.

"I told you already," Kane huffed. "The bitch tried to kill me."

"Listen," Styles began. "Don't say shit else to me until we go our separate ways," he said as he headed down the street.

"Where we headed?" Abel asked once he caught up with Styles.

"To my crib," Styles answered as the rest of the crew got their stroll on.

They finally reached Styles' house.

"What the fuck!" Kane huffed when he saw a police car parked in the driveway. "So you a motherfucking cop?"

"Fuck outta here," Styles said, looking at Kane like he was crazy. "My wife is a cop," he said as he stuck his key in the lock and unlocked the front door.

On the couch was a sexy, dark-skinned woman with a long, expensive-looking weave.

"Hey, daddy," Lisa sang happily as she got up and slid into Styles' arms. "Why didn't you tell me you were going to bring guests home?"

"Sorry, baby," Styles apologized. "Shit got a little messed up, so I had to bring them here," he told her. "Plus, these are the people that are going to help us pull off this job at the end of the week."

"Where's Jimmy?" Lisa asked. Just by the look on Styles' face, she already knew what time it was. "Y'all hungry?" she asked, looking at her new guests.

"Yes, please, I'm starving," Monica said with no shame in her game. She hadn't eaten anything since breakfast.

"Make y'all selves at home," Styles said as he went in the kitchen with Lisa. He handed her the duffle bag full of money as the two embraced in a long, sloppy kiss. "You don't even wanna know what I had to go through to get that money," Styles said.

"Just know it will all be over in a few days," Lisa told him as she kissed him again.

Abel sat on the couch and saw luggage packed by the door. He figured that after the bank job, Styles and Lisa were going to leave town. "You all right?" he asked, looking over at Monica.

"Yes, I'm fine," Monica replied. She was just ready for all this madness to be over so she could get back to her regular, normal life. She also didn't like what the promise of money was doing to Abel. She could see the money already changing his decision-making.

"Y'all come eat," Styles said as he made everyone's plate. Once everybody was seated at the round table, they all began to eat.

"Did you go over the plan with them yet?" Lisa asked as she shoveled mac and cheese in her mouth.

"No, not yet," Styles replied, biting into his chicken. "I will after we finish eating." He wanted to make sure he had everyone's attention when he did go over the plan. Styles' whole life depended on this one plan, and he couldn't afford no fuck-ups.

Once everyone was done eating, Styles led them down to the basement, where he pulled out the blueprint and layout of the bank. "Here's the plan," Styles began. "We got two people working for us on the inside, so they'll be standing right next to the silent alarms when we hit the bank, which will be at 8:45 a.m. on the dot. So now we don't have to worry about no alarms or no cops, we'll only be inside the bank for five minutes," he said, looking around the table at everyone.

"Our person on the inside will have the key to the vault." Styles paused. "Inside the vault it should be two to three million." He smiled. "All we have to do is go in there, get the money, then walk right back out the front door. A piece of cake."

"You—" Styles said, looking over at Lisa. "All I need you to do is be posted up in your car about a block away. Once you see us leave the bank,

I need you to quickly pull up and go inside the bank. Once they see you, the people inside the bank will think they're safe. They won't bother to call the cops because you're there, giving us just enough time to get away," Styles said with a smile. "No way this shit can go wrong."

Styles knew his plan was a bulletproof one, and he couldn't wait to pull it off. He and Jimmy had been pulling off jobs for years, just waiting for their big break, and now the time had finally come. Even though Jimmy was gone, Styles still planned on giving his half of the money to his family.

"That sound like a good-ass plan," Kane said, rubbing his hands together greedily. His whole life he had been a fuck-up; now he was finally about to get paid, and he couldn't wait.

"So what do you need us to do?" Abel asked.

Styles smiled. "Y'all have the easy job. You—" he said, looking over at Monica. "All I need you to do is be the driver. Can you handle that?"

"Yeah, I can handle that," Monica replied.

"Good." Styles smiled as he looked over at Abel. "Your job is to watch the door. Once we're inside, I need you to tie the door shut until it's time for us to leave."

"I can handle that," Abel said with a look in his eyes that said he was ready.

"And you—" Styles said, looking over at Kane. "All I need you to do is fill up as many duffle bags as you can with money in four minutes, while I hold the customers and employees down."

"I got you," Kane replied, visualizing how much money was going to be inside the bank.

"And don't fuck nothing up," Styles warned. "Because if you fuck something up this time, I'm going to kill you."

"Man, ain't nobody going to mess nothing up," Kane said, waving him off. "I'm just trying to get paid like everybody else."

"Let's go get this money then," Styles said as he and Kane shook hands. "I'm going upstairs to get some rest. We take the bank down in two days. Make y'all selves at home," Styles said as he headed upstairs with Lisa.

Once Styles and Lisa were gone, Kane spoke. "Damn, we about to be paid," he said excitedly. The look on Kane's face said that he was excited about finally being able to have some money for once in his life. "I'm going to buy Mommy the biggest house."

"Please just stick to the plan," Abel said. "The plan is a perfect one. Don't mess it up."

"Oh, so that's how you feel too?" Kane asked, feeling slightly offended.

"You been fucking up ever since you got out of jail," Abel reminded him. "All I'm saying is don't fuck this up for all of us. It's bad enough you already got us involved in this bullshit."

"Don't worry. I won't fuck up your little perfect life," Kane huffed as he grabbed his jacket and headed for the door.

"Where you going?" Abel asked.

"Out!" Kane replied as he left.

Two minutes later, Styles came down to the basement. "Who just left?" he asked with a .38 in the palm of his hand.

Abel just shook his head. "Kane," he answered.

"I swear your brother is going to make me kill him," Styles huffed. "We supposed to be laying low until the bank job," he fumed. If he didn't need one extra man for the job, Styles would have definitely killed Kane and not even thought twice about it.

"I'm going back upstairs," Styles said with anger in his voice. "Y'all all right?"

"We good," Abel replied as he watched Styles exit the basement.

"Your brother is crazy," Monica said out loud. "It's hard to believe that you two are even brothers."

"I know," Abel said in deep thought. He had a funny feeling that somehow Kane was going to mess up the perfect plan. He hated to say it, but his brother belonged behind bars. Some people just weren't ready to be out in society, and Kane was one of those people.

"What you over there thinking about?" Monica asked as she rested her legs across Abel's lap.

"What you going to do with all this money?" Abel asked as he began to massage Monica's feet.

"I don't know." Monica smiled. She had never even imagined having that much money in her lifetime. "I guess buy us a nice house. Then we can go get married in a nice place like Hawaii or somewhere."

"Hawaii?" Abel repeated with a smile. "Now that I'm about to be rich, I'm not sure if I still want to get married."

"Oh, really?" Monica said as she playfully kicked him. "I just can't wait until this is all over, then we can finally not have to worry about nothing anymore," she said. No more worrying about bills, no more living from check to check, and no more headaches. It would be just good times from now on, and Monica couldn't wait.

Upstairs, Lisa lay across Styles' chest as the two watched an episode of *The Wire*. "You sure we can trust them?" she asked out the blue.

"We have to," Styles replied. "They the only ones who can help us pull this off."

"Abel and Monica seem cool," Lisa said, "but I don't trust Kane. It's just something about him."

"Don't worry about him. This plan is so good that not even he can ruin it," Styles said with confidence. "There is no way this plan can go wrong. Simply no way!"

Time to Get Paid

Abel heard a noise and his eyes quickly shot open. He looked over at Monica and saw that she was still asleep. Abel flicked his arm and looked down at his watch. It was 6:20 a.m. Seconds later, he saw Kane walk through the basement door.

"Where the fuck you been?"

"Calm down," Kane said nonchalantly. "I was just out having a few drinks."

"For two days?" Abel said. "For a second I thought you was going to miss the job."

"And miss out on my big payday?" Kane said, looking over at Abel like he was crazy. "You must be smoking."

Seconds later, Styles appeared at the top of the basement steps, wearing all black. "Glad you finally decided to come back and join us," he said as he descended the stairs. "You ready to go?" he asked as he and Kane stood face to face.

"I'm ready," Kane replied.

"Here, put these on over your regular clothes," Styles said, handing each person a blue mechanic jump suit.

Seconds later, Lisa joined the rest of the crew in the basement, wearing her police uniform. "Everybody set and ready to go?"

"Yeah, we ready," Abel answered quickly.

"Here," Styles said, laying a bunch of guns out on the table. "Pick whichever one y'all want," he said as he grabbed the M16. Kane followed his lead and also grabbed an M16.

"Damn, I always wanted to shoot one of these joints," he said, admiring the assault rifle.

"Well, keep hoping," Styles said quickly. "With a plan like this, won't no gunfire be necessary."

Abel grabbed two 9s off the table and handed one to Monica.

"What's this for?" she asked. "I don't need that. All I'm doing is driving."

"Just take it anyway. I'll feel more comfortable knowing you have it," Abel told her.

"Okay, baby," Monica said, taking the gun from Abel's hand and sticking it down in the pocket of her jump suit. All Monica could think about were the sunny beaches down in Hawaii. She kept telling herself over and over again that everything was going to be all right.

"This is what we will be wearing on the job," Styles said, removing four evil-looking clown masks from a bag. "Try 'em on," he said and then watched the trio try on their masks.

"Damn, it's hard to breathe with this shit on," Monica complained.

"Don't worry about it." Styles smiled. "You won't have to wear it for long. Five minutes and you'll never have to see me or that mask ever again."

"Amen to that," Kane said loudly.

"Here's where we going after the job," Styles said, handing everyone a small piece of paper with an address scribbled on it. "That's the warehouse where we going. It's three cars already gassed up and ready to go there." Styles paused. "We going to go there, split up the money, then we can each go our separate ways," Styles said, shaking everyone's hands.

"I love you, daddy," Lisa said as she kissed Styles on the lips and walked out the front door.

"In two hours, all of our lives will be changed for the better," Styles said with a smile. "Everything is going to go smoothly. But," he said, looking at Kane, "if one of them guards try to be a hero, you know what to do."

Twenty minutes later, Styles walked out to the stolen van that sat parked in his driveway. "I hope y'all ready," he said as he hopped in the back seat along with Kane. Abel took the passenger seat, and Monica got behind the wheel.

"Y'all ready?" Monica asked as butterflies began to form in her stomach.

"Let's do it," Styles said with confidence.

With that being said, Monica quickly backed out of the driveway and headed toward the bank.

What the fuck did I just sign up for? Monica thought as she cruised down the highway. The closer she got to the bank, the more nervous she became, and the more she wanted to back out of the deal.

"You a'ight?" Styles asked, noticing the nervous look on Monica's face from the rearview mirror.

"I'm fine," Monica replied, winking at Styles through the rearview mirror.

"Everything is going to be fine," Styles assured her. He knew she was nervous, and she had a good reason to be. If they got caught, she would definitely spend the rest of her life in prison, so Styles totally understood her mind frame.

Abel sat up front in the passenger seat, sweating bullets. He, too, was a little nervous, but he knew it was too late to turn back now.

Fifteen minutes later, Monica pulled up a block away from the bank. "What you want me to do?"

Styles looked down at his watch that read 8:09 a.m.. "Just chill right here until I tell you to move this motherfucker," said Styles, his voice all business. He quickly slid his clown mask down on his face. "It's almost showtime," he said as he pulled out his M16 and made sure everything was locked and loaded.

Abel pulled out his 9 mm and said a quick prayer before sliding his clown mask down over his face.

"What we waiting for?" Kane said, tossing his mask over his face, clutching his M16.

Styles didn't reply. He just looked at his watch that read 8:11 a.m. He looked out the window and saw Lisa's squad car parked over in the cut at the beginning of the block. He gave her a head nod, and she quickly nodded back.

Two minutes later, Styles looked down at his watch again. "Time to go get paid," Styles announced as he tapped on the back of Monica's seat.

Monica slid her mask over her face and stepped on the gas. There was a screech of brakes as the van jerked to a halt in front of the bank. The side door on the van slid open, and Styles and Kane quickly jumped out and entered the bank. Abel gave Monica one last look as he hopped out of the van and joined Styles and his brother inside the bank.

Styles walked straight up to the guard, who was getting ready to reach for his weapon. "Don't even think about it!" Styles yelled, getting the attention of everyone in the bank. The guard slowly placed his weapon on the floor and lay face down.

"Back the fuck away from the counters!" Kane yelled, jumping over the counter and forcing everyone on the floor. "Move and I'll blow your fucking head off!" he yelled as he violently shoved a white man with Coke bottle glasses down to the floor.

Once Abel got inside, he tied the front door with a thin rope. When he finished that, he walked over to where Styles had his M16 trained on the guard.

"Tie this motherfucker up!" he ordered as he ran and jumped up on top of the counter. "Everybody listen up!" Styles yelled, pacing back and forth on the counter. "Everybody follow directions, and nobody will get hurt. We're not taking your money, we're taking the bank's money!" he told them.

"You, get up!" Styles said, aiming his gun at the bank manager.

"This the manager?" Kane asked, roughly grabbing the man by the back of his neck and forcing him over to the vault. "You got fifteen seconds to open this motherfucker up!"

As Styles walked back and forth on top of the counter, he secretly nodded at the people he had working on the inside. He was a man of his word, and he planned on giving them their proper cut for their participation.

When the bank manager finally got the vault open, Kane violently shoved him down to the floor and then rushed inside the vault.

Once Kane stepped inside, he couldn't believe his eyes. He had never seen so much money in his life. Kane removed the three big duffle bags from around his neck and quickly began to fill them all up.

Styles looked down at his watch and yelled out, "Two minutes!" as he continued to pace back and forth. Styles looked over at Abel and gave him a head nod, informing him he was doing good.

Monica sat outside in the getaway van with a nervous look on her face under her mask. This was the longest five minutes of her life. She kept looking around for any signs of police. She looked out her side mirror and saw Lisa sitting parked a block away. "Hurry the fuck up," she thought out loud.

Kane piled as much money in each bag as he possibly could. Once all the bags were full, he began stuffing money down his drawers and in his pockets. "Fuck that. I ain't gon' never be broke again," Kane said to himself as he heard Styles yell, "Forty seconds!"

Kane stuffed a few more stacks of money down in his drawers as he stood up and dragged all three of the bags out of the vault.

Styles smiled under his mask once he saw Kane come out of the vault with the three big duffle bags. "Come on. Let's go!" he said as he jumped down off the counter and slid a duffle bag across the floor over to Abel.

Kane picked up one bag and tossed the strap to the duffle bag around his neck, and Styles did the same thing.

"Didn't I tell you this shit was going to be a piece of cake?" Styles said as he and Kane walked backward to the front door. "Everybody stay calm!" Styles said as they got closer to the front door.

Abel quickly jogged over to the front door and untied the rope that held the doors shut. "Come on!" he said in a high-pitched voice.

As soon as Kane reached the front door, he quickly raised his M16 to the back of Styles' head and squeezed the trigger, blowing his head clean off.

"What the fuck are you doing?" Abel screamed once he saw Styles' lifeless body hit the floor.

"More money for us," Kane huffed as he struggled to carry two duffle bags and his M16.

When the bank manager heard the gunshots go off, he quickly crawled over toward the counter and hit the silent alarm button.

"Come on, man, we gotta go!" Abel hurried him.

Lisa sat parked in her squad car when she heard the shots go off. "What the fuck?" she said out loud. She just prayed that nothing had gone wrong and those shot were just warning shots.

Seconds later, Lisa heard on her police radio that the silent alarm had just been pulled. Immediately, Lisa knew something wasn't right. She stepped on the gas as she turned on her siren and called for backup.

"Yes, I'm downtown on Fourteenth Street. We have a bank robbery in progress. Backup requested," Lisa said into her police radio.

Seconds later, she saw only two men exit the bank. Styles was the taller man out of the three. When she didn't see him walk out of the bank, she immediately knew that Kane and Abel had set up her man.

Lisa quickly sprang out of her car and sent shots in the direction of the two men.

"Come on. We gotta go!" Abel said as he hurried out of the bank. He stopped dead in his tracks when he saw Lisa standing with her gun trained on him. Seconds later, he heard a series of loud shots, followed by two hard blows that hit his chest. The next thing he knew, he was on the ground, looking up at the sky.

Kane looked down and saw his little brother laid out on the floor, and he just snapped. He dropped the two bags, aimed his M16 at Lisa, and squeezed the trigger, waking up the morning streets with rapid gunfire. Kane held on to the trigger as he continued firing shots.

He walked over toward the squad, watching Lisa's body jerk and dangle like she was a puppet on a string, until he finally ran out of bullets. Kane quickly reloaded his weapon as he saw two more cop cars pulling up. Kane didn't waste any time as he opened fire on the two cop cars.

When Monica saw Abel hit the ground, she quickly hopped out of the van, ran to him, and kneeled down by his side. "Oh my God, baby, are you okay?" she cried as she snatched off his mask so he could breathe better.

"I'm okay, baby. Grab that bag," Abel whispered, pointing to the bag of money.

"Fuck that money!" Monica yelled as she struggled to get Abel on his feet and help him inside the back of the van.

Once Kane was sure that both cops were dead, he quickly reloaded his M16 and ran back to the front of the bank. He grabbed the two duffle bags and tossed them in the back of the van. He then quickly ran over and grabbed Abel's duffle as well. Kane tossed the last bag in the van and then quickly hopped behind the wheel and sped off.

Kane weaved in and out of traffic at a fast speed. He didn't want to admit it, but he knew he had fucked up big time. But it was too late to turn back. Kane zoomed down the street, taking all the back roads, trying not to get caught.

"Please drive this motherfucker!" Monica yelled from the back seat as she held Abel's head in her lap.

"Is it bad?" Abel asked, looking up into her eyes.

Monica looked out the window as she replied. "It's not that bad. You going to be fine," she lied.

Abel's whole blue mechanic jump suit was now red from the amount of blood he spilled. "Please drive faster. We have to get him to the hospital," Monica yelled as she saw Abel's eyes start to roll in the back of his head.

"A hospital?" Kane echoed as he snatched his clown mask off of his face as he zipped through highway lanes like a NASCAR driver. "We can't take him to a hospital," he told Monica while looking at her through the rearview mirror like she was crazy.

"If we don't get him to a hospital, he's going to die!" Monica yelled. "He's your brother, for God's sake!"

Monica knew if she wanted to get Abel to the hospital, she was going to have to make a move. She quickly reached down in her mechanic jump suit and removed her 9 mm. "Take me to the hospital right motherfucking now!" she demanded as she pressed the barrel to the side of Kane's head. She had heard stories of how grimy and low-down Kane was, but right now she was witnessing it firsthand.

"Bitch, you gon' pull a gun out on me?" Kane growled as he quickly stomped on the brakes, causing Monica to come crashing to the front of the vehicle. Immediately, Kane grabbed the gun, trying to pry it from Monica's hand.

As the two fought for the gun, it accidentally discharged. *POW!* Kane violently elbowed Monica in her face as he snatched the gun from her hand.

"Dumb-ass bitch!" he huffed then opened the door and kicked Monica out of the truck. He pulled off, leaving her lying there bleeding on the concrete.

Monica fell out of the van and rolled on the concrete for about seven seconds before finally coming to a stop. She immediately reached for her arm. The bullet had managed to graze her.

Instantly, a crowd began to form. Monica hurried to her feet as she jogged over to the subway and trotted down the subway steps.

When Monica made it down the steps, she pulled a paper out of her pocket. It was the one Styles had given her, with the address to where they were supposed to meet.

Monica quickly removed her mechanic suit and walked all the way to the other side of the platform. She nervously waited on the platform until the train finally came.

"Stupid-ass bitch!" Kane barked as he pulled over to a quiet block and slid out of the driver's seat of the van.

Kane never meant for his brother to get shot on the job. He had fucked up, and he knew it was all his fault. Kane quickly slid out of his mechanic jump suit and kicked it underneath the van. He slid the van door open and saw Abel looking dead at him.

"Help me, please," Abel begged, holding on to his chest.

"I can't," Kane said, trying his hardest not to make eye contact with his brother. He knew it was all his fault that Abel was lying there with two bullets sunk in his chest. The plan went just as it was supposed to, until Kane's greediness fucked it all up.

"Please," Abel whispered. "Don't leave me here like this."

"You'll only slow me down," Kane said as he struggled with all three duffle bags. Kane knew what he was doing was wrong, but the only thing on his mind was getting away before the cops caught him. He planned on leaving town and never showing his face ever again.

"Don't do me like this, please," Abel begged.

Kane looked down at his younger brother, lying in the van with two holes in his chest because of him. Kane slid the van door shut and power-walked two blocks, where he flagged down a cab.

Kane hopped in the cab and quickly slid down in his seat as he gave the cab driver the address that was scribbled down on the piece of paper that Styles had given him. Kane knew that at least a getaway car would be there for him to hop into, and then he could ride off into the sunset.

As Kane sat in the back of the cab, he thought about Abel. He hated to have to leave him for dead like that, but he told himself he had to do what he had to do.

Kane pulled out the .45 that he had tucked in his waistband. He made sure he had a full clip before sticking it back in his waistband. "Stupid motherfuckers," Kane laughed as he watched cop cars flying past in the opposite direction.

"The only person I can depend on is me," Kane told himself when the cab pulled up in front of the warehouse. "Good looking," he said, slipping the cab driver a hundred-dollar bill.

He slid out the back of the cab with his three duffle bags. Kane struggled with the duffle bags until he entered the warehouse. Inside, Kane saw three cars parked, just like Styles had promised. A bright smile spread across Kane's face as he began thinking about how he was going to spend the money.

He quickly popped the trunk on the Acura and dropped the three duffle bags inside, then slammed the trunk shut. Kane looked over and saw a few bottles of champagne resting on a table. He guessed that was for them all to celebrate once the job was done. Kane popped open a bottle and turned it up.

Before he could put the bottle down, he heard the door to the warehouse open. Kane quickly spun toward the door with his .45 already in hand.

"What the fuck?" he said with a confused look on his face as he saw about twenty Chinese men enter the warehouse, all holding automatic weapons.

"Fuck is all this about?" Kane yelled out.

"I'm sure you remember me," Charlie Young Fat said with a smirk on his face. "What, did you think I wouldn't find you?"

"Listen," Kane said, tossing his .45 down to the floor. "I'm pretty sure we can work something out. How much is this going to cost? Just name your price."

"I don't want your money," Charlie Young Fat replied. "I have my own money. I want your soul."

"I could have killed you if I wanted to, but I didn't," Kane said, trying to play that card.

"Your mistake," Charlie Young Fat said, raising his hand, signaling for his shooters to open fire.

The bullets ripped and chewed through Kane's body like a shark leaving blood chunks everywhere. His body was left in the warehouse, smoking.

"Black people are so stupid." Charlie Young Fat chuckled as he exited the warehouse with his hit squad, leaving Kane's body there for the police to find.

Monica sat on the train, clutching her wounded arm. Other people on the train just stared at her. They didn't understand why the young, nice-looking woman was crying her eyes out.

Monica just couldn't believe how Kane could do his own brother the way he did. From the first day Monica met Kane, she knew he was nothing but trouble. Monica didn't know how, but somehow she was going to kill Kane.

As she continued her ride on the train, all the good memories that she and Abel shared flashed through her mind. The memories brought a smile to her face, as the tears continued to stream from her eyes.

"Get yourself together," Monica told herself, wiping her face dry as her stop come up.

Monica stepped off the train, reached down in her pocket, and removed the small pocketknife that she always carried. She didn't know how she was going to kill Kane with a pocketknife when he had an assault rifle, but she was willing to die trying.

Monica jogged up the steps and quickly headed down the street with her pocketknife in her hand. She tried to stop them, but she couldn't control the salty tears that streamed down her face.

Monica stood across the street from the warehouse and then took a deep breath as her foot left the curb and she headed across the street.

Monica stepped foot in the warehouse, and the first thing she saw was Kane's body sprawled out across the floor. At first she thought she was dreaming, but with each step she took, she became more sure that it wasn't a dream.

When Monica finally reached Kane's body, a smirk danced on her lips. Monica kneeled down next to Kane's body and plunged her pocketknife in and out of Kane's neck at least fifty times. She knew he was already dead, but that made her feel a little better.

"That's for Abel," Monica sneered as she spit on Kane's dead body.

Next to Kane's hand lay a car key. Monica picked up the key and stuck it in each car until she found out that it belonged to the Acura.

"Where the fuck did you put that money?" Monica said out loud as she popped the trunk to the Acura. All she could do was smile when she opened up one of the duffle bags and saw all that money looking up at her.

"Thank you, Jesus!" she yelled as she hopped behind the wheel of the Acura and started up the engine. As soon as the engine came on, R. Kelly's song "I Wish" was pumping through the speakers. Monica sang the song to Abel as she pulled out of the warehouse and headed straight for the highway, never to be seen or heard from again.

ORDER FORM
URBAN BOOKS, LLC
97 N18th Street
Wyandanch, NY 11798

Name (please print):_____

Address:_____

City/State:_____

Zip:_____

QTY	TITLES	PRICE

Shipping and handling-add $3.50 for 1st book, then $1.75 for each additional book.
Please send a check payable to:
Urban Books, LLC
Please allow 4-6 weeks for delivery

ORDER FORM
URBAN BOOKS, LLC
97 N18th Street
Wyandanch, NY 11798

Name (please print):_____

Address:_____

City/State:_____

Zip:_____

QTY	TITLES	PRICE

Shipping and handling-add $3.50 for 1st book, then $1.75 for each additional book.
Please send a check payable to:
Urban Books, LLC
Please allow 4-6 weeks for delivery